ELIZABETH STEPHENS

THE BONE KING AND THE STARLING

Copyright © 2025 by Elizabeth Stephens

All rights reserved.

No part of this publication may be reproduced, distributed, or transmitted in any form or by any means, including photocopying, recording, or other electronic or mechanical methods, without the prior written permission of the publisher, except as permitted by U.S. copyright law.

The story, all names, characters, and incidents portrayed in this production are fictitious. No identification with actual persons (living or deceased), places, buildings, and products is intended or should be inferred.

Paperback illustration by:

Hardcover by: Maldo Designs

Dust Jacket by: Maldo Designs &

Sprayed Edges by: Maldo Designs

Interior Formatting by: Maldo Designs

TO THE BLACK GIRLS
STILL IN LOVE WITH
RAGNAR LOTHBROK
AND ERIC NORTHMAN

I SEE YOU AND
I RAISE YOU
KING CALAI
OF WRATH.

TRIGGER WARNING

This book contains dark themes, including a Black woman in the position of thrall (Scandinavian serf or slave during the Viking age), graphic depictions of torture, non-con, and discussions of early childhood abuse. A full list of warnings can be found on my website at www.booksbyelizabeth.com/standalones

Prologue

THE STRANGER

I watch the young thrall wash blood off of her hands in the fountain, enrapt. She does not see me in the shadows. I do not want her to. I don't want any of them to. Not yet. For now, I've come only to watch.

The wind picks at the cloak disguising my armor. I pull the hood low as much to protect from the wind as to hide my face. The thrall wears no such cloak. She wears only a battered dress and shoes that look ill-fitting when she takes a few steps back towards the house she was thrown from. She stops, turning at the sound of laughter.

Before her abrupt arrival, I had been watching the drunks in the town square fall over each other as they exited the longhouse. I'm pretty sure one of the men was the chief of this small village, but I would need the morning's light to know for certain. The thrall disregards the men now, but she still does not return to the building she was thrown from. I wonder what evil or ill keeps her at bay. What fear does she have that is greater than the cold? From the little of this town I have seen so far from the anonymity afforded to me by cloak and shadow, I can only guess.

The town is poor. That does not surprise me. When I first told my men I wanted to host the next games here, despite the many larger cities that may have been more suitable, many grumbled and spat. I did not have many volunteers interested in crossing the western woods by horseback. One of the only villages that is not accessible to Ithanuir by boat. It was a nuisance, and yet, I do not question the gods, for it was their hands that guided me. And I am surprised, confused even, by what I have found.

Though the poverty of this place may not surprise me, what does surprise me is how poor the poorest are compared to the town's wealthier inhabitants. The thrall, for example. Her hair is a natural riot of curls unlike most of the other villagers in this place, yet where many others have tight patterns of intricate braids in the common style of this region, hers hangs long down her back, few braids that there are, tattered.

Her skirts look dirty, even in the moonlight. I cannot see much of her face as she watches the doorway to what looks like a kitchen, though I can see the face of the young male villager who approaches her from the back.

Blond and well fed, laden with muscle, he wears a cloak similar to mine and hide boots that glint in the moonlight as he makes his way across the square. He catches the thrall by the elbow as she idles near the fountain and pulls her around to face him, as if it is his right.

An unpleasant feeling stirs low in my gut, seeing her touched. The fact that she does not enjoy his touch only amplifies it. She rips her arm away from him, but he pushes her chest, forcing her back towards the fountain. When the backs of her skirts brush the stone lip of the fountain and she wobbles, he grabs her by the throat and shoves her backwards, holding her suspended over the shallow water.

I am moving, though I had no intention of doing anything more than watch tonight. Intervening here could jeopardize all of my plans for this village, for these games. But as I move, it is as if I do not have a choice. My bones have begun to sing, telling me to close in, stop this. Closer, I can hear this boy's harsh words on the wind, "You will not deny me much longer. And when I finally have you, the things I will do to that little cunt..."

I grab the boy by the shoulder, wrenching him back and bringing my wrist down hard across his forearm, though not quite hard enough to break it. I shove him off of the thrall and he stumbles towards the hall. The expression on his face as he turns his gaze up to me is positively laughable.

"You dare," the boy shouts at me — *me*.

The sudden splitting reminder that he cannot see my face or identify me by my armor catches me off guard. I chuckle. I am unused to being treated as only a man.

"You dare laugh at me? I am Tori, son of Gilead, and this whore here belongs to me."

"I'm not a whore," the thrall says, surprising me.

"Don't talk back to me." The boy called Tori advances on her as if I'm not even there, like he doesn't even see my body, he is so fixated on the girl. He has hate in his eyes, more than desire. I pity her for the things he will do. And he will do them. Males like him in villages like this live unrestrained. At least, they *did*.

I punch the boy in the gut as he lunges towards her. The pressure of my fist is enough to cause him to buckle and collapse onto the cobblestones. I wait for him to rise. He does not. He merely continues to spit insults up at me and writhe there like a wounded animal, so I grab him beneath one arm and leg and toss the whimpering coward into the fountain.

A group of drunks standing nearby laugh and I chuckle with them at how long it takes the stupid, malignant parasite of a boy to remove himself from the icy water. As warm as this fall night is, he still cannot afford to be outside more than moments. For that reason only, I imagine, he spews a few more foul curses in my direction — leveling another curse at the thrall, too — before staggering off down a street to the left, taking him away from here. Away from her.

"He will be back," I tell the girl, turning to face her while making sure to give her space.

She is looking after the boy, tracking the alley he disappeared behind and keeping her back to me as she does so. And when he's finally gone, only then does she let her shoulders droop. "I know. Thank you, sir, for intervening. He has grown more bold with the games so close."

She turns around and tilts her face up to look at me. I know she cannot see me beneath my hood, against the light of the bright white moon. It is full tonight.

But I can see her.

Beneath the shimmering, supernatural light of the gods — gods who already took their sacrifice from my men and women on this night — I see her face in full clarity and everything, simply everything in the gods' expansive earth, comes together.

Time unwinds like a spool of thread. My body grows hot beneath my armor and I know that I will have many more gods to thank for this before the night is through. Raya, goddess of small creatures, for sending me the raven from the east — the first sign I received to come to this small village when I could have used a much larger, more important town to host these games. Aquenius, god of water, for laying the watermark on the map. Resenia, moon goddess, for showing us her most precious gift in all its fullness here in this square right now so that I might see this female before me in the light and marvel. To Ghabari for what will come next.

I swallow and choke, surprised by the sudden way my throat works.

The female tilts her head and squints. "You are not from Winterbren, sir." Her voice is pitched as a question, so delicate and strong in equal parts. Her hands fiddle nervously in her apron-covered skirts. The brown of her skin appears silver in this light.

She is simply beautiful.

Though to be sure, there is nothing simple about her beauty. The way she has been put together is unlike anything I have seen, and in the capital Ithanuir, I see all kinds, all shapes, all colors. She has brown skin, though it's difficult to assess the exact shade. Her hair is dark curls that cling to the beauty of her face. A few loose braids hold the mass back so that I can see her clearly. Ragged though they may be, I'm grateful for them now.

She has high cheeks and eyes that tilt up towards her hairline. Her brow is soft, as is the slope of her nose, which is perfectly proportioned and round. Her mouth is full. So full. Her upper lip is tiny compared to the bottom. My hand twitches in my cloak. My thumb aches to drag across her mouth, to test that softness with my own rough skin. To feel it crumble beneath me like an army beneath my axe. I want to conquer her.

The thought is as harsh as it as consuming. I want to conquer her. But it is true. I have never wanted anything more.

Perhaps, one thing.

To be conquered by her in return.

"I...am not," I bluster, embarrassed in ways I have never been. I am unused to this. To being received as a man, only, and in the presence of a female so lovely the gods have grown jealous of her. That they would send her here, to this place at the forgotten end of the world, where she would be made to work at the lowest tasks and be treated by the villagers with cruelty as she does it, it is a disgrace. Only redeemed by the fact that the gods sent me here to fix it all, and to find her.

"Are you of Wrath?" Gods, her voice is saccharine-sweet. She is too soft. Too small. Too decadent a creature for the likes of me.

And it matters not. I clear my throat, my hand twitching again. I move it to the handle of my axe to keep from reaching out and grabbing her, no better than the boy who came before. "I am."

"Are you passing through?"

"In a sense." I shift my weight uncomfortably between my feet.

She edges back, undoubtedly put off by my uncertainty. I want to ease her, yet I open my mouth to say something, anything that will keep her here, and find nothing. My lungs are dry. The gods who have brought me to her feet forsake me now.

She takes a step away from me, towards the longhouse. "I should return to my duties, sir. It was very nice to meet you. You have been very kind. I will not forget such kindness." When I do not say more, she turns from me with a short bow.

She does not know that the gods have interceded, changing her fate forever.

I have already overstayed my time in this village, but I linger, waiting until the darkness is thicker than syrup, long after the fires have grown cold, after the drunks have crawled off to bed and the thralls have taken their rest among the rushes.

I slip into the hall and position myself near another group of travelers. They eye me warily but grow more comfortable when I pay them no attention, but instead watch the thralls huddle together for warmth in this drafty place. A disgrace. And it is not only because she is here among them. No one deserves the humiliation of having to sleep here, in this. I can only imagine what these travelers think, being welcomed into Winterbren like this, and I snarl under my breath, drawing the eyes of a young girl sleeping between her parents among the other travelers.

She looks directly into my eyes, despite my hood and offers me a small wave. I wave back.

The girl's mother notices our exchange and directs the girl's attention away from me and I smile. If only the thrall I am after had someone to watch over her as this young girl does. Because, as my gaze finds the dark swath of her curls among the other thralls asleep on the floor, I watch her shiver and know. This thrall, who has nothing to protect her from the cold as she nestles amidst the rushes with not even a thin blanket to cover her will find shelter soon enough. I will be her shelter. And yet...

Doubt hovers over me like a cloud.

This poor thrall has nothing and no one. She is young and abused, clearly alone. It will take time for her to understand what I already know.

She is destined for me by the gods.

She will be frightened and unsure when I return to stake my claim. I will need to restrain myself with her. I *will* restrain myself with her, I assure myself, even as my disobedient cock swells in my trousers at the thought of having her pretty face turned up towards mine — *her on her knees, my fist wrapped in her curls, restraining her so that I may do what I like and take my time.*

My desire is not a beast I have often — if ever — lost a battle of wills to. But I struggle now. Struggle to remain against the wall, watching, when I want so ardently to go to her, pick her up and take her back to my camp, have her among my things, as a Viking should. We are not a people who wait and watch, but raid and take. At the very least,

I long to go to her now and give her my cloak, my fur, to shelter her from the cold. I am failing her already.

Wait. *Wait*... Tomorrow. This is her last night like this.

I itch with yearning, but I know that I must wait to reveal myself to her in the daylight. For tonight, I watch her sleep. And then I wait longer, long enough that I know my warriors will have begun to worry, but I want to ensure that she remains unbothered by the blond fool.

Finally, when I feel the familiar irritation resulting from sleeplessness begin to set in, I rise and leave the great hall that is many things but not great. I find my horse, who is displeased to have been kept in these unfamiliar stables for so long, and return to my camp.

There, I find the prisoner we took from among the bandits that attempted to raid our caravan two days prior. We originally took three prisoners, but two were sacrificed in the full moon ritual. I take the last and sacrifice him to Raya and Ghabari, carving his skin from his flesh methodically while he screams.

I bathe in his blood beneath the light of the full moon and offer my thanks to the gods for bringing me here to this small village on the outskirts of Wrath where my wife has been waiting for me.

The Thrall

STARLING

I'm cold, but that means nothing in Wrath. It's cold all year and we are just entering the very cold season. As a thrall, I'm not allowed furs, so I wear my only wool dress layered atop a long canvas tunic. Both are drab enough, they capture the color of the ominously low sky, and both are too thin, having been worn by the village chief's three daughters many times before they came to me.

All three of our chief's daughters have been promised to their future husbands, though only one has wed. The eldest now lives in the neighboring village. The youngest is pledged to Viccra, a good man, though the second oldest is pledged to Tori. I would pity her had she not spent so much effort being needlessly cruel to me and to the other thralls, Mirabel in particular.

I wrap my hands around my elbows, squeezing my arms tight around myself to try to stop shivering. Ebanora, standing at my side, makes a short snickering sound that causes me to look at her, but her gaze has lowered to my chest. I look down and realize I'm squeezing my arms so tightly that it's pushed my breasts to the upper edge of my dress and I snort, elbowing her in the side. I relax my posture as much as I can without freezing entirely.

"I'm sure my brother doesn't mind the view," she whispers in my ear and I laugh even harder as I glance past her at her brother. He's one of the warriors set to participate in the games and he isn't looking at me at all — he's never noticed me much, which doesn't bother me in the slightest — but right now I feel nervous for him. I want him to do well in the games, not just for him but for Ebanora and her entire family. Though she and I are separated by status and three years, she's the only thing close to a friend I've ever had. They are poor farmers. Her brother being selected as a warrior trainee by the king would elevate their status considerably.

I smile back at her cautiously and when she snickers audibly, I tense. A hard glare is cast over a broad shoulder. Tori is our prized village warrior, slated to be chosen this year. If he is, I don't doubt he will choose me for his prize — his future wife, be damned. Each of the chosen warriors are allowed whatever pleasures they like on the eve of their selection. The only reason he has not had me yet is because our chief — more accurately, the chief's wife Rosalind — knows of Tori's desire for me and has held it over his head as a motivation to keep him in line.

I don't wish to lose my virginity to Tori, especially not after the threats he made against me last night. I was grateful to the large stranger that intervened…at the time. But in the light of the morning, I worry about Tori's retaliation. It will be against me, given that the stranger is likely gone now, and it will be terrible. That's all I can think as his hard stare turns to a wicked smile. His gaze drops down to my chest and he runs his tongue over his white teeth.

I shudder even though I don't mean to. For as unenthusiastic as my reactions are, I know how they excite him. I have seen him in the village picking on smaller boys — and some girls — of lower status before. He is excited by their tears — by my tears — my displeasure. My pain.

I find it somehow even worse that he is an attractive male, coveted in our village for his looks. He could have any female he wants easily with just a kind whispered word and yet he chooses to withhold all of them. Perhaps, they do not even exist in his vocabulary. The stranger, on the other hand, I didn't get a look at, hidden as he was beneath his cloak and positioned in relief against the moon's brightness. He is probably an ogre for as gentle as his words were and the easy way with which he stood up for me. It would have been nice to look into his eyes once, to thank him. Instead, I am left to suffer Tori's cruel stare alone now.

Tori's skin is tan layered over white. His hair is blond, like most in the village. Winterbren is generally a homogenous place, which is why I stand out so strikingly. My mother was taken during a raid from a distant land across the sea of sapphire. She boasted dark brown skin and tight, black ringlets. My father looked like Tori and was just as mean. I came out looking like both of them. Long, dark curls and waves that hang tattered down my back to my rear. Medium brown skin that darkens quickly in the sun. The same dark eyes my mother had when she was alive.

I know that there are many males in the village who want to sample me to see if I taste any different than the pale-faced blonde and brunette females of the village, but Tori has staked his claim and frightened them off. But after the games...after the selection is made and Tori is inevitably chosen to leave our small village for the capital, I don't doubt he will take my virginity with him. Then, I will be free for use by anyone.

I have been drinking the root's essence with the other thralls since I turned fourteen. It will keep me from getting pregnant — at least, it has worked for the other girls — but I don't have plans to prevent what will be inevitable. The chief's wife who has only ever been fair with me — if quite short of kind — assured me that it is my role within the tribe to comfort our warriors however they like to be comforted. That it will be my only role of significance.

While her words frighten me, I *am* already twenty. For the fact that I did not lose my virginity the moment my parents died six years ago — or as most thralls do, in my adolescence — I am grateful to the chief and his wife for naming me as their ward, even if I have the status and perform the duties of a thrall.

I also know that, while whoring is not the future I envisioned for myself as a child, it is possible to earn a little extra coin from the men of our village, or passers through, like the kind one I met last night. For as much as I don't relish the idea, I do look forward to hopefully one day purchasing my very first fur along with my freedom. And if not that, at least a pair of new shoes.

I wiggle my toes in my boots. When my parents died, I had nothing. So, even though my clothes are threadbare and my feet are cold in my leather slippers, I'm still grateful. That I wasn't cast out in the cold entirely was a blessing from Raya. Short of my limited utility as a young female and a passable cook, I still don't know why the chief and his wife took me in at all. Most in my village in my circumstance would have been left to the cold. If that had happened...

I glance at the back of Tori's head until the distant pounding of horses' hooves cause his head to swivel back around. I keep staring, wondering about my fate — what it will be like in three days after the games — when I am handed over to him. Will he come for me in the great hall and drag me to the stables where males are known to rut lowborn females? Or will he knock on Chief Olec's door? Will Rosalind hand me over herself? I wonder if, after it's over, he'll gift me anything at all...

I jerk at the sudden sharp pressure above my elbow. Ebanora is watching me, her sapphire eyes alight. She smiles at me, her cheeks pink and her white-blonde hair clean. Three years my junior, she will likely be married off in the next year, hopefully to a good man, though most likely to a farmer — a warrior farmer if she's lucky.

She is excited for today and in small part, I echo that feeling. I've never seen the games before and I've certainly never seen the king. The procession has just begun and I lean in when Ebanora's shoulders turn towards me, her fur tickling my cheek.

"Here he comes, the bone king." The king of blood, the king of bone, I know what they call him and why they call him that and it makes me shudder even as Ebanora continues. "Unlike the village chiefs or the southern kings, King Calai leads the procession himself. He always has. Only true rulers lead their armies into battle. False rulers hide behind their warriors. That he leads the procession instead of idling at the back is a testament to that."

I nod along, soaking up any knowledge of anything at all that she seeks to give me. She has regular lessons but after my parents passed, I was no longer permitted to join Ebanora and listen in to what she was taught.

"What's it like? The capital?" I whisper, knowing that she's had the pleasure of traveling the long road to Ithanuir with her parents and older brother once. He will participate in the games, though I'm not sure that is his true desire. Like his sister, he hasn't a fighting bone in his body, but he is almost sixteen and strong. Chief Olec insisted and even I know that, for his poor family, it would be a great honor were he selected to train with the king.

But I do worry... If he is selected to live in Ithanuir for a year, would his family — or even just his sister — accompany him? Ebanora is smart and beautiful. She would surely find a husband in the city who could provide for her better than the males here. And then I'd never see her again...

Ebanora speaks animatedly and I feel a terrible guilt that I would deny her excitement for my own selfish reasons. I quickly plaster a smile on my face and give her my attention as she says, "It's grand. The longhouse is ten times the size of the chief's, sturdy, elevated from the ground by a short staircase. The floor is made of boards that sit above the ground so it never floods when it rains. And the market is incredible. All kinds of people from all over Ithanuir pass through it. The temples are beautiful. The temple to Raya and Ghabari's love is sensational. It would be a true honor to even witness a wedding take place there."

My heart beats hard, and it's hard to push aside those feelings of longing. They're girlish thoughts and by the end of the games, I'll be a woman. There won't be time for those kinds of thoughts then, so for now, I suppose it might be alright to let myself idle in them.

"And what of the king?" I say, the pounding of distant hooves making it difficult to be heard.

"He will certainly marry there. Though there seems to be no indication that he will soon take a wife..."

I chuckle under my breath. "Is that all that consumes your thoughts?"

Ebanora's cheeks grow ruddy then and I feel sorry for her. "I am a great burden for my family. I hope I can find a good match..."

"You will." I take her wrist. "And let's not talk about that now. The king, I meant what is he like?"

"Larger than life. Truly. He is one of the most imposing males I've ever seen. My family never had the pleasure of an introduction, but we did see him in passing several times and each time it was frightening. He doesn't ever smile.

They say he picks his teeth with the bones of his enemies. That he drinks his ale from their skulls."

"The bone king." I shiver.

"The people love him for it," she says, nodding in confirmation. "The prisoners he takes are not known to live long and his punishments are terrible. They say it's because his father was too kind, he was backstabbed by his uncle." I've heard the story. The one that ended with eighteen-year-old Calai skinning his uncle alive and retaking the crown his father lost. "He's violent to ensure that none dare cross him."

"I'm glad he isn't staying long."

Ebanora pinches my outer arm again and I jump. I give her a scolding look and she laughs. "Don't be so frightened. He is also very generous. To take our warriors from us and then return them *trained* is a generosity the kings before him did not extend."

It is true. These games are new and widely celebrated. Each year, King Calai calls as many as a dozen young warriors from each village to compete in a series of games. The winners of the games from each village travel to Ithanuir to train with the king and his warriors directly. A year later, they are returned more capable of defending the outer villages.

It's been seven years since our village on the edge of Wrath was last raided by one of the western tribes, but when they came, it was Torbun's eldest son Viccra who was seen to have fought the most bravely. He had just come back from his year in Ithanuir.

Each year, King Calai oversees the games in a different village personally. A small village of only six hundred, it's an honor to receive the king here. He's been king since I was born and has only overnighted in our village once since then. I was only six and not allowed out of the house to see him. And this is our village's first time hosting him for the games.

"You're right."

"Of course I'm right," she says with all of the sass of a much older woman. I can see her mother in her easily when she smirks at me in such a way.

I bump her hip with my own. "But that does not mean that *I* would like to be anywhere near him."

She makes a nervous face at that. "Neither would I." She hesitates, looking like she wants to say more. "He caught an assassin from Eccaron while my family was in the capital. He sacrificed him to Davral." The goddess of pain. A sacrifice to her is said to guarantee victory in battle. But Davral only accepts sacrifices in one way...

I freeze over. "He performed the ritual?"

She nods.

Bile tickles the back of my throat, but I press it down. I shake my head. "That's terrible."

"And there are other rumors..."

"What?"

"That he tortured raiders just outside of Winterbren on his way here."

I shiver even more violently. "I'm grateful I'm a thrall then, and won't merit an introduction."

"Good thing we are but lowly females," she whispers, a grin overtaking her face. "We won't have to talk to him or risk incurring his wrath, but that does not mean we can't still look— Look! Here he comes." She squeezes my wrist and I can feel the tension and excitement of the townspeople around me as the crowd suddenly surges forward.

Jostled from the back, I cling to Ebanora's arm and push myself up onto my tiptoes, though that hardly helps. I'm not tall, shorter than most of the women and shorter than all of the men. "Here, stand here." Ebanora grabs my shoulder and yanks me to Tori's left, where a small gap allows me to see the reddish-brown snout of the most incredible horse I've ever seen as it carries the king of Wrath — *our* king, the king of bones — down our small village's largest street.

The horse alone is enough to distract me. Its hooves sound like the clack of lightning layered against the deeper thunder of the horses behind it, traveling like a thick cloud. Its coat is fine and well cared for, bridled in black. The creature stands taller than any man here and it's because of that that I have no problem at all seeing the king as he suddenly flashes into existence. I could have been standing directly behind Tori and still seen most of him. Now, he's all I can see.

The three rows of people that stand between the king and me vanish. I see him in all of his glory, even though he does not see me. Ebanora had not been telling tall tales. He's a beast of a male. More beast than the one he rides atop. Broad and muscled everywhere, his size is only accentuated by the plush brown and black furs lashed across his breadth. He wears leather beneath that and, for his sake, I hope cotton or wool below that because without it, he'd have to be cold. Then again, he's not a male who looks like he gets cold. While his skin is the same white color of most Winterbren's villagers', he has a heavier tan laid atop that base color than most. Sunlight clings to him. As does flame.

His hair is red and vibrant, the least common color in our village. It's a handsome color, though I would never dare to describe the king as handsome. He looks far too savage for that. He has scars on his bare hands that disappear beneath his vambraces. His neck is thicker than my upper thigh. His face is severe, the bridge of his nose slightly bent — at least, it looks that way in his profile — his brow prominent, his eyes dark beneath it. His cheeks and jaw are cut hard, making his entire countenance appear mean and angry. And big. My head feels so small by comparison.

I reach up and touch the side of my scalp, scratching my fingers through my hair. It's matted in patches and I drop my hand immediately, feeling ashamed as the king swings his massive head on his massive neck and looks down at us from atop his massive steed, gazing over his massive, muscled shoulder.

"My lord, I will fight for you until the last breath! Wuah!" Tori shouts loudly and I flinch. The king's gaze lands on him and as several of the other warriors clap for their bold friend, the king does not break his pace. He only dips his chin once before sweeping his gaze from Tori over the crowd. Then he's off again.

While the rest of the caravan of riders moves on — I lose count of them at thirty — and Tori receives cheers and congratulations for catching the king's notice, Ebanora leans in towards me. "Is it just me or did the king's gaze seem to linger over you?" Her voice is taunting, meant to inspire fear — I can tell from the way her tone goes up at the end. And despite knowing all this, it works.

I get chills and shudder. She laughs and I steer her away from Tori as the crowd begins to disperse frantically — the feast is about to begin in the great hall and it will be the largest this village has ever seen. While I won't be in attendance like Ebanora will — with a place at one of the six long tables — I will be there nonetheless, serving.

"You are blind as a winter bat."

She laughs and loops her arm through mine.

"He was looking at Tori," I add as we round the next set of houses.

"Tori is an idiot," Ebanora whispers.

I snicker, not wanting to agree with her and be heard. That will certainly get me another beating. "Thank you for making me come and watch," I tell her as I bring her to the door of her home. A squat wooden structure, it's only two rooms, but to me it seems like a labyrinth.

"I'll see you at the feast." She kisses my cheek.

"I'll try to serve at your table."

"Please! I'll sneak you all my sweets."

I giggle and kiss her back and am off to the kitchens.

The Prize

STARLING

Ale sloshes over the sides of my pitcher as I move quickly between tables. My arms ache with the weight. My legs ache for other reasons. I've banged my shins and knees multiple times on the edges of the bench seats as I squeezed between the narrow gaps between the tables.

It is my least favorite duty because the more the males drink from their horns, the more lecherous they become — and the king's men are rowdier than ours, which only heightens the debauchery. There must be over two hundred people crowded into our village hall. It's much too small to fit all six tables, but crammed in here they are, so I have to squeeze between seats that are nearly pressed together.

The high table is positioned in front of the throne, parallel to the back wall. All of the other five tables are organized horizontally to it, pressed together bench to bench to fill the full width of the hall. Only a small pathway for the thralls and kitchen staff to run along files down the wall leading connecting the back wall to the front entrance.

Wedged between two of the tables now, I pour ale to every outstretched horn and cup that shoves itself towards me, being careful to avoid the high table as well as the seats nearest it where the highborn warriors sit alongside their families. I feel Tori's gaze on me at several points in the night. He hails me with his horn, but I pretend not to notice. Each time he does that and I look back at his face, I catch his smile widening. I quickly shuffle on.

Sweat drips down my back, staining the collar of my dress. Washing it will be a difficulty, but I am overdue a wash. I stink and I know it, even more now with how much ale has spilled over me tonight. Finally brushing the back of my wrist across my hairline, I pour my last cup from this pitcher.

With the good excuse that my pitcher is now empty, I make my way towards the entrance of the hall. It's still hot in here despite the fact that the only fires that have been lit tonight are the torches. For once, I welcome the icy breeze that wafts through the open doors.

Thralls and other cooks dash around me, adding to the feeling of frenzy. I know I can't be caught dawdling, but the festivities are magnificent. I glance at the array of tables smushed from wall to wall and inhale deeply, marveling at it all and knowing that I will see no such sight again in my life. This is likely the only time anyone of such importance will ever grace us with their presence here in Winterbren and I will likely remain in Winterbren until the day I die.

I long to look at the king but nervousness prevents me from staring. I spare him only a quick glance. Positioned in the center of the high table, the king's red hair stands out. He stares forward, Chief Olec leaning in towards him and speaking into his ear. Despite Chief Olec's boisterous laugh, the king's stare remains flat and uninspired. I shiver, remembering what Ebanora said and looking towards her. She is seated on the edge of the table closest to the entrance where I stand now, and when she meets my gaze, she flashes me the white cloth she has hidden in her hand. I smile.

She gives me an excited little wave and, as I brush past her, she slips me a little folded square. She's done this three times already and each time, it's been a sweet cake — my favorite, though far too high a delicacy for any thrall to have. I've only ever tried them thanks to her. My parents had never given me one to sample before they passed away. Even when they were alive, my position within the tribe had been little higher than a servant's. My father had been a farmer and a warrior, when required, but hadn't been very good at either. We'd been quite poor.

My mother had been a talented seamstress, but the first time one of the village ladies paid her for one of her designs, my father hit her so hard she lost a tooth. It was a higher payment than he'd received in a year and he'd been insulted. She didn't sew again after that and any designs she had made, I didn't inherit. I believe Rosalind took and sold those that there were. I've never seen them since and wouldn't ever have dared ask about them.

I scurry against the outer wall, passing by dozens of other thralls carrying trays and carting pitchers of water, flagons of wine and tuns of mead, eager to get to the back storeroom where the alcohol is kept so I can eat my treat while I refill my pitcher.

I'm jostled by an older male thrall and slam against the wall. I drop my pitcher with an audible "ooph," but keep my treat in my clenched fist. The male doesn't turn to look at me, but limps off. I know better than to expect acknowledgement, let alone an apology. We are punished if we are caught flagging or seen making conversation with one another.

Massaging my shoulder, I reach for my pitcher. As I do, Torbun's booming voice calls out, "Silence all, quiet, quiet!" Torbun is our chief's second in command. As such, I have waited on him at Chief Olec's often, but I'm not sure he's ever much noticed me. His wife is the great beauty of the village, even now that she's well past her prime childbearing years, and he's always looked at her with affection.

I snatch up my pitcher just as my back is pressed against the wall by another thrall, Elena, who moves to stand in position directly next to me. My shoulders brush servants on both sides. Both stand taller than I do. Elena by only a little, the male by quite a lot. I hold my pitcher tight to my chest and look towards the high table. With everyone seated now but those of us serving, it is easier to see the chief and the king seated beside him in the position of honor.

The king is relaxed in his seat now, leaning back, a horn of ale in his fist that he brings to his mouth as his gaze sweeps the space, never landing. His expression is indecipherable. His eyes are dark. His red hair looks even redder in the light of the torches that gleam across it. He's removed his furs, tossing them over the back of his chair to reveal a scant smattering of leather, concentrated mostly over his chest and leaving his arms bare.

I swallow hard. He is a frightening male to behold. I can picture Ebanora's stories clearly now. I can see how he could have performed the ritual of Davral, which if true, would have ended with him bathing in and drinking his enemy's blood.

His shoulders and arms are even larger than they seemed atop his horse, no longer hidden beneath his furs. His biceps bulge with each movement of his hand to his mouth, veins streaking across them. All of his warriors are twice the size of the largest of ours, but he's largest. All but one other male seated at the high table is dwarfed in size compared to the king, and that warrior male is rotund and built like a boar, laughing riotously into his wine cup.

Torbun claps twice and raises both hands. The chatter dies slowly. I glance sideways at Elena, who offers me a small shrug, her stare returning forward. Torbun already made introductions, so I can't fathom the reason for the interruption at this late stage in the evening. Still, he smiles. He has a large smile.

His voice is booming as he speaks. "We are grateful for King Calai and the bounty he has brought to our village, are we not?"

A great roar goes up and I can't help but smile myself. Though I haven't yet had my chance to partake, King Calai was generous and set aside a large feast for us helpers specifically. Very few guests we've had have come bearing gifts and none have been so generous.

Torbun claps again, demanding silence. "The king has brought us a feast for the ages and in three days, will be taking warriors from our small village to train in the great capital of Ithanuir, returning them in one year so that we can remain protected and safe." The hall cheers again. "If there is a way we could repay our great king's generosity, should we not take it?"

The roar is loud enough to make me want to cover my ears, had I any hands to spare. Instead, I laugh and nod along at Torbun's words. He's riled up, riling all of us, and earns another loud whoop from the crowd when he gets up and stands on his chair.

He throws his arms to the side and says, "But His Highness Calai is king of all of Wrath and we are but a small village on its farthest edge. What could we possibly have that he cannot find elsewhere in greater, grander quantities?" Whispers rise up. Torbun fans them like embers. "Does anyone have a guess?"

A few guesses are thrown out — mead, ale, fish, fur — but Torbun shakes his head. "You men should know better than any what we have that the other villages of Wrath do not..." He pauses and when there are no further guesses, he shouts at the top of his lungs, "The most beautiful women!"

A cheer goes up loud enough to bring down the hall. A violent wind would have had a less catastrophic effect. Elena hisses beside me and shakes her head. "Fools," I catch her mouthing. I might have laughed, but I'm distracted by Torbun again. "Our king has requested the company of a willing female for the night. If any such unmarried females exist in this hall, please stand so that King Calai may take his pick. Fathers, release your daughters without fear, for King Calai is a generous male and intends for a great honor to be bestowed on his prize — undoubtedly riches that will make this feast seem paltry."

This time, female voices squeal and screech. Limbs are shuffled and elbows are thrown as a dozen — no, *dozens* of women find their feet. I watch as Lucildeth — a widow of fifty — pulls her neckline down and her breasts up at the same time that Ebanora tentatively rises from her bench, her mother's hands fixing her hair while her brother stares on slack-jawed and angry and his father restrains him.

Ebanora looks at me and I widen my eyes. Her cheeks tint pink. She only just got her moon blood earlier this warm season. The king is over thirty-five. I believe he may even be older than Ebanora's father. And the stories she told me. He is a cruel, beastly male. She cannot want this...

My lips part but my throat is dry. I know how the world works and despite the fact that Ebanora feels like royalty from where I kneel so far below her, I know she is far from wealthy.

The promise of riches for her family in exchange for their only daughter's virginity is too great a chance for Ebanora to remain in her seat. And she is beautiful. I can only hope that the king carries an ounce of honor in his body, that he wouldn't take someone so young and innocent. I glance at Lucildeth again as she puckers her mouth and hope — pray to Lohr, the god of lust — that he prefers a woman with more experience.

"And what a fine selection we have here for you, my liege. On behalf of the chief, his beautiful wife, and our entire village, we welcome you to take your time inspecting our array of willing females, each guaranteed to offer you a pleasurable night." He gestures at the risen women and my gaze strays from Ebanora's flushed red cheeks to the king. My heart sits like a dagger in my neck.

He rises to his feet, pushing his chair back. It groans under his displaced weight. He drops his empty horn on the table and begins to walk with purpose. There's no way he'd be able to stick his meaty legs through the narrow gaps between the benches, so he does the reasonable thing and comes down the servants' aisle. The one Ebanora is currently standing far too near to. It'll put her directly in his path.

My stomach clenches as I watch him. His heavy feet are wrapped in fur-lined boots. The leather and fur of his pants strain against his powerful legs. His weapons knock against his thick thighs as he takes step after step, moving down the row lined with servants, closer and closer to Ebanora while his gaze sweeps to his right, across the tables where so many eager women have risen.

Those nearest to him look so hopeful as he approaches them, and their hope is immediately crushed as he continues, his steps sure, his stride unfaltering. His red beard catches the light, shimmering brown and burgundy and orange. As does his hair, the top half of which is bound back away from his face, a few loose braids woven through the mass that falls down to his shoulder blades.

His large head swivels and his massive breadth storms forward. Ebanora and I stare at one another. Her expression has fallen slack and I don't quite understand why she's staring at me in such shock until it hits me that the king has come to a stop directly before me.

Me.

The immense presence of the king of Wrath tramples me like a horse and my gaze is wrenched from Ebanora to the male standing above me. His shoulders twist smoothly to face me, and his head turns away from the risen women, gaze finding my face and focusing on it like it's the first face he's ever seen.

His black eyes move over my forehead and nose, cheeks, chin and lips before dropping down to my chest. He looks my body over briefly and then returns his gaze to mine. Face tilted up, I disgrace myself by not looking down quickly enough. It is not appropriate for one of my station to look at him directly, and yet, he does not punish me. I stare down at his legs, waiting — hoping — for him to ask me to fetch him something. I am a thrall. That would be my duty. Anything more I am not prepared for.

Beside me, Elena stiffens while the male to my right edges away from me, putting space between us. What is happening? Heat hits the backs of my eyes as I wait and pray to Raya for mercy.

And then he takes a step. There can be no mistaking the fact that he's standing in front of me now. Any cowardly hope I might have had that his focus was on Elena beside me is gone. King Calai's enormous body eclipses the world behind him. I take a tentative glance up to his chest and warily eye the leather straps that crisscross all over it. Beneath them, scars shimmer. He has a cut on his stubbled jaw where no hair grows. It's small but glistens silver when he tips his chin down to look at me. I shame myself by glancing into his eyes a second time. *Fool*. If he hadn't intended to punish me before, he certainly will now.

He edges forward another step, and then another. My back is plastered to the longhouse wall, yet his chest is almost against mine, separated from it by only the pitcher between us. And then…not even that. I flinch when he takes the pitcher by its open mouth, using just one of his massive hands to remove it from my grip and hand it absently to the male standing to my right. The bone king then reaches for my left hand, clenched around my treat. It shakes. I cannot control it.

His large, leathery fingers skim the outer edge of my wrist. His hand is so big, it doesn't look real. I've never met anyone as big as he is. He deftly turns my palm over in his. Lingering over the veins in my wrist for a moment, he opens my fingers with his thumb. They're dirty, my fingers. His are callused, but clean as they stroke my skin. All of his movements are sure. His thumb moves down towards the heel of my hand and flicks one edge of the folded napkin with his short nail. I don't dare try to keep my treat from him. If he came to punish me for having it when I shouldn't, I won't resist. Whatever punishment I shall receive, I'll live.

He makes a soft sound through his nose, one I can't interpret. Then his thumb pushes my fingers back around my sacred, stolen morsel.

"Are you willing?" he says, his hand still cupping mine, holding it aloft between us. He rakes his thumb over my knuckles, the gesture strange and familiar even though he doesn't know me and I exist in a world apart from his. He is as distant to me as the gods. At least...he was.

I still do not believe that he could be talking to me. I want to glance to someone — anyone — for aid, but I'm too frightened to look away from his hand closed around my trembling fist. I gnaw on my bottom lip, too afraid to answer.

"You are standing," comes his low brogue, "so I will assume that you are."

I'm a thrall. I'm not allowed to sit at a feast. He knows that. He has to know that. There's a male standing right beside me. But who am I to tell him any of that? I open my mouth but a whimper is all that I emit.

"Look at me."

Oh no. I can't do that. It's a flogging offense for a servant to meet a king's gaze directly like this.

"I give you permission." His hand releases my fist and it drops like a stone. I am unbearably attuned to the brush of his fingers on the outside of my dress. His fingers trail up my forearm, past my elbow. He picks a loose string — one among many — off of my dress before he reaches my shoulder and touches the place where my shift meets my skin, tracing the edge with his calloused fingers. He moves his hand along my clavicle, his knuckles brushing over it so softly, yet with so much threat. He could break the bone with just that hand, I'm sure of it. And I feel like sobbing at the realization.

"I require it, little bird."

I shiver from head to toe despite the heat of the hall — and the even greater heat he emanates. I may be a thrall, but I have never been touched like this before, not on my bare skin, so intimately, with such implied intent. My lower lip trembles as his hand moves to the side of my neck, which he strokes gently with his rough thumb, up and down my quivering muscle.

"Shh," he says. "Be still." He touches my jaw and then forces my chin up, but I keep my eyes closed, much to his disproval, because he clacks his tongue against the backs of his teeth. "Little bird, look at me."

I swallow hard. His hand momentarily fists around my throat as I do. I struggle to lift my gaze past his beard and take several short, hot breaths to build the courage. I finally take in his nose, but he loses patience and tips my chin even further up with his thick thumb, giving me no other choice but to look into his dark and violent stare or up at the patchy thatch roof above his head. I don't dare defy him again and choose the more frightening of the two options. I meet his gaze.

Later, I will wonder if what I heard was true or a conjuring of my frightened imagination, but in the instant our eyes clashed, I could have sworn I heard the king take in a sharp breath, as if I'd startled him. But I will never know for certain.

In the next moment, his cheeks turn ruddy and his naturally pink lips take on a more striking carmine color, flushed from wine or something else. A vein throbs across his forehead and a muscle in his neck jumps. His hand flinches around my throat, making me jump. In a moment of silent shame, I drop my sweet bread.

I wipe my now sticky palm off on the rough material of my threadbare dress as my gaze passes between his eyes, trying desperately to decipher if the corners of his mouth and the stitching of his prominent brow betray ease or an edge. Right now, I feel all of his sharp edges stabbing and jabbing into me as I wait and pray for whatever ill is to befall me, but when he speaks, he does so gently, his voice taking on a tone that tickles my sense of familiarity once again.

"Have you bled?" His words are low and soft.

Startled by the question, I answer in truth with a shallow nod before the humiliation of his request can wash over me.

His brows pull even closer together, as if he is displeased with my answer, or unsure if I'm telling him the truth. "How many years?"

I hold up one hand with my thumb, pointer, middle and ring finger lifted. My pinky finger I keep lowered against my sticky palm.

His full, pink mouth tightens and he speaks in a gruff voice that cuts like broken glass, "Does another soul here hold your heart?"

I shake my head even though I am confused by the question.

"Where is your family?"

I shake my head more quickly, my hair shifting around my shoulders. He reaches up and grasps the end of one curl. His nostrils flare. I wonder if he smells my stench. I am embarrassed...humiliated...confused. My stomach is in knots and if it would not have embarassed me further, I suspect I'd have lost control of my bladder the moment he touched my arm.

"Are you claimed by another?"

I shake my head.

"Are you promised to another?"

I hesitate and before I can think of a more acceptable, decent answer, I stutter, "Not for a w-wife, my king."

"Hm." He is twirling a single curl around his finger, watching it with fascination before his gaze slowly passes from my hair to my shoulder beneath it, and then across the top of my dress. His hand tightens just a little around my throat in a way that can only be interpreted as a threat. Is he...is he going to kill me here? Like this? Perform the ritual of Davral on me right now?

"My king..." I whisper. "Mercy. Please..."

I haven't led a particularly beautiful life, but it's mine and I intend to see it through. I might not have much, but I have hopes...hopes for furs, for clean shoes, maybe even one day, if I get really lucky, a poor farm boy to take me for his...and if I were truly to be spoiled by the gods, maybe even with him a couple children to raise and to love and to shower with all the affection I didn't receive from my own kin. Yet the king does not release me. Instead, he closes his eyes.

"Mercy," he repeats. He repeats it two more times.

His eyes open and his gaze grows distant as it lingers on my ear. He tucks the curl he'd been toying with behind it and says so softly I strain to make out his words, "How can I offer what the gods have denied me? The gods do not intend mercy on either of us."

"Please," I say again, heat pressing at the backs of my eyes. "I have nothing to offer."

His gaze snaps to mine and his hand drops halfway onto my chest. He rubs his thumb across the thin bones of my sternum. "Would you like to come with me?"

I freeze. Panic consumes me. "I'm just a thrall," I whisper brokenly.

"I can see that." His gaze travels down over my clothing all the way to my feet. His hand falls with it, exposing my throat and landing on my shoulder, which he squeezes. "You will come with me," he says in an even deeper tone. "That I allow you to believe you have a choice in this is a gift that I now revoke. It has been decided. Come. You must be hungry."

He takes my sticky fist in his, swallowing it whole in his palm and begins to pull me away from the wall. My feet are blocks of stone as they drag behind me, passing all of these people *staring* at me as if I've grown seven heads. The king retraces the path he took and pulls me to the front of the room, to the high table where only the favored sit, and then pulls me down onto his lap as he retakes his seat beside the Chief of Winterbren.

"Tell your females to be seated. I have made my selection," he grunts as he settles me on his lap, positioning my legs across both of his so that my outer right hip is pressed right against his abdomen and my rear uses his thick thigh for a seat cushion. He ignores Chief Olec and the other men and women seated at this table.

Rosalind, seated at Chief Olec's other side, stares at me around the chief's body with menace in her eyes. Torbun and his family sit on her other side and strain to see over the top of her immaculately arrayed hair to look at the king and me. Behind me sit a smattering of King Calai's warriors. I cannot see their expressions to interpret them, but I can hear the easy way they continue to speak and laugh amongst one another, as if this is something to be celebrated. Then again, they know the king best. Perhaps, he does this type of thing all the time, at every village he passes through. Maybe, they are simply animated because they are used to it.

Chief Olec meets my gaze fleetingly before I tear my attentions to the heavily decorated table. King Calai stretches both arms around me to reach his plate, which is clear until he ladens it anew. He cuts a piece of turkey off of the bone and surprises my wits out of my temples when he does not eat it himself, but instead brings it to my bottom lip.

"Open," he says, voice easier than it was.

I obey and take the succulent turkey off of the tines with my teeth, noting that this is the same fork King Calai used and now, we are sharing it. He takes the next two bites and, as I finish chewing my first, has another piece of meat ready for me. This one, ox. I've prepared ox many times before, but I've never tasted it and I nearly moan with the pleasure that glides through me at the rich and fatty texture.

"You like ox?"

I nod and then in a trembling whisper, add, "It is my first time." I glance up at his face, hoping he understands what I'm trying to tell him. The fork in his hand dips, his brows furrow, he opens his mouth, but it's Chief Olec who speaks.

"Your choice is surprising, my liege," Chief Olec offers with a loud laugh.

The king continues staring at my face, deep into my eyes like he's trying to mine for some precious resource, but he should know, I don't have anything. I break his gaze first and after another weighty silence, he resumes skewering pieces of meat from his plate and alternatingly eating a bite and feeding the next to me.

"I make no choices. I am merely led by the gods," the king says in a way that nearly sounds dismissive as he surrounds me with his body and his attention, sparing Chief Olec little. "Do you prefer wine or ale, little bird?" he says to me.

His chest lines my shoulder and arm, his body cupping mine so intimately. His head is positioned high over mine and the fact that he didn't seem to register what I was trying to tell him before makes me especially apprehensive. My mouth is dry and I am thirsty enough to try either wine or ale, whichever is offered.

"Wine, I think?" I've only had a few sips of ale and found it unpleasant. I've never tried wine at all, but I'm hopeful it won't taste worse than the ale I sampled.

The king hails both and they arrive in a large flagon and a pitcher just like the one I'd been carrying around the room. The irony is not lost on me as a thrall called Mikas pours ale into the king's wooden cup now. I reach for the pitcher of wine to pour myself a cup, but the king bats my hand to the side.

Successfully scolded, I feel my cheeks warm. The king says gently, "Apologies, little bird. I did not mean to dismiss you, I just wanted to be the one to pour your wine." I watch him do just that, an act that I can see draws eyes from the warriors seated at the front tables closest to us. My blush is pronounced, I'm sure. "Do you forgive me?"

I sit up straight, as if stuck by a pin, and meet his gaze. He's smiling at me softly and brings the wooden cup to my bottom lip. "O-of course, my king."

His nostrils flare slightly as he offers me wine. Alarmed and uncomfortable as I am, I drink from his cup gluttonously. I drink nearly two cups of wine in between bites of meat, potatoes and other vegetables. I'm slowing, my stomach heavy with how much I've eaten. My back is more arched and I find myself, appallingly, leaning more and more of my weight against his chest.

He does not comment on it. Instead, he calls to the thrall that passes. "Sweet cake for my female."

It's Elena. She doesn't look at the king as she follows through on his command. She doesn't look at me either as she sets the flat braided loaf down on the table before the king and me, and I feel terribly alone. Elena is of a higher position in the village than I — most everyone is — but there's no chance she has ever had an entire sweet cake to sample before. Guilt makes my stomach roll as Elena bustles off. Looking past her, I try to see Ebanora in the crowd, but she's too far in the back of the room.

The sound of something falling pulls my attention to the table nearest the high table and the warriors seated along it. Tori catches my gaze first. He is seated right there at the end of the table, glaring at me and the king's hand on my shoulder. The king doesn't notice, but continues kneading my upper back in a way that feels like trouble. All of his subtle ministrations are working together to make me feel more and more relaxed. So relaxed that I do the unthinkable. I place my cheek on the king's shoulder and use his body and beard to block Tori from sight.

The king tenses beneath me, but only for a moment. "Are you tired?"

"No, my king," I whisper. And it's true. My body may be relaxed, but my mind is racing, my heart is pattering. I am a bundle of nerves.

"Shall I serve you your sweet cake?" the king prompts, but I shake my head. He picks my sticky hand up from my lap and smooths his thumb across my dirty palm. "You treasure it when it comes from your little friend, but not when it comes from your king?"

I feel like I'm being trapped, slowly cornered by a much larger predator. And I fear how he knows where I acquired my treat. Will he punish Ebanora? Was he watching her? No. I already know the answer to that. He was watching me.

I should just eat. It's an enormous offering, one I likely won't ever get again. But my stomach — irrespective of the guilt and the nerves — has been filled with more food than it ever has been before in one sitting. I can feel the bulge of my stomach below my belly button. It's strange, and inside, the pressure borders on unpleasant.

Holding my stomach, I dare a trembling whisper, "I have never eaten so much, my king. I want to, but I don't know how I could eat more without being sick."

He makes a gruff sound, his arms shifting around my body even tighter. He holds me fast against his chest while my head spins and my body fights against this strange sensation... Ease. If I let myself, it would be so easy to imagine that this was real, that he was a male I could trust, that here in his arms, Tori could never touch me. That I'd never feel hunger or cold again. That I'd be safe. The sensation is so powerful it nearly brings tears to my eyes and I sniffle.

The king suddenly grabs my jaw and tilts my face up. He glares down into my eyes, his mouth severe, and he hisses, "Have I upset you, little bird?"

I shake my head, feeling caught and very much like I will cry. "No, my king."

"Speak to me truthfully. I wish to make no mistakes with you. Some are inevitable, but where I can avoid them, I plan to." His arm on my back pulls me in tight and I do something terrifying — more terrifying than trying to make sense of what's happening.

I give myself a small gift, a luxury unlike any I could have ever fathomed this morning. I...pretend. I pretend that I'm not a thrall and that this isn't wrong and confusing, and I pretend that Tori can no longer bother me because I am safe here. I no longer dwell on the fact that I will likely, hopefully, be well compensated for whatever the king should choose to do to me tonight. I pretend that I'm not afraid of losing my virginity to such a large, virile male and pretend, for just this moment, that this is okay. I let myself feel all the warmth and contentment I've been too frightened to feel.

It'll just be this once.

Just this once.

And then never again.

So, for now, I can allow myself this gift, one I'm gifting to myself. The ability to enjoy the king's warmth and to enjoy this fullness and contentment.

I blink quickly and suck in a shaky breath and then I...smile very slightly. The king tenses, but I don't think too much about that and say, "It is only that...I am not used to feeling like this, my king."

"Like what, little bird?" He sits up straighter, forcing me to lean back to see his face. His huge arm braces my spine and his hand comes up to support the back of my head.

"Sheltered."

The king shudders visibly from his head to his toes. He emits a low growl in the back of his throat, tilts his face up towards the ceiling and whispers words under his breath too quietly for me to catch before abruptly returning to me. He swoops down, arching his back so that he can press his forehead to mine directly. I gasp. We are so close, nearly nose to nose. His eyes are closed and his lips are slack and smell like the rich spices from the wine.

He tips his mouth down and it suddenly occurs to me that he's seeking...asking...for a kiss from me. He...wants to kiss me. I don't know why that comes as such a shock —

it is, after all, the reason he wanted a female for the night — to rut. A surge of nerves pass through me and I clench my knees together tight, clench my skirts in a fist and inhale. *Pretend*. I pretend that I've done this before, many times. I don't want to displease him. But the truth is that I've never kissed a male before in my life...

I tilt my face up, hoping he'll take control and show me what to do, but the moment his dry lips alight on mine, he abruptly jerks. The king pulls back and looks over his shoulder and I sit, stewing in the butterflies that have overwhelmed me as I watch Chief Olec clap the king on the back again. The king does not look pleased and I don't miss the grunted laughter from the king's warriors seated at the table behind me. Embarrassment washes over me.

"I was just talking to Torbun here about the power females hold over us. Remarkable, isn't it? That the lesser sex could turn the heads of even kings!" Chief Olec brings his ale to his mouth and spills half of it down his chest and beard.

"You've made a fine choice, my liege," Torbun says, leaning past the chief and his wife to be seen by King Calai. "My wife has always said that with a bit of cleaning up, this young thrall would make any man a fine companion." A fine companion. Not a wife. I drop my gaze to my knees as pretending becomes a little more difficult.

"Hm," the king says and it is the only answer he gives. I don't expect him to defend me, but to be discussed like this still hurts. I may be a thrall, but I still have some pride.

"She certainly holds a draw for the boys," Rosalind says, her voice cool. I glance up and watch as, seated on Chief

Olec's other side, she cuts into a large flank of meat. She glances up at the king, gaze not landing on mine. "I'm sure you don't see many like her in Ithanuir, my liege." Her voice carries hints of a question.

One he responds to in brief. "In Ithanuir, we see all kinds, Lady Rosalind."

Rosalind gives me a look that I don't like. I look at the king's hand resting possessively across my knees. "You may need to clean her before you use her, my liege. She is unwashed."

I tense, stung.

"Is it common for you to instruct males of your village on how to occupy themselves with their females, or do you make exception for me?" Behind me, I hear a lady warrior snicker while the males buck with laughter. All his warriors, it would seem, are listening.

Rosalind gives the king a stare that frightens me, so diffident and defiant and cold. Chief Olec, seated between them, makes no move to intervene. He merely continues eating, glancing between his wife and the king as if confused by what's going on. I'm not sure how much he's had to drink, but he does not seem coherent. It is not uncommon for him.

"Apologies, my liege," she says slowly. "I meant only to inform you as she is our ward."

"A ward you keep unwashed?"

Rosalind bristles, "It is not our priority to keep all orphans and thralls washed. And she is of little utility to the village. It is a gift that we allow her to remain here at all. I hope it is not too presumptuous for me to assume that we will be compensated, as her keepers, for the time you choose to spend with her tonight. She is ours, after all, my Liege."

"I thought you just said she is of little utility? Should she not then, be free for my use?"

Rosalind is much smarter than her husband. She is, from what I've seen, the smartest person in our village. But the king, this big brute of a male, seems to so easily entrap her. She flounders in ways I have never seen before. "She will be of greater use when you have claimed her honor and shown her the ways of pleasure. Then she can tend more fruitfully to the other males who have requested her. We will have no more reason to keep them at bay anymore, my king."

"And yet, if I am increasing her value to the community by having her for the evening, I wonder why I should then be expected to compensate you for her time."

Rosalind doesn't respond. She merely purses her lips.

The king shakes his head slowly and clicks his tongue against the backs of his teeth. "You certainly do have an unusual way of doing things here in Winterbren."

And then Rosalind's voice grows dark. She snaps, "My king, this thrall is a virgin. She is not going to be able to satisfy a male of your appetite. I suggest you choose another female — or two or three — to occupy yourself with tonight and return her to the barns where she belongs."

My shame is a raw wound that Rosalind picks at with each sharp word from her tongue. I don't know what I've done to deserve her speaking of me like this. She's never spoken to me like this before, so hatefully...

I wedge my palms in between my clenched thighs. The king, meanwhile, palms my low spine, rubbing circles through my dress that may intend to provide reassurance, but do nothing to reassure me. His hand spans the full breadth of my waist. It makes me nervous when he squeezes, as if demonstrating his size compared to mine and making sure I am also aware of it.

And then he ducks his head and whispers into my ear directly, too quietly for Rosalind to hear. "Does she tell truths? Are you a virgin?"

I nod. I had already tried to tell him as much. And even if I did not want him to know, there would be no point in lying. He would find out soon enough — as soon as he tried again to kiss me — and even if he still wanted me after that, Rosalind would skin me alive for trying to lie to their honored guest.

His palm splays over my knee. He soothes his thumb over my thigh. "Shh," he says to me softly. And then to Rosalind, he says in a voice that's louder than need be, "I think you may be right, Lady Rosalind." I tense. "My little bird could use a bath before I claim her. Why don't you draw her one?"

I dare a glance up when she does not respond to the *king*. And for a moment, I fear for her, until I remember that she is the chief's wife and that affords her security. Then, I fear for myself. She is displeased and since he is the king and that affords *him* security, I do not doubt that she will turn her displeasure towards me.

"Certainly," she finally says, elongating the word. "Elena," she calls, but King Calai interrupts her.

"No, Lady Rosalind. Not Elena. *You*."

Lady Rosalind doesn't move. I feel the tension. I hear the chuckling from his warriors at the other end of the table. Lady Rosalind's lips pull together in a tight scowl and her left eye twitches. Torbun pretends to be deep in discussion with his wife on his other side. She has not looked up as Rosalind spoke. I don't dare look at Rosalind, either. I *know* that I will be punished for this severely as soon as the king sees fit to release me. The manner of my punishment, I do not as of yet know.

Quiet hangs over my head like an axe. My feet don't touch the ground and my dirty slippers start to slide off of my feet. I don't make any move to keep them on. The axe is falling.

"Rosalind, my love, did you not hear the man?" Chief Olec slurs loudly. He claps the king on the arm, making me jump. The king holds me closer. "Go on, draw a bath for the king and his pretty thrall." Chief Olec slaps his palm down towards my knee and I brace, but the king catches Chief Olec's wrist. He squeezes it and Chief Olec's blurry red eyes round. He makes a face and looks at the king with incredulity before returning his attentions back to the flagon of ale. It's empty now. He hails another while his wife begrudgingly gathers her skirts and gets up from the table.

"Are you alright?" the king whispers in my ear.

I nod, even though it's a lie. The king's hand freezes on the place where my prayer hands are wedged between my thighs. I suck in a startled breath when he pulls on my wrists to extract them, and then slips his hand into the place mine just were, in between my legs, high on my inner thighs. His fingers curl into my skin and I feel my whole body flush. I look up at his face. His mouth is relaxed, as if to spite the tension, and he gazes down at me with eyes half lidded.

I open my mouth to tell him something, to warn him about my inexperience, to beg him to apologize to Rosalind and the chief so that I may be spared a later punishment, but I don't say any of that. Instead, I gasp. His fingers crawl higher, towards the juncture of my thighs and when he pulls me tighter to his chest, higher onto his lap and grunts...I can no longer ignore the bulge between his legs. My weight settles further over the hard length pressing at my bottom from below. I feel myself swoon slightly forward.

"Rosalind spoke truths, my king. I don't know about any of this." I cling to the straps covering his chest and he bites his bottom lip.

He makes a sound, a deep coo in the back of his throat. "That you are a virgin does not displease me."

"But I may displease you, my king."

"It is not possible," he murmurs.

"Choose another."

"No." His other hand shifts up my back to apply gentle pressure at the nape of my neck. His hand fits fully around my throat. He bends down, inhaling as his nose drags up behind my ear to my hair. The smell of him, sweet bread and wine and leather, is pleasing to me in ways I'm unfamiliar with. My thighs are trembling where his hand is locked between them and I feel and unfamiliar *heat* pooling at their juncture.

"I promise you, my king, I do not know what I'm doing...in this..."

"And I promise, little bird, you need not worry about that."

His hand crawls higher up my legs. He will reach their juncture soon and I choke, afraid by the surprising pang of *pleasure* I feel. I don't understand it. "Please." I grab his forearm.

He presses our foreheads together, a new and sudden urgency in his touch. "You fear me, little bird?"

"Yes, my king."

"I understand why, and I am sorry for it. There will be time for me to reassure you," he snarls against the side of my face. "But not tonight. I cannot and I will not wait."

He proceeds with none of the gentle caution he did before, allowing me the chance to seek his mouth with my own. This time, his lips swoop in and gather mine up like a prize left out in the grass, so ripe for the taking.

He crushes his warm, dry lips to mine, angling his face so that he can devour me fully. His tongue licks the seam of my mouth and I gasp, surprised at the startling sensation. His tongue slips between my lips, past my teeth and gently strokes the roof of my mouth, my tongue — anywhere he can taste. At the same time, his hand shoves up my dress to where my thighs come together and he touches me *there* where no man has touched me before. The feeling is dangerous and scary and I feel humiliated anew at both the fact that he intends to rut me *here* and the fact that I no longer am pretending when I release a wild and needy mewl. My head falls back on my neck and I gasp for air.

"Fuck," he curses, separating our mouths as he catches me. His hand kneads my mound through my dress and all I can think to do is spread my legs for him to grant him further access. It feels...too much and not enough. I am going to cry out of need and frustration, for I do not understand this, how to make him stop or how to make him give me more of it.

He comes for my mouth again, kissing me ruthlessly at the same time that he stops his ministrations on my mons. He removes his hand and I twitch violently, panting against his mouth, my wine-laced breath mingling with his.

"Come," he grunts against my lips.

Before I understand what he means, he lifts me up in a cradle hold and I'm distantly aware of the sound of his warriors — and then everyone in the entire great hall — cheering as he carries me away to the room behind the throne where the chief and Lady Rosalind ordinarily sleep.

I'm clutching his leathers for dear life while he hugs my body high on his chest. He kisses me feverishly, cupping the back of my head. I part my lips, allowing him entry as I pretend that this is real and that he truly wants *me,* not just another receptacle for his seed as he's known to take as he passes through all of Wrath's villages. As I saw tonight, there is no shortage of females available to him.

He bites my bottom lip and a crazed energy compels me to want to match his violence. Or at least, to try. I move my lips around his upper one, nip at it with my teeth and, when he releases a strangled groan and pauses, I stick my tongue into his mouth to taste him like he tasted me.

He breaks our kiss and staggers into Chief Olec's chambers. He leans heavily on the wooden posts lining the threshold and tilts his face up again to the thatch again. My face is hot with embarrassment that leaves my body in a rush when he pants, "I thought you said you'd never been with a man before."

"I haven't, my king. I've never even kissed one before. I would not lie to you, I promise."

He shudders and whispers, "Mercy," before looking down at me with a startlingly dark expression. Like he's debating not whether, but how, he intends to kill me. "Then how is it that you feel as if you've practiced on a thousand men before with the express intent to learn how to kiss me?" He rubs his thumb roughly across my mouth, punishingly, as he takes another step. "You taste *made for me* by the gods."

A warm pressure fills my chest and it is enough to distract me as he sets me down on shaky legs and moves behind me. He pushes me forward and my hands fly out to support myself and catch a support beam in the center of the space. There is a large bed in the nook to my right, a small eating area to my left. There are two more rooms branching off of the eating nook, but I cannot see what they hold as they are covered by drapes.

I glance towards the bed, wondering if I should move towards it, when the king suddenly grabs the back of my dress and yanks hard on it. I gasp and shiver all over at the brush of cool air against my spine and realize in the jerky way he moves that he's *cutting* my dress in two. A fleeting despair at the thought of no longer having clothing is replaced when I feel his warm, heavy hand alight on the center of my back.

He makes a choking sound and for a moment, doesn't move. Doesn't say more.

"M-my king?" I nervously breathe after a moment has gone by, in which he's pushed my dress down my arms and then shoved it down over my hips so that I stand facing away from him, hands braced on the beam, naked all over with my clothing pooled at my feet. He must not be pleased with my body...I think, and flush.

His fingers skim my spine and then move back up to the nape of my neck. His hands start to trace patterns and I realize what's troubling him a moment before he says, "You've been beaten?"

I exhale, glad that is all that's concerning him. I nod.

"With what?"

"A whip."

"Made of what?"

"Wire."

His fingertips trace some of the marks. They should be fairly pale — I haven't been struck in a while — but I also haven't taken the time to look at them in a long time, either.

"I'm sorry if they offend you, my king."

He hisses and then I jump when his body suddenly comes up behind me. Right behind me. So close, his heat is pressed against me from neck to heel. He brackets my feet with his boots and I know that if he were to make a misstep in his shoes, he'd likely break my now bare toes. Everything about this feels so dangerous for me. Pretending not to be frightened takes more work as I inhale shallowly.

"You do not apologize to me, little bird. Least of all for this. You do not apologize to me even when you do something wrong." He pulls on my hair, tilting my head back until I can see his eyes looming over me. "Do you understand?"

Tears come to my eyes at the pressure, the overwhelmed way I feel. Truthfully this time, I shake my head. "No, my king."

He reaches around my body and cups my left breast. I gasp when he pinches my nipple. "It is alright." He kisses my forehead. "You will soon."

His hands move over my body, touching me everywhere, starting at my breasts and chest before moving down my stomach to the flare of my hips. As he removes his hands from my body, I hear the unmistakable sound of the clasps on his leathers being unbuckled and I shudder. I know I should offer to help him, but my hands shake too badly.

"You are," his low voice rumbles, and I worry about what he will say next. How could his assessment of my nudity be favorable when he is used to bedding highborn women? Women afforded baths every week, if not every day, those who don't bear dirt smudges on their forearms, fading bruises on their legs, filth caked beneath their fingernails because they don't do and have never done manual labor.

"*Exquisite,*" he exhales deeply, his entire chest rising and falling against my back.

His *bare* chest.

I open my mouth to thank him, but no words come out.

I see leather pieces fall to the floor. His vambraces, his chest pieces, his remaining furs. When his arms wrap around me next, I see that they are fully exposed. And when he presses his body against mine again, I can feel his beastliness outlined in every ridge of his pectorals, every hard line of his abdomen, his massive rounded shoulders, his impossibly hard, thick thighs when he finally unlaces his boots and trousers and steps out of them.

I gasp as his erection presses against my back and he moans. I shudder, shivering in earnest now. "Shh," he says in my ear. "I know you are nervous."

His assurance does nothing for me. I continue to quiver, proud of myself that I manage to remain upright at all as he rubs his length slowly along my back, bending his knees considerably to lower his erection to my buttocks and sliding the rock-hard, yet deliriously smooth appendage in between the crease.

"Have you seen a man bare before?" he says, his voice thicker than it was.

I nod. Of course I've seen men bare before down at the river. It's where the thrall's wash.

He makes a ticking sound in the back of his throat and grabs mine, offering it a squeeze. "Who?"

I can't speak and am ashamed of my reaction. Females are bedded by males all the time. This is not a Davral ritual. I am not to be flayed alive. And if I leave here injured, I can and will survive. "Just the um...the..." I can't speak, can't think, not with the way he spreads my ass cheeks apart with his hand and prods the head of his cock at my other entrance. Does he plan to...rut me *there*? I wasn't even aware that was something males *did* to females.

"I grant you leniency because I know that you are afraid, that you are a thrall, that I have done this all wrong, but when your *king* asks you a question, little bird, I expect an answer."

He is reprimanding me and I shudder as his cock withdraws and one of his fingers moves between my ass cheeks and presses at my tight, tight entrance. I suck in a hard breath as he breaches my tight opening, sparking tears in my eyes. It feels...so strange. His other hand drops from my neck between my breasts, over my belly, moving around my front to cup my mound and when he burrows his fingertips into my curls, he finds a section of very, very soft skin and so, so gently, strokes it.

I make a terrible, embarrassing sound as my skin — all of my skin — alights in sensation. My knees don't want to hold me up anymore and I all but wail, "Just other servants, my king. We bathe in the river together." My voice is hitching and unstable.

"Good girl." Abruptly he kicks my feet apart while his mouth comes down to my shoulder. He bites me hard enough to make me cry out. "I will bathe you..." He grunts between kisses strung between my shoulder blades. He's rubbing his whole body up against mine like a beast in rut, meanwhile I can scarcely catch my breath. "After."

And then his hands are everywhere — roaming across my breasts, squeezing them hard, passing over my stomach, roughly cupping my buttocks. And then I feel him working at something. His huge arm wraps beneath my stomach and he lifts my feet clear off of the floor in order to notch the head of his penis at the entrance of my vagina.

"My king," I gasp, shocked at how quickly he's accelerated things, and I brace, terrified, my fingers clutching the pole, my legs dangling uselessly beneath me. He starts to shove against my body, but I'm not able to take him. I'm a little damp, but the friction is painful as his erection drags against my lower lips, probing at my mound. It hurts and I release a desperate wail.

He surprises me when he withdraws and pants into my ear. He places my feet back on the floor and his meaty fingers delve between my folds to find my center. His other hand spans the width of my stomach and I can feel his fingertips digging into my skin as I wince again and clutch the pole, holding onto it as if it were my sanity.

His finger delves past my mound, spreading my lips wide to find the heat of my body. He slides a single finger into my core. I tense. I can feel my legs shaking and wish he would let me fall. I wish he would let me go, but I think we're past that.

His large digit swirls inside of me, pressing deep into my core, touching places that no fingers have ever reached. And then he stills with one finger inside of my body, the other now in my hair. He gives it a slight tug and I realize he wants me to look back at him.

Carefully, I open my eyes and I'm surprised to see the expression on his face. His cheeks and mouth are both blood red. "You are a virgin," he says, and chokes. "Much tighter than I expected."

I nod rapidly, surprised by his confusion — I told him this before, didn't I? And I imagine that he's bedded his fair share of virgins before. He hisses, sliding his finger further inside of me. He attempts to add another but I push up onto my tiptoes. The pressure is too much. "Please, your highness, it stings."

"Calai," he corrects me. "You will call me by my name." He kisses my temple then, in a surprise show of I don't know what, because it cannot be affection, before dropping his mouth to mine. I jerk back, though I don't mean to, but instead of rising to anger, he whispers, "The gods are testing me."

He slowly slips his fingers free of me and I sag, the wine cleared from my mind. I try to stand on my own, but the king is crowding me. He turns me to face him, pinches my chin and pushes me down. I don't understand what he wants of me until I'm already on my knees, looking up at his face past his enormous erection.

I gasp at the sight of the appendage between his legs knowing that it cannot possibly go where I think it will. His penis is stiff and pulsing, pale skin flushed an angry color. The enormous erection he boasts looks more like a weapon than the swords he wore on his belt. I wonder how many females he's raped in raids, how many whores and mistresses he keeps in Ithanuir. I imagine it would take an entire stable of females working all hours of day and night to keep that thing sated. And right now, all he has is me.

He presses the purpling head of his cock to my lips. It tastes salty. There's a slight stickiness coming from the slit. My tongue passes over it as I close my lips and he makes a choking sound in the back of his throat. I look up at him as his hand keeps working his length.

His words are choppy as he grunts, "Just one kiss."

The head is bloated and the veins are pronounced against his shaft as he passes his hand over it once, twice, and then faster. His testicles, covered in a light dusting of red hair, are clenched tight against his body. He reaches out to touch my hair and has to bend his knees significantly to be able to brush his penis over my face. I don't expect the skin to be so soft or so hot as it touches my cheek like a caress.

I don't know what I'm doing, having never kissed a mouth before, let alone *this,* but I mimic the motion he made against my own lips and lead with my tongue as I press my parted mouth to the slit along the top of his penis, kissing it like he asked.

He makes a snarling sound and I jerk back, worried I've hurt him, but his hand on my hair keeps me close. "Again. Please," he says. He *begs*.

Feeling strangely...powerful...I lick his cock from tip to base, finding that I enjoy the way he seems to struggle. He has ahold of the post in the center of the room and looks, from this angle, just as shaky as I felt when I was leaning upon it.

I lick him all the way down to his testicles and, in a daring attempt, I pass my lips over those, peppering them with kisses. He starts to pant harder, his chest heaving. "Please. Put it in your mouth. I need to feel you surrounding me."

I open my mouth as wide as I can and feed his head towards the back of my throat. The moment I close my mouth around his erection, laving the underside with my tongue, King Calai cries out. He rips his cock from between my lips and I start as ropes of murky white fluid gush from the bloated head all over my cheeks and forehead and lips.

The surprising liquid pours from my forehead into my eyes, causing me to blink rapidly before I close them altogether and I can only feel from then on as more of the liquid comes to cover my bare chest. I didn't realize it, but I'd reached up to brace myself on his thighs. My nails curl into them now while his tight, almost pained-sounding groans loosen. I can hear his heavy breath and I know that he's dropped down to crouch in some way before me when I feel a wall of heat come against my front, and then the pressure of the hand that follows after.

He drags his fingers through the fluid he's sprayed over my sternum, bringing it down and ringing it around one nipple, then the other. I arch back, surprised by how pleasurable that feels. And then I whimper audibly — *loudly* — when he replaces that finger with his mouth. The hot, sucking pressure of his mouth cleaning away the fluid he just decorated my nipples with is scandalous, but he does not stop.

He cleans one of my breasts with his mouth before moving to the other, sucking as much of my breast as he can get into his large mouth. Nerves dance across my heart, never having been handled this way before. It's rough, but the sensations... My chin tips back and I reach for him blindly, grabbing and clinging to his shoulders as my back arches and I thrust my breasts further into his mouth.

"Augh," he moans as he pulls back. I reach up to try to clear away the cream in my eyes, but he catches my wrist. "I worry I am not strong enough to pass this test," he whispers. A cloth of some kind moves over my eyelids one at a time, but he uses his finger to clear the rest from my forehead. "Open your mouth."

I open my eyes and my lips part automatically. I watch as he moves his cream-covered finger towards my mouth and feel it glide against my lips and taste the strange musky flavor on my tongue. I suck on instinct.

He hisses and withdraws his hand completely, then sweeps in and kisses me, holding my face between his enormous hands before he just as abruptly wrenches back and picks me up. In a cradle hold, he carries me to the room behind the right curtain, and I am surprised to find that it holds a very large bathtub full of steaming water that smells of rich bath salts and oils.

The king nuzzles against my temple. "I will seed you tonight. I am sorry, but I will not be able to stop myself." His voice is shaky and his words perplex me. I had thought that was what he brought me here for, but I don't question him as he takes me to the gorgeous wooden bathtub in the center of the room.

Candles are lit all around the chamber and the water is *hot* as he sets me inside of it. I jump. The temperature is heavenly, but I am unused to it and I grip the edges of the bathtub when he releases me, as if in fear of an underwater monster rising up from the black bottom of the basin and swallowing me whole.

Though I suppose the only one likely to do that tonight is him, I think to myself as he sloshes into the tub and sits heavily against the basin across from me, taking up any and all space that was left. He's holding onto the edges of the tub as well, but his eyes are honed on me like I've captured him with wicked sorcery. Like he's trying not to attack.

He stares at me. I do not know where to look. His red hair turns dark in the water as he dunks his head. Wiping his face, he gestures at me with two fingers. "Come."

There is nowhere for me to go, but when I don't move, he sits forward and grabs my left arm. He yanks me towards him, turning me around, and my back lands against his chest. Tension threads the liquid surrounding us as he slowly begins to work soap over my skin. He kneads my shoulders, my back and then picks up a soft cloth and washes my face, my arms, my stomach, my feet. He takes particular time cleaning the undersides of my fingernails with a small pick and then using a fresh cloth to clean me *there*, between my legs.

"Sit forward." He then takes time washing my hair. He uses a blunter pick to comb the knots out of all of my curls. It takes some time. "Your hair is beautiful."

My stomach clenches and I hold onto my knees, not complaining at all as he combs oil through my hair and, on the next pass of his fingers, they drag through clean. My eyes feel hot. It's been...a long time since I've been able to pull my fingers through my curls like this and the delicate way he worked...I could pretend easily that he cared.

"Thank you, my king," I whisper.

"Calai."

I only nod. I couldn't get the word out if I tried.

Finished, the king hauls me against him, draping one arm over my shoulder and using that hand to squeeze my opposite breast. I arch again on instinct and King Calai groans, "I do not know where you came from, but if I had never found you, I would have missed you." The king slips his other hand between my legs. I squeeze my knees together, but his hips scoop mine and he presses his knees between my own and spreads them to either side of the basin, leaving me fully open and exposed.

He starts to massage my core, where I am most sensitive, and I do not know whether to enjoy the sensation or retreat from it. It feels deeply vulnerable and intimate. But his hand is on my breast again, flicking my nipple and he is biting and kissing and suckling the side of my neck. My hands are gripping the edges of the bathtub, holding on for dear life as my excitement starts to build and I start to gyrate against the cock beneath my ass.

He bites my ear and I surprise myself when I turn my face to the side, my lips seeking. He is so responsive and immediately ensnares my kiss with an even more demanding kiss of his own. Meanwhile, his hand picks up speed between my legs, flicking that patch of exceedingly soft skin between my curls until I cannot bear it.

"King," I shout, afraid. My whole body is feverish. I start to thrash. "What is…"

"Shh… Do not fight this. Surrender to me."

I do not know what he means until it happens to me for the very first time. I become wild. I try to keep quiet, but it's difficult as my breathing picks up and my stomach muscles spasm. My legs squeeze the outsides of King Calai's, losing a battle I didn't know I was fighting. I'm trembling, gasping, my hips are jerking and I'm suddenly submerged in pleasure. My whole body bucks, curling up, no longer terrified but purely elated as an intense wave of pleasure adorns me and takes me away.

"That's it, Starling, come for me." He calls me by my name and yet, I'm so enrapt, so lost to the feeling of his hands on my body that I don't even notice until hours, perhaps days later.

I scream and my body spasms one final time. I jerk as the wave I've been riding finally crests, making it possible for me to access reality in a way I couldn't the moment previous. All at once, the pressure of his fingers in my curls is too much. The oversensitivity of my skin is painful. I pull away, but there's nowhere for me to go and I whimper.

"You did beautifully," King Calai says, his hand traveling lower, away from my sensitive skin that sings. He reaches my mound, spreads my lips and presses a finger inside of me, then two… The pressure is bearable in a way it wasn't before, his fingers sliding in and out of me easily, pleasantly…more than pleasantly. I start to feel the fever pitch coursing through my entire body build anew.

"K-King Calai," I moan.

"If you keep making those sounds, I will lose myself to this," he grunts in my ear as his fingers slip out of my body.

I mewl, surprised by my own disappointment at the loss and, before I can censor the lewd, unladylike words that slip from my mouth, I whisper, "I don't understand it, my king...but I don't want you to stop."

"Fuck." His big hands shove me forward until my legs are straight beneath me and my body is bent over them. I reach out and catch myself on the edge of the tub's heavy basin. The wood is warm beneath my fingers, the steam creating droplets on the wood that disperse beneath my hands. The candles billow in the wind my body makes as I am maneuvered wherever the king intends. I feel my shaky lower half held up by arms stronger than the steel that had been strapped onto his belt.

And then I feel the pressure of something much larger than his fingers at the entrance of my core once more. My mound pulses, feeling hot and slightly swollen even though he's barely touched me yet at all. I'm panting and he's grunting as he lines his erection up with my core a second time and, without warning, thrusts forward.

I gasp as he successfully breaches the barrier of my body that had been too tight, too dry for him to enter before. It helps that I'm soaking wet in a way I know has nothing to do with the bathwater. My body's natural lubricant eases his entry but still, the enormous erection that he shoves into me meets resistance. I don't feel pain, but the pressure borders on it. I feel unholy sensations zinging through my core, through my soul, and I don't know how to interpret any of them. Tears prick the backs of my eyes and my arms threaten to give out on me. I shake, but he holds me steady.

"Look at me," he says as he presses his penis inside of me another inch.

I look back, straining to see him over my shoulder. It's frightening, meeting his gaze. He is grimacing, clenching himself together very tightly. His chest, dusted in red curls, bulges and flexes with each of his movements, no matter how slight. His palm slaps my outer hip before he takes it in a rough grip.

"You're tighter than I believed possible... Tighter than anything I've ever heard stories about." He moans loud and beastly.

And I am just as loud as I respond to him in whimpers and gasps, breathy moans and deeper, more animalistic sounds. He pushes into me even more, more, the pressure so huge, the feel of his cock so damning, claiming. His erection is long, bigger than I knew a man's could be, and I worry that he hasn't entered me fully yet. He groans. I groan. His hand is on my shoulder, the other on my hip, keeping me from collapsing.

"Do you feel pain?"

I nod. The pressure has tightened as he's reached an impassable point in my body. His hand massages down my back and he slows. "I'm going to seat myself fully. You'll feel a momentary pain, but it will quickly fade."

I bite my bottom lip and nod jerkily, pretending I'm not frightened. He leans forward and pulls my lip free of my teeth. He drops over me, blanketing my back with his scar-riddled chest. He braces his hand outside of mine to hold himself up on the tub while his other hand cradles my cheek gently.

His lips feather over my cheek, finding my nose and kissing its tip before dropping down and capturing my mouth. He sucks my bottom lip between his teeth in a way I find disorienting, and it is a calculated action, I realize in the next moment when his hips jack forward and a sharp burning sensation fills me up.

I gasp and release a wild, pained mewl, but he doesn't retreat. He thrusts shallowly, his erection moving in and out of me slowly, until finally, after some time, the burning starts to fade even as the pressure remains. His hand on my face brushes away my tears before snaking around my hip. I feel him suddenly combing through the thatch of short curls guarding my sex until he finds that point just above my opening that feels so raw still from when he touched it earlier.

"You're so brave, little bird. Taking my cock so well. Being such a good girl." He grunts in my ear as his fingers pick up speed and my legs start shaking in earnest. "Have you ever experienced pleasure before, my prize?"

I shake my head and squeeze my eyes closed.

"Look at me."

I open them and meet his gaze. He's far, far too close. I can see the darkness of his eyes, feel the heat of his breath. He smells like wine and sin. I imagine that this is what fucking the god Lohr himself might feel like.

"Have you ever touched...yourself to orgasm?" he grunts on each thrust.

I shake my head. I don't even really know what he means.

His brows come together over his once broken nose. "I am your first in all things?"

I nod.

"Gods." He leans in and presses his mouth to my temple. Vaguely, through the roaring wave of conflicting pains and pleasures that assail me as his fingers start to move at a perilously fast speed and his shallow thrusts, too, move faster and faster, I hear him say, "Raya, I owe you a second sacrifice for this." He speaks to the goddess of soft things, the one males like him are not meant to worship. Males like him speak to the gods of war and mayhem, debauchery and lust and I know that it is to Lohr, that lustful god, that I offer my thanks in this moment.

My face twists. Euphoria comes for me again. I grab for him anywhere I can, wanting to batten myself down as I prepare to wade through the storm. My hand hits his wrist. I grab onto it, clutching it for dear life as a dizzying wave of *need* cuts through the rougher sensations rumbling through me.

"Calai...King Calai," I correct in my desperation. "Please..."

"Please *what*, little bird? Tell me. What do you need from me?"

A warbling sound chokes my throat and I all but scream. "Let me come for you. Please..." My head hangs in defeat. "Take me."

He roars out a battle cry and starts to slam into my body in earnest. The feeling of my body gripping his cock is salacious and wonderful, his girth filling me up like a fist. I am so wet, his penis moves through my body easily despite my inner muscles straining around him, fighting him out no longer, but welcoming him in.

One of his hands on my breast squeezes and the other between my legs flicks wildly and roughly until I fall apart in his arms. I orgasm for the second time in my entire life, for him, the waves of pleasure something I couldn't fathom getting used to.

The pressure zings through me, harder and longer than it did the last time. I scream — *scream* — the sound more animal than woman. I'm vaguely aware of a slighter, softer pain as my core clenches and releases in spasms around his length without me meaning for it too. I worry he doesn't enjoy it when he groans and curses even louder. He leans over me and bites down onto my shoulder. I buckle and before I can regain strength enough to support my own weight, his thrusts lose their rhythm and he collapses.

We crash into the bath, water sloshing over its smooth edge. He lands on his knees with me still on top of him, my body still impaled on his erection. One of his hands clutches my hip bruisingly, the other arm still lining the front of my body, that hand wrapped around my throat.

He makes a sound twice as loud as I did and a thousand times more animalistic as his body goes tight and hard beneath me. "*Mercy*," he says, roaring the word up into the sky, "Teffina, thank you for this." He calls out to the goddess of pleasure and love, another goddess whose name I am surprised to hear leave his lips.

His thrusts are hard and powerful, the seat of my behind crushed against his lap as he hammers into me three, two…one final time. His hands are clenched and when I hazard a glance over my shoulder, it's to see that his eyes have rolled back. He looks like a male possessed.

He releases one final primal cry before crushing me to his body like he wants to keep me so close I absorb into his skin. His fingers are like crude, blunted claws where they clutch me, and I know they'll leave bruises visible tomorrow…cruel reminders that will linger days after he's gone, taking with him all of his power, all of this magic.

"Lohr take me," he whispers again as he pulls me tight into his chest. His hips jerk upwards, my whole body jolting with each spasm. This goes on for some time, the king holding me tighter and tighter until I can hardly breathe.

And I don't mind.

Tears press against my eyelids, demanding sacrifice. "Thank you," I say to no one, to everything. I've never felt like this before and it's a terrible feeling. This fear that leaves me shaking. This hope that will leave me crushed. This brief lapse in time where the gods have decided to show me what it is like to truly be wanted is too much.

The king's beard is rough against my cheek. "You are too exquisite for this world." His voice is a dark threat and an utter contrast to his words. His hand finds my breast and fondles it absently. His other hand cups my jaw, his thumb feathering gently over my lips.

"You please me so well, little bird." His voice is the rumble of a storm. "I've scant desire to leave your warmth." His hand hooks around my body and feels between my legs. I stiffen. "I don't intend to."

He begins massaging the back of my neck, his thumbs hard and powerful against my nape. It feels so good. So *fucking* good. I moan audibly.

"Gods," he groans. "The sounds you make." His hand tightens around my throat and his fingers between my legs start to move faster. "You make even the most inexperienced male believe himself a god to women." He chuckles against my cheek. "If I didn't have your virginity smeared across my cock right now, I'd have guessed you very experienced in this."

I shiver.

He *bites* my cheek, nipping at my skin hard enough to worry he truly does intend to devour me. And then he lifts his hand from my abused mound, where he's feeling along the seam where his cock disappears inside of my body. "You're bleeding a little, my love." I tense at the term of affection, feeling slightly *betrayed* by it. He shouldn't call me such things. And I must remind myself that, despite what he says to me, *he* is the experienced one and he knows what to say to please. "Do you need a break?"

He rubs his fingers together and I see the clear liquid smeared over the whorls of his fingertips is, indeed, tinted pink. "Yes, Your Highness." I nod, needing a break more from his words than from the movement of his body.

His fingertips slow over my sex again and his other hand releases my throat. "Give me a moment," he says in a murmur, almost as if he were speaking to himself. "Eghh," he moans, making a deep, guttural sound in the back of his throat as he slowly lifts my body off of his lap.

I wince as his length leaves my heat, leaving behnd a gaping hole inside of me. I mewl. "Shh," he whispers and gathers me to his chest. I'm grateful for it, for my own legs provide all the support of splinters.

"Come to me, little bird." He leans against the back of the tub and pulls me against his chest, my back to his front. The water comes up to cover my breasts and I sink into its warmth, and the greater warmth of the male behind me. I try not to focus entirely on the feeling of his legs parted around my lower back and the brush of his softening cock and the hair that shrouds it pressing against me, and press against me it does. He's still...thrusting...and it's affecting my thoughts.

"Relax. You've done so well, taking me like you have." He pulls my hair over my shoulder and coaxes me into looking up at him. He's so close.

His lids are hooded and he smiles at me and it's a frightening thing only because it feels so intimate. I can imagine that this is not a male who smiles often. I don't know what I've done to deserve him sharing one such smile with me.

I blush. My face burns and he chuckles, the sound causing his entire chest to vibrate, me along with it. "You are..." He looks me over, eyes on my forehead, hairline, nose, lips... He rubs his face roughly and laughs and I flinch. The sound is shocking because it's so loud, so unabashed and so pleasant. I'm embarrassed. And I'm sore. I can feel the tingling in my lower half telling me that I will see bruises when I arrive before a mirror.

"You need not cower from me. I will not hurt you." He seems so sincere but I don't understand why. I am nothing more than a whore he's paid for for the night. Maybe, a whore he won't even pay at all.

I bite my lips between my teeth as his hands start to work over my back, massaging and kneading. I can smell soap, pine and bergamot, decadent flavors, but I still struggle to relax as his fingers work up the nape of my neck and into my hair. He adds more of the same oils he did before, combing them through my curls with his fingers.

"You have thick hair. I'll have to ask the bonesmith to fashion a suitable comb that I can use." That he can use? I wonder what he means though I don't ask. I remain tense, uncertain if I should allow myself to do as he says and relax against him, or if I should prepare to be dismissed. I do not know this male. His intentions have, thus far, been confounding and I do not trust him.

"Honey and sweet butter," he breathes against the shell of my ear. He hugs me to him in a way that makes me feel...warm. A warmth that has nothing to do with the temperature of the water. I don't think anyone in my whole life has ever hugged me like this before. "I am a male reborn."

We lie there for a while, simply basking in the water. The steam rises up like a shield against the cold that threatens to crawl in through the wooden walls as night comes for us all. He's so calm, lazily stroking his hands up and down my arms. It's hard not to feel like I should be falling asleep...but I am far from it.

"Can you stand?" he whispers in my ear, voice coaxing and gentle.

I nod, though I know that's only a partial truth and get to my feet at his prodding. My legs are shaky and weak, but I don't dare tell him as much. Instead, when he says, "Turn," I do as he commands until I'm standing knee-high in the water, my sex at his eye level.

I flinch when I see the blade. Short but gleaming, it looks sharp and I'm afraid when he brings it between my legs. "Spread your legs. I'm going to remove some of the hair. I intend to feast for hours and when I do, I don't intend to get your curls stuck between my teeth."

His words are shocking and I don't know what they mean. It all sounds alarming and scary, but he simply chuckles and drags his blade in easy strokes over my hair, not removing it, but trimming it short. He's a meticulous male and I cannot help but spare several glances down at his face as he works.

He's biting on the inside of his cheek and his gaze doesn't stray from his task. He has a small cloth in one hand pressed beneath his area of concentration and uses it to catch all the small hairs. When he's finished to his satisfaction, he places the blade and folded cloth outside of the bath, leans back and bites his bottom lip hard enough for the colors to change beneath his skin.

"You're swollen here..." His thumbs return to prod my mound, parting it, and I hiss at the shock of air against my sex. "Are you in pain?"

I shake my head, but I hesitate. I know he sees. "I am a restrained male," he says, though the expression on my face must convey what I'm thinking because he chuckles lightly, leans in close and licks a dangerous line through my folds. I buck, caught off guard by the sensation, and barely hear him as he whispers, "But not with you."

He licks me again, this time cupping my entire sex with his mouth and lips, his tongue laving my swollen, bruised, *wanting* flesh. I gasp, my hands fisting again and again as I struggle to remain upright. I cannot do this. He asks for too much. I release a warbling cry and his head drops back. "I will need to feed this madness. Lohr will not be sated by what I have taken from you so far."

Panic zings through me as he opens his eyes and looks up at me from between my legs. Prostrated like this beneath me, it is a frightening scene to behold. I can see the madness the king speaks of shining in his black gaze. He presses his mouth directly to the bundle of nerves he touched so vigorously earlier and I waver.

"Are you ready yet, to take me again?"

I can barely understand him over the sudden surge of blood through my temples and the whooshing in my ears. My mind knows that my body is weak, perhaps, too weak to take any more. But my body knows only the pleasure he's shown me thus far.

I am only here for the night. The one night. I exhale. *I will never be here again.*

My hands fall nervously to his shoulders. To touch him without his express command could see me badly punished. But...I do it anyways, finding a small stone of bravery amidst the rubble of my virginity and clinging to it. And I am rewarded.

He leans in closer until I can only see his face by staring directly through the valley of my breasts...and it has softened. His eyes are so bright, so clear. I'd never have been able to guess that he'd had any ale or wine at all this evening and for a moment, my mind thinks of my own leader here in Winterbren. I don't think I've ever seen Chief Olec's eyes so clear or aware as this.

The urge to touch the king's hair is so strong in me, I flex my fingers and relinquish the little honor I have left, if there is even any at all. I whisper, "My king, may I touch you?"

In a blink, his eyes round and his lips go slack before he returns to me with a grunt, "Freely."

Surprised by his answer, and that he isn't upset with how forward I am, I take an unfathomable liberty and gently brush my king's red hair away from his forehead. His eyes flutter and he leans into my touch. The strands of his hair are surprisingly thick. His hair is rough and knotted around the braids. Several of them are woven throughout the loose strands, and now they're all tangled together. I used to do my mother's hair, and she would do mine, but I've never touched a man's hair before. It's an intimacy I never even realized existed.

Growing slightly more bold when he closes his eyes, I stroke my hand through his long locks, all the way down the back of his neck. He tips his forehead forward against the soft skin between my hips, moaning low in the back of his throat. And when I repeat the motion again, he presses his mouth against my sex.

His tongue peeks between his parted lips and flattens against my swollen nub. I shudder and whimper, gripping his hair now instead of stroking it, needing the support. He says nothing, but licks me again, the rumble in his chest wrapping itself around my knees as I waver. His mouth opens wider. His tongue draws slow circles around my soft, battered skin and then he lifts his hands and spreads my mound away from my lips, baring me entirely to his hungry gaze. He plants sweet kisses on my lower lips, my mound, over my sensitive skin that beats with its own pulse.

I wobble on my feet, but his hand presses against my lower back and holds me up against his face as two fingers of his other hand slip between my thighs, gently stroking the tender skin. I didn't realize how raw my inner thighs were before, but I can feel now all the places his rough leg hair and skin abraded mine. It hurts a little, but his hand feels so nice. And then...

I gasp as he slips his fingers inside my body, one, maybe two... My head falls back. His tongue doesn't increase in speed, but instead, continues to lazily taste every inch of my sex until...until...

His fingers hook in my body and he presses against a place in my core that simultaneously makes my legs tremble. A few moments more, and I'm done. I orgasm standing upright, the pressure of trying not to fall almost painful against the sudden way my head spins. The fire between my legs burns and sizzles while I ride a wave I hope never crests. I gasp, moan, shout to my king for mercy. And when I come back to reality, it's to see him looking up at me, watching me as if hypnotized.

His fingers leave my body and his hands come to my hips. I realize only then that my hands are both tangled in his hair pulling it hard. "S-sorrry, my king," I say, releasing my hold.

He doesn't seem to have heard me. He seems hardly present as he rises to his feet and lifts me up. "Here, doveling." He sets me down outside of the tub and picks up a towel hanging on the post in the room.

"Thank y…" I start to say, reaching for the towel, but the king wraps it around me and dries me himself. He takes particular care when squeezing out my hair before roughly rubbing the towel over his. "Shall I…" I try again, reaching for the towel to help him dry the rest of his body, but he doesn't hear me again.

Instead, he steps a foot directly between my legs, knocking me off balance. When I fall, he catches me, lifts me up and carries me to the room with the bed. He tosses me onto the pillows and begins to prowl up my body, moving my splayed legs apart until they are so wide, he can fit his immense shoulders between them.

Lying on his stomach, he presses a kiss on my lower abdomen. "How many males have brought you pleasure like this?" I know he speaks of his mouth on my mound and I feel heat ravage me thoroughly.

"N-none, my king," I whisper.

"And none ever will." I don't know why he'd say words so cruel to me when I am already at his mercy. "When you think of pleasure from now on, I am all that you will see. My body, my cock, my seed. I plan to empty inside of you several more times before the night is through, if you can take me?"

He's asking me? I don't quite understand, but remember, *only one night. One night is all I get.* I nod. "Yes, my king."

"Calai," he corrects.

I don't respond. He closes his eyes and nuzzles his nose into my stomach. "I want your virginity in all ways tonight, little bird. I have had your mouth and your pussy. I will take your asshole next, but I will be as gentle as I'm able."

His words rile me, as salacious as they are, and I feel a clenching in my lower abdomen, muscles working I did not know existed before. I gasp high and breathy and lock my hands on his shoulders as he comes to cover me and begins kissing me in earnest once more. I notice that he did not ask me when making his last request — no, proclamation.

I am delirious with pleasure and panicked as his body rubs over mine. His cock is hard again and slides easily inside.

"I can feel your sex clench around my cock," he says in between kisses up and down either side of my neck. "You may not be able to walk tomorrow, but you will not need to. I will ravage you tonight, but I will not leave you to ruin." His words are shaky — a warning for me or a reminder for him, I am not certain which.

Then he picks up the pace, his cock hot and hard as it slots into my body cleanly, my inner muscles shoved roughly aside to accommodate his massive girth.

The juncture of my thighs is sore and angry as he shifts his hips, picking up speed as he pounds up and into me. From this angle, looking up at him in the darkness of the candle-lit room, I watch as his face darkens to a deep red hue and the vein jumps over his forehead. His neck bulges and his burly chest flushes and I bounce beneath his cock, my front rubbing madly over the red hairs layered atop his muscled body. The friction against my lower half is so much...it's too much...

"Are you coming?" he says, brows drawn.

Our eyes are locked and my mouth is open, but I don't answer. I just nod and mewl desperately as another pleasure sensation roars over me and I lose myself to it. "Fucking hell," he grunts, turning to steel. He jerkily slams his hips into mine, his balls slapping the underside of my body. He buckles a little as his head drops into the curve of my neck and he roars so loud it makes my ears ring.

I feel a surprising surge of wetness between us and afterwards, his body softens. He kisses me everywhere, lips slow at first before they pick up speed. He kisses and kisses me and my slow lips merely accept the offering, too drugged to keep up. "Now for your other hole," he says, and I don't know what he means until he slips his cock out of my vagina, leaving his juices to leak lower between my ass cheeks.

He maneuvers his hand between us and my whole body startles when I feel the sudden press of one of his large fingertips against my rear hole. "This..." I start.

"Shh," the king says, sounding almost angry. "I won't rut you fully, you're too tight. But I will seed you here." His gaze flashes to my lips. "And maybe your mouth one more time."

His finger pushes inside of me all the way and I flush with pain. I cry out. The king captures my cry with his mouth. "You're pleasing your king so well."

I gasp as he forces me to meet his gaze. "That's it," he whispers. "Tell me who's inside of you right now."

Tears wet my eyes. I don't understand how I can feel so brutalized and so treasured all at once. His finger in my...where I never ever would have thought I'd be penetrated...feels larger than his cock did in my vagina when he took my virginity. And now he's come for the rest. "M-my king..."

"No." His finger starts to move inside of me, the lubrication of his seed the only thing making this possible at all. "Answer incorrectly again and I'll add a second finger."

"King Calai," I whisper in a panic.

He shakes his head and the pressure in my bottom increases two-fold when he stretches my ass hole with the addition of another digit. "Shh, little bird. Relax and it will be less painful." He brushes my hair back from my face. "I am sorry for this, but I need to claim all of you tonight. I will be easier on you tomorrow, should the gods allow it.

But tonight, my need is too strong. Tell me who is inside of you and I will help you come."

He sits back onto his heels suddenly and his other hand starts to gently rub the place on my body that feels like lightning. Swollen and prominent now, my spine arches the moment he touches it. And then the brute tortures me by removing that hand and sliding the fingers in my rear end all the way inside of my body up to his palm.

Burning fullness fills me and I wail, "Calai! Calai... Calai, you're inside of me."

"Yes, I am, my love." He removes his hands from my rear hole all at once, climbs over me once more and plunges his hot, hard length easily inside of my vagina. "You take me so easily now," he grunts on his next thrust. "Just a wet hole for my pleasure." His words are unkind, so why, then, does a fist in my chest clench? I feel my hips tilt up to meet his next thrust as his mouth comes down onto my own.

I kiss him back until he wrenches away from my lips and hisses, "My little virgin whore. So well used now. A bed for my cock and receptacle for my seed and mine alone. I will lie in bed with you every night and seed you a thousand times over until your belly is full with my heirs." Heirs, he says, not bastards.

My jaw starts to tremble. He grabs it. His touch may border on severe, yet is nowhere near as cruel as his hollow words are as he makes me promises that he has no right to make. He cannot simply claim a wife by choosing her from a crowd and fucking her. There are permissions to be obtained, doweries to be paid, ceremonies to be performed, sacrifices to be made. He offered to take me for the night and keep me for the night alone. When this is all over, I may very well be pregnant with his bastard and he will be gone, to begin this cycle anew in the next village he comes across.

That sense of betrayal washes over me again and for the first time tonight, I'm able to ignore the voice in my mind freeing up my insecurities and enabling me to enjoy this. *It's only one night*, I think bitterly and I turn from him, moving my face away when he tries to kiss me again.

His touch turns rougher. He grabs me beneath the jaw and forces me to look up into his face. "You're mine." He sounds upset. Angry even. *Mad*. "Your cries are mine, your breasts are mine, your whimpers are mine, your hot cunt is mine, your ass is mine, your future sons and daughters are mine, your skin, your hair, your hopes, your fears, your wants…desires…it's all *mine*. You are mine, little bird." His thrusts are uneven, but that doesn't matter. He's rutting into me fast, at a pace my quivering thighs could never hope to match. His fingers dig into the soft flesh of my ass and I cannot…hold on…

"Every part of you is mine," he whispers, voice softening as he pecks at my lips while I utter little whimpers. "And I am yours. Calai belongs to you, Starling." He savages me and I am ashamed to be consumed by it, because the pleasure has battened me down like rope to my wrists and ankles and I cannot move except to scream and lift my hips, arch my back and release for him with tears in my eyes and wounds on my heart.

Distantly, I hear him continue to speak. "You come for me like the gods designed it so because they did. Lohr and

Raya working hand in hand. I'd have combed all of Wrath in search of you if I knew you existed. My perfect…little…" And then he says one word, one treacherous impossible word, and it skewers me like a dagger in the night. "*Wife.*"

My orgasm crests at the feeling of him leaving my heat and suddenly he's lower, fingers lubricating my ass with my slick before the pressure increases a hundred-fold. His erection pushes into my body, into my impossibly tight rear end. He grunts above me, throaty and loud. "Augh! You are too tight, little one. Fuck…"

"It…hurts…" I try to say, but my voice is starched and inaudible.

He pushes deeper, the head of his penis fully inside of me, but little more than that. He can't come in more. He'll split me in half.

Fortunately, he holds where he is, hips retreating on each thrust, but not edging inside of me any more than that. He holds himself up on his arms, his ribbed abdomen clenching and rippling and dripping with sweat. His forearms bracket my head and his face twists. "Ach, little bird. Would that I were sorry for this, I could stop now. But I am not…"

His hips are rocking slowly and his face is twisting in passion. He closes his eyes and presses our foreheads together. I can smell the scent of my sex on his skin. I whimper and he groans, "I'm about to release. Tell me again, tell me who owns you."

"Calai," I whisper.

"Yessss," he moans. His body stiffens and he arches up and his shoulders bunch by his ears and the strangest sensation fills my ass hole as his erection enters into me with another little shove and the bright burst of his semen spurts into me in a blasphemous, erotic way.

I don't like it, but cannot help crave it. I want to do more for him, anything he wants, knowing that it's *my* body driving him to such destruction. But I also know, and remind myself, that this is only just this once. His words are lies, because there is no such thing as forever. There is not even tomorrow for us.

He moans and as he comes, he kisses me all over my face, rubs my body, massages my breasts. I cannot know how much time has passed. All I can do is hang on for dear life as the surge of heat pulls through my body and the king roars loud enough I'm sure they can all hear him throughout the hall — if not the entire village.

He's panting by the time he drops onto me, slightly to the side, just enough so that I can breathe. My chest is heaving even though I was still by comparison to the heavy labor he just performed, the war he waged over my flesh.

"I have taken you everywhere, little bird," he moans, his cock sliding out of my ass in a way that makes me clench. I lie there in the bed, his seed decorating my body like blood on a battlefield. I am utterly spent, my lower lip trembling from exhaustion and from the mental anguish brought on by his words.

"Gods, I cannot believe I waited for so long." He tilts his head towards me in the bed. We lie on our backs side by side. I ache all over. My heart is beating so hard. "It was worth the wait." His eyes crinkle at the corners when they meet mine. "You are sensational. An exquisite being. To have had your virginity in every way it counts is the greatest honor."

His chest moves like a wave with each of his labored breaths. I feel myself tearing up. I don't know what to say. "Thank you, your highness."

He flinches and then his brows crease. He reaches for my face and it is my turn to flinch. He growls and suddenly, he's rolling closer to me. He presses his lips to my forehead and then each of my cheeks, the tip of my nose, and finally, my swollen lips.

He pulls blankets and furs up over me, but he himself slides from the bed. He's angry again, brows drawn, and presses on my chest when I try to sit. "Sleep. You need it. I will return with water and wine, some food, too. Are you hungry?" I... I don't know what to say. I thought he was upset. "You must replenish yourself. I will return shortly, my princess. Don't leave the bed unless it's to use the bathroom. And don't wash up. I like the sight of my seed spilling out of you."

He brushes his thumb over my bottom lip and I watch him walk out of the room, bare-assed. I hear the whooping and hooting from the great room as he enters it and I frown, unsure of what it all means.

I try to puzzle through what he said to me at so many different points in the night, try to make sense of how I'm feeling, but it's all too much and the moment I close my eyes, I fall asleep to a single thought.

He called me princess, not queen.

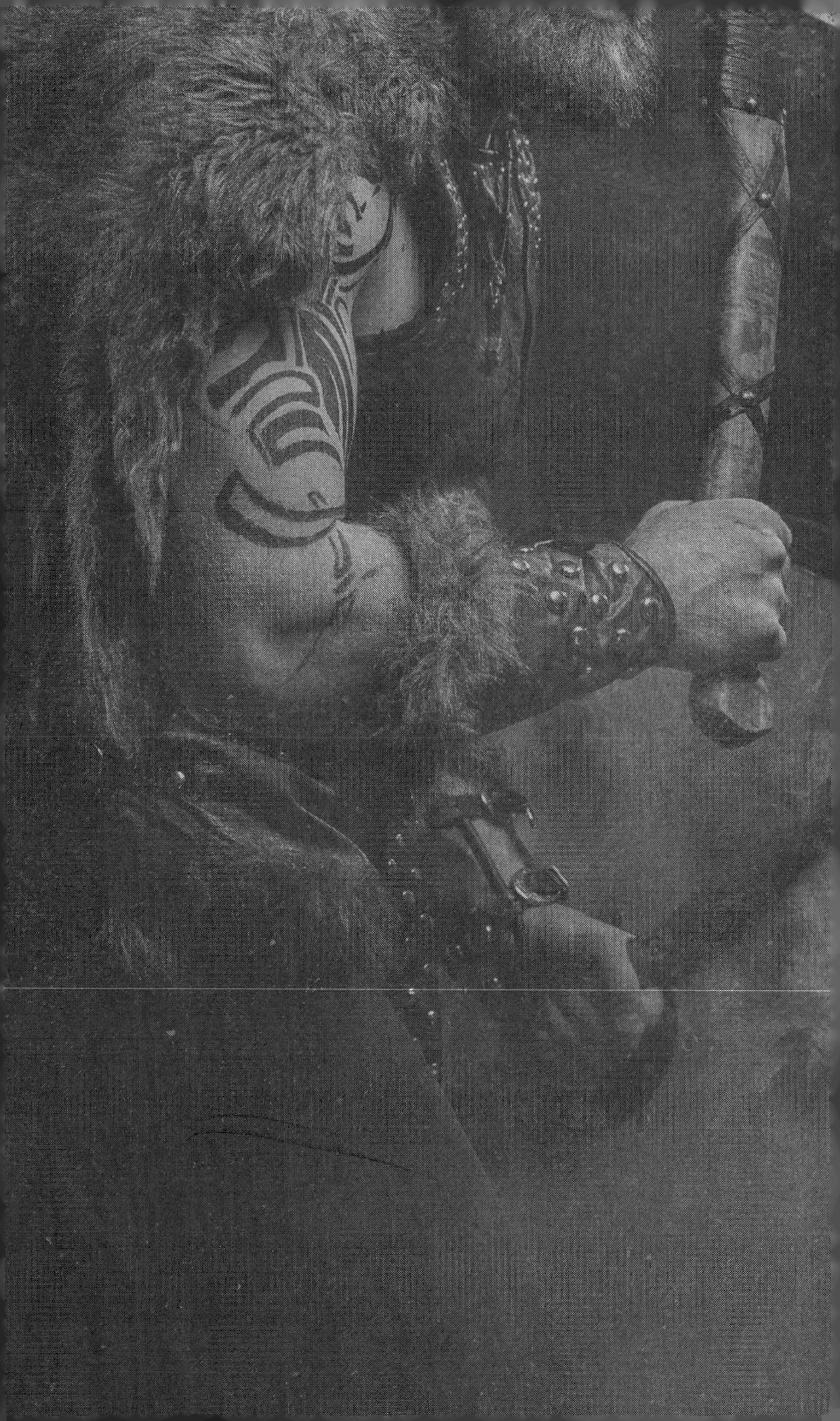

The Virgin
CALAI

"The gods are merciful," I roar, my arms stretched over my head in triumph as I reenter Winterbren's hall. The hall has been cleared of most people, three of the tables already cleared and packed away to make space for the thralls laying rushes out. A bonfire has been newly lit in the center of the space and my warriors sit around it stoking the flames. "And the gods are merciless…"

A few lingering souls sit scattered at the remaining two tables, though I note with displeasure that Olec is still among them. He sits with his man, Torbun, though their wives are absent, and Olec is half asleep, slumped over a table while Torbun laughs riotously at something he or some other schmuck has said. He hails me when I appear, cheering with the others, but I ignore him and move towards my warriors at the fire.

"You there," I call to the nearest thrall. "Ale, wine, a platter for my female and me." The female looks at me with enormous eyes before nodding once and scurrying off.

I slump onto the floor while my warriors laugh at me and shake their heads. "Where is Puhyo?" I ask Daneera, snatching her ale from her fist on its way to her mouth.

She snorts. "Making himself at home with a female in the stables."

The other men snigger at that. "You've lost several good men and women this evening."

I glance around — there is only one other female in my party besides Daneera — and laugh, "Hilde has found herself a companion as well, then?"

Another chorus of cheers go around. My thirty gathered are twenty now, with those who've sought lush pastures elsewhere for the night. I mind not, so long as the majority of my warriors remain together to defend against any who might think to ambush us. And I need the additional guard tonight.

I drain Daneera's ale and toss the goblet aside, leaning back fully onto one elbow and letting my cock flop against my inner thigh. "I do not know how you men get anything done, and if it is half so pleasurable for a female, how you lot get anything done, either."

More sniggering. Fuzier shouts at me from a few places away, "So does our sweet young queen know she's taken her king's virginity yet?"

I grin, feeling a surprising warmth in my cheeks. Am I blushing? "She does not need to know. I'm certain my ministrations have frightened her enough without her knowing she's the only female I've ever claimed."

"It did not sound like she was disappointed," Daneera laughs. The other males laugh with her. "Her screams could be heard to Ithanuir."

My smile nearly splits my skull, it is so large. "The sounds she makes. Gods, the sounds... Lohr did not tell me it would be like this."

The thrall has returned, quicker than I suspected she would, with a platter piled high with foods from the feast and a full flagon of ale, a full pitcher of wine. I thank her and bid one of my men to pay her with coin — there will be no more of this thrall business here or anywhere in Wrath. I abhor how my wife has been treated in the days I've known her and how I expect she was treated her entire life. The surprise on the thrall's face when he hands her a silver makes my heart clench. Tears come to her eyes. She looks at me, looks at him and stutters, "Th-th..."

"No thanks needed, young one. Enjoy your rest this eve," I say and she scuttles off while my warriors laugh once more.

"Can it be? Is the bone king no more?" Daneera crows, her pale face alight with color.

"King of bones? Perhaps king of lambs," Fuzier adds.

"He's soft as a peach," Dolar says and the males devolve after that as I lumber onto my knees, steeling myself for the shock of seeing her in bed again and trying to will my cock into submission so I don't rut her. The last time was too much for her, I know that — knew that — but I was a virgin bastard and lacked the restraint. I will do better going forward. I hope. I pray.

"You're damn right I am. You'll find me next on the battlefield, armed not with an axe, but with flowers," I grunt.

My warriors are laughing in earnest now and I grin around at all of them, rise to stand with my lady's tray in hand and arch to stretch out my back. My cock, only half erect now, hangs heavy between my legs. Hektor points at it. "She really was a virgin then."

I glance down and grin broadly, but then my smile wavers. There is a streak of blood on my cock. Pride hammers in my chest, along with an unfamiliar concern. "Should I have Hilde look at her?"

"Ah, that's normal, my Lord." Hektor is young, yet still more experienced than I am with fucking, particularly in that he fucks both males and females. "A little thing like her would have bled naturally, opening her legs for that monstrous snake you're wielding."

I nod, strangely reassured by the much younger warrior.

And then Fuzier, a male my age with light brown skin and dark hair streaked with grey, says in that same chipper voice, "And is she pleased to know that she'll be coming with us after the games? Back to Ithanuir, that is."

"How could she not be?" Daneera says. "Have you seen the way they treat their thralls around here? Disgraceful. It is a shock Raya has not yet struck down this foul place." She speaks loud enough I know that the table full of Winterbren's so-called warriors can hear her. In any other city or village, I might reprimand her disrespect. But not here. Now, I do not even look up.

But I do frown. "Of course. I told her many times what she means to me, to you, to us all."

But my warriors don't laugh. Instead, they exchange glances that seem to speak a tongue I do not. "Speak, the lot of you. I may be the king of flowers for her, but for you all, I will be the king of flayed corpses if you don't open your mouths."

Ale and wine are running freely through the group. Hektor, a dark-skinned waif of a man who doesn't look like a warrior at all, yet ranks among my most lethal, drags his wrist across his burgundy mouth. "You mean to say, my lord, that she *does* know that she will become queen? That she does know you intend to wed her?"

"Yes. I was clear."

"You are a lucky male then." Fuzier sits up and hands me the pitcher and the ale flagon.

I take both in one hand, brow furrowed. "How do you mean?"

Fuzier scoffs. "My wife would take my stones in the night if I had her before making her an oath before Ghabari."

"Many males take their wives in raids," Daneera insists.

"This isn't a raid," Hektor responds, and he's right. Unease stirs in my belly. "But I'm certain she'll go easy on our virgin king." He grins, but the doubt has already been sowed. I kick him in the thigh and he buckles around the blow, laughing as wine dribbles down his chin. "I mean no disrespect, my liege."

I turn to Fuzier. "You think she will be displeased?"

Fuzier actually looks thoughtful, his eyes growing distant as he stares in the direction of my chambers. "Did you inform her she would be your queen or did you ask her?" He tugs at his wine-stained bottom lip.

My skin prickles. Despite the heat of the fire, I can feel the chill of the drafty hall in ways I could not before. I shudder and glance over my shoulder, the pull to return to her side and ensure that she is pleased with me strong.

Fuzier continues when I remain quiet. "She is likely not a female who's been given many choices in life." He shrugs as if he has not obliterated the coherency of my thoughts.

"And you are *certain* that she's aware of her new status?" Daneera adds. "If you're not certain, there is always time then to change your approach and ask."

I rub my bearded chin, feeling the wetness of her slick still coating it in parts. And loving it. "Perhaps, I will ask."

"Good. She won't say no. You are king, after all, and you certainly seem to know how to please a female if her cries of pleasure were any indication."

"Anyone would be pleased by a sword like that," Hektor barks, pointing at my groin, and my warriors devolve again into laughter.

My smile returning in part, along with a sprig of hope that sprouts in my chest, I take a step away from the group, giving young Hektor another swift kick.

"When will you inform the chief you'll be taking his thrall?" another of my men calls.

"Not anytime soon," I mutter, not loud enough for the chief and his men to hear, though I return to tell my warriors, "I have plans for the chief and his wife, but I need more time to ruminate on them."

A low, excited murmur whispers among my warriors. They know of my plans and I can see the delight of bloodlust shimmering in many of their gazes.

"She won't say no, my king," Daneera calls at my back as I turn from the group and round the ornate throne raised on the dais. "You are the bone king, after all."

I do not respond to her as I return to the room to find my queen asleep on her back. Her body is so beautifully rouged, brown skin glistening with the product of her exertion. She sleeps soundly, the slow rise and fall of her chest stirring emotions deep within me, emotions I haven't felt for some time. I think of my mother, strong woman that she was, and wonder what she would think of this female here now.

I smile, knowing that she would like her. My father may have been king once, but it was my mother from whom I inherited my fierceness. It was she who protected me and provided for us after my uncle took the throne. She hid us away in a remote village of Wrath, not entirely unlike this one, until I was strong enough to return to Ithanuir. She fought at my side, even, when I took my uncle's life and earned my name.

This female is very different from my mother, not just in terms of appearance. Delicate, where my mother is a strong, robust woman, yet no less a warrior. I know my mother will respect that. However, I wonder now over my warriors' words. Have I gone about this all wrong?

I sit on the edge of the bed and place my covered tray and alcohols on the table, ignoring them for now in favor of stroking my fingers over her hair. She tips her face towards my touch in her sleep.

I reflect on our past exchanges, on the words I've said to her, and I know in my chest that what I told my warriors was untrue.

Even though it seemed so clear to me, I never once outlined her new role within Wrath. I never told her expressly that I planned to wed her in Ghabari's temple in Ithanuir before all of my people — our people, now. I simply took her and showered her with praise she deserved for the higher plane she took me to this night. I called her mine. I assumed she would understand that I do not make trite statements. I do not offer false hope.

But she does not know me. She knows her drunken lord, whose word is as shallow as a puddle after a light rain. She will not believe my words easily. I will need to show her and yet, I only have three days.

If I offered her a choice, would she come with me? Or would she choose to stay? And even if she said yes, would she agree to the offer of marriage from her king? Or from Calai?

A small prick fills my chest with a terrible pain. I will offer this female a choice, perhaps the first she's been given in her life, but…what will I do if she says denies me? My eye twitches along with my swordhand. I know the answer to that question. If she says no, I will take her anyway like a warrior in a raid. She is mine. It is up to me now to ensure she understands. To ensure she feels the same.

I slide beneath the furs I have layered atop the bed and wrap my limbs around her, trapping her to me beneath the sheets as I plan to trap her to me for the rest of my days. Gods forgive me.

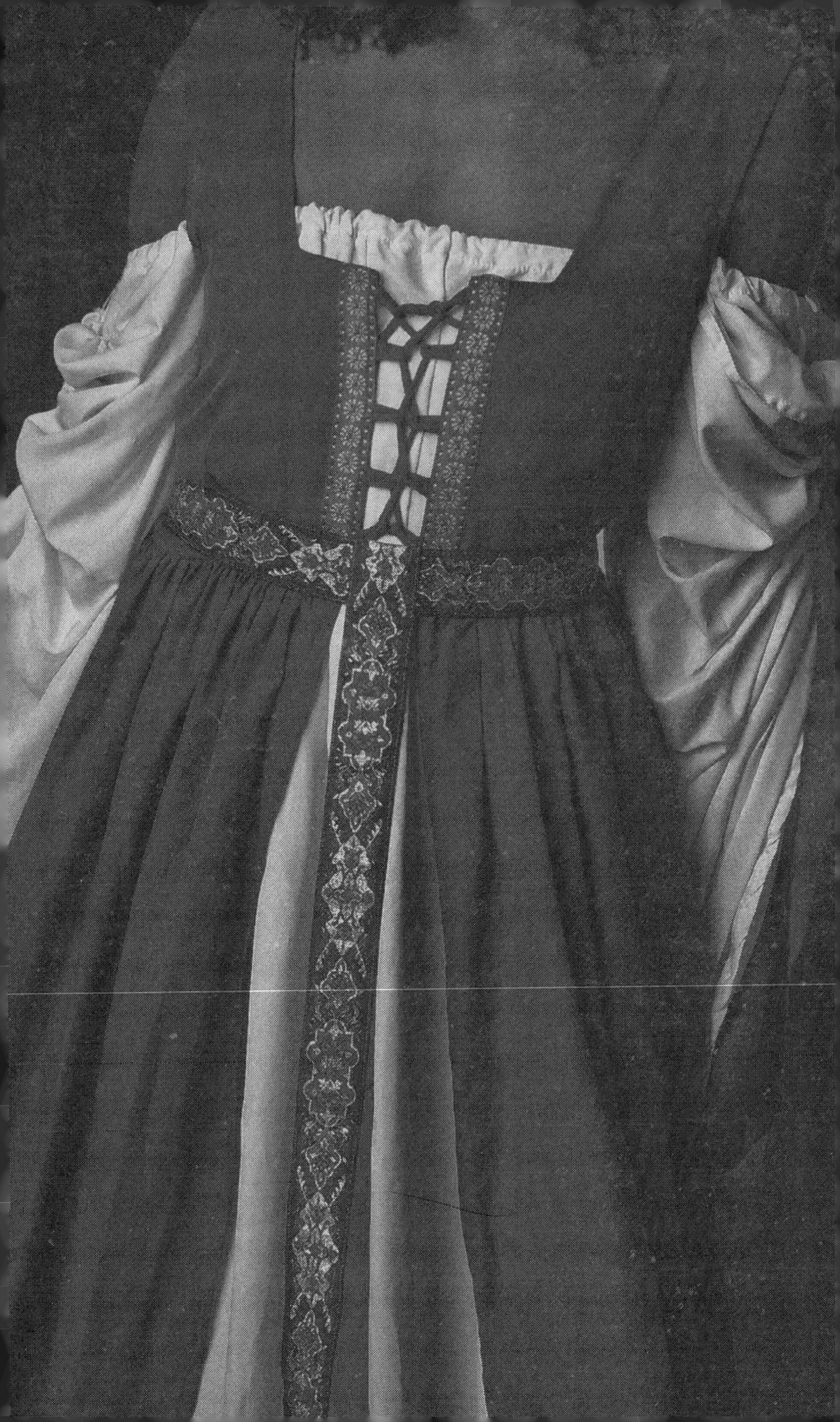

The Coin Master

STARLING

"Psst...psst!" A light tapping on my outstretched fingertips is what causes my eyes to finally open. I see a blurry outline and I don't understand where I am or what's happening. It's Rosalind, but this is not the great hall, nor are these the stable rushes where I sleep when the hall is full. I am not cold. No, I'm not cold. I am warmer now than I have ever been, even if I do feel pains all over my body. What...where am I?

Rosalind stands near the edge of the bed — a bed that I'm lying atop — placing linens on the dresser. She motions for me to come. My head rolls to the left and I start. King Calai is in my bed — no, I am in his — no, we are both in Chief Olec's bed because last night he promised me riches in exchange for my virginity. He took the latter, but made no mention of the former.

One of his arms and legs are draped across my front. His face is turned towards me and he looks angry, even in sleep. I shudder. The enormous size of him has not diminished with the night. I wonder what time it is — if I'm late for my duties. Perhaps, that's why I've been woken up.

With great difficulty, I manage to slide out from beneath the king's impossible heft and off of the bed. I land on the cold, hard-packed earthen floor on shaky legs. I walk to Rosalind and she holds out a shift for me to dress in. It must be one of hers because, as I continue moving, my memories come back to me in rapid flashes and I remember that he cut my dress and shift off.

Rosalind's dark grey gaze is cold as it roams down my bare body. Shivering in the cold air of her chamber, I pull her shift over my head. She doesn't betray her reaction to my mottled skin and enflamed, puffy sex. I don't inspect myself thoroughly, afraid of what I might find. Instead, I simply take the painful steps I need to follow after her when she gestures me out into the great hall where King Calai's men and women are fast asleep.

She leads me down the servant's path against the wall until we reach the alcove where drink was stored last night. I walk with a limp. She glances down at my left, offending leg when she turns and lifts the curtain, cocking her head for me to enter. We step inside and she wastes no time in turning to me and speaking, though it takes me several tries to understand what is happening. I feel like I've been beaten. But I also feel...full. Sated. For the very first time in my life.

Wrapped in his arms, overwhelmed, it had felt...terrifying...exhilarating...an experience I will never forget even though I am far too afraid of him to ever want to repeat it. Not that he would offer. His words were intense and yet, I know that they were only that. Words. Not worth anything. I've learned over the course of my lifetime not to count on words for anything. Words offer no warmth. Words have no taste. Words are like the wind, empty and fleeting.

"Wh-where is what?" I stutter, catching only the tail end of what she's said.

She gives me an annoyed look, her blonde braid frizzy and long and draped over her shoulder almost all the way down to her waist. "The prize he awarded you? Chief Olec and I are entitled to a fair morsel of it. Without us, you'd have been put out, whored out, or died six years ago when your parents did. Now, hand it over."

The chill that inches across my chest moves like a spider, slow and spindly. I never had a particularly warm or affectionate relationship with Rosalind or Olec, but I did not foresee her ever trying to do something like this to me. I thought she *wanted* me to be free. I think back to the strange tension between her and the king last night though and my stomach pools with uncertainty.

I shake my head and whisper, "He didn't give me anything."

The sound it makes is the first thing that alerts me to the strike of her hand against my left cheek. My head whipping to the side is what confirms that I've been struck. Then comes the ringing in my ears and the flickering pain last, which lets me know that I've been struck hard. She hit me.

She's hit me before, only once or twice and only because I'd done something wrong. I dropped a wooden plate, spilling hot food all over the ground. I broke a guiding rod on her loom. I spilled red wine on one of her shifts. Perhaps more than once or twice, but fewer than ten times. She'd never been overly cruel but this? Tears well in my eyes and my nose begins burning.

I cover my mouth with my hand and keep my gaze trained on my feet while she hisses in a rage, "You will get coin from the king if you have to steal it. Do you know how many males had already bid on your virginity? Do you know what Tori paid for it?" She sneers. "Cry all you want, but that will not change the fact that I have protected you from what males like Tori have wanted from you for years with this bidding war. Tori has won and now I cannot pay him back.

"You will need to pay, or I cannot be responsible for how he chooses to punish you for letting the king ruin you in this way. And you are ruined, make no mistake. You are too clearly used, even by a whore's low standard. It will take weeks for those bruises to heal and Tori expects payment in three days. You will need to come up with eighteen silvers and nine gold coins to cover his payment alone, and you will need to pay me at least twice that for orchestrating it all and caring for you these past years.

"Do you understand me?" she says after a long pause in which I say nothing.

I shake my head, my fingers still clenched across my lips. "I... That is too much. I cannot come up with that."

"If you bed every male in the village twice over, you might be able to pay Tori his fee. You will need to steal from the king to get more than that."

I'm still shaking my head, flustered and confused. "Steal from the king?"

"Yes. Now, drop your shift and turn around."

Panic assaults me. I take a half step back and meet her gaze. It is blood-red with fury. Her lips are twisted into a cruel line. "Did you really think I would let you humiliate me like that last night in front of the entire village? Drawing a bath for you? An orphan thrall? Turn around, you ungrateful little whore. I will not say it again." I watch her pull a wire lash from between her robes. My lower lip trembles. She brought it here for me, intending to punish me all along. I haven't done anything wrong…

But that does not stop me from dropping my shift to my waist and letting her slash her wires across my back once, twice, a third time. The pain burns, a ripe stinging that feels like the cool brush of nettles. I fall forward against the wall, thankful that she's finished and didn't hit me more. I've seen her hit other thralls with wild abandon, until their legs gave out and they collapsed onto the floor.

"Good," she says at my back. I can feel my heartbeat in my fresh wounds and taste humiliation and fear in my mouth. "Now, get yourself cleaned up. You smell. And you're dripping seed all over my floor like an animal. Go see Bruna about root's wart as well. I will kill any bastards you produce, rather than help you care for them." She's gone in a flurry, the scent of blood lingering in her wake like a perfume.

After she leaves, I take a moment to sit on the ground and weep before following through on the tasks she's assigned to me. But when I rise, it's not regret that fills me. It's not despondency, either. For the very first time in my life, my whole body comes alive with a cold, cold rage.

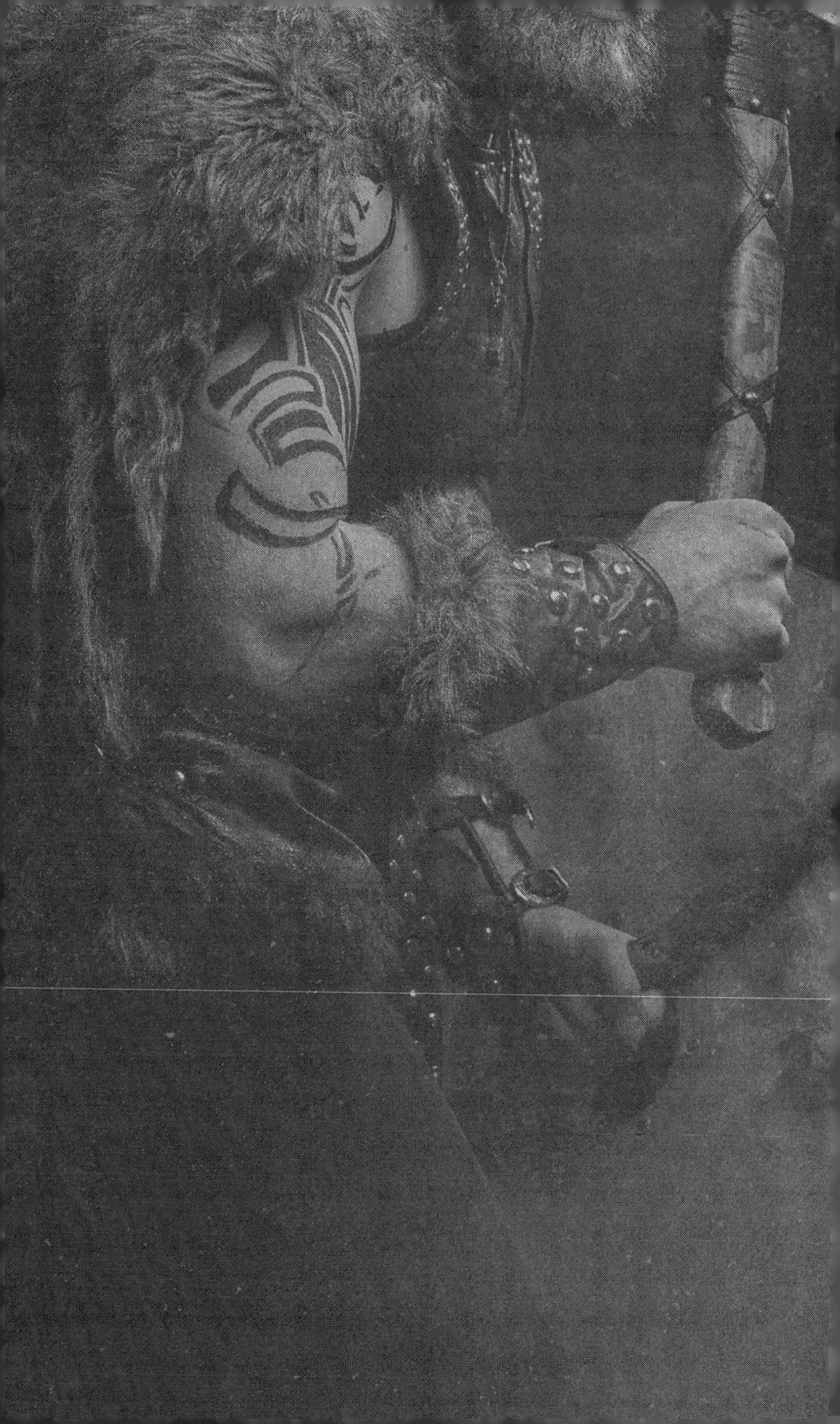

The Runaway

CALAI

"There you fucking are," I grumble unhappily as I finish lacing my boots.

"You did not have such a good night then, my lord?" Puhyo's dry tone does nothing for my sour mood.

He leans against the post in the center of the entryway, looking in on me seated at the edge of this pathetic scrap of a bed. I glare at my second in command and debate his worth relative to my desire to bleed him dry in this moment. His worth wins out. Barely.

"That is not what I heard," he continues when I merely grunt, stand and lace up my trousers. "I heard that our king has earned himself a new title. The king of lambs. At least, that was last night. Did something happen this morning?"

"She left." I snatch the nearest fur off of the mattress and toss it against her pillow angrily — a pillow that was cold this morning when I woke needy and desperate to sink into the softness of my wife once more in the daylight.

Only to find her absence.

"Ah."

I latch my weapons belt around my waist and affix my axe to the holster around my shoulders. It is the first day of the games and, though I do not intervene or participate in any way, it is important for the men that I look prepared for war. I am the bone king. What incentive would it be for them if their king arrived carrying flowers while asking for bloodshed? And I will ask for bloodshed. Many times over.

"The men did say there may have been a...lack of communication between yourself and my future queen." His irreverent tone is undercut only by the words that he calls her.

My hands fumble the next buckle that affixes my furs to my chest. My chest swells on my next inhale and holds.

"The fact that she has no idea she is to be made queen does explain why I saw her out in the village before dawn laboring to carry water to the kitchens."

"You saw her this morning and did not think to wake me?" I rattle out my next exhale, fury coating my limbs as I finish tying my furs to my body.

"Yes. I had no idea what had passed between you."

I snarl and start towards him, "Where was she?"

"I saw her only once, briefly and from afar when I went out to take a piss. I take it by your...general aura that you did decide then?"

"There was no question, Puhyo. I will cut out your tongue, no matter how much I otherwise enjoy hearing your jokes, if you speak ill of my wife again."

"I do not speak ill of your wife, my king. I speak ill of you." He beams, his skin a darker shade than mine, his hair black. "She'll make a fine queen."

"It does not matter if she makes for the worst queen in Wrath's history, she is mine and you'll deal with her just as you put up with me."

He laughs, his head cocked back. "No easy task. Though if she has you making jokes and getting out of bed this early in the morning, I imagine her shortcomings will be easy to forgive."

I exhale, my shoulders rolling back. "Yes. She is so soft, Raya would be jealous." I want that softness here. I want to take her again. Ravage her all day. Forget about the games. Demand her acceptance of what I want from her. Be sure she knows her place is at my side and always will be.

Puhyo whistles between the gap in his front teeth. "I am happy for you, my friend." As I move to pass by him, he claps me on the back. I meet his gaze. His dark eyes are shining with laughter. It eases me, though I'm not certain why. "The bone king deserves his softness."

"I want her at my side, never to be parted from her again." I want to touch her, hold her, squeeze her, speak to her...do what it takes to have her look up at me through those thick, curly black eyelashes with nothing but trust and affection.

"Do not worry, my king. She will need to come back if she intends to receive the *reward* you promised her." He sneers the word.

Puhyo had counseled me to wed the female the moment I saw her in the village yesterday morning. It had been to him I'd confided after I saw her the first time, that fated night. He had counseled me away from announcing that I wanted a bed whore for the night in exchange for riches. I had thought otherwise. It seems he'd been right.

"That was a foolish ruse, my king."

I laugh through my nose and rise to my full height. "I did not want to announce my plans to the room."

"You insinuated a willing female would receive gold, when the true prize was a kingdom."

"You have seen these people," I tell him as we step out into the Winterbren hall. I gesture around the space. Dilapidated and in disrepair, despite the emeralds that sit fat on Lady Rosalind's neck. "I will marry once, and I do not take mistresses or bed whores. The chief and his wife need disrupt the sanctity of my bond with her, nor the other villagers. That is between us and the gods."

"Yes, I know. And Ghabari shines down on you with affection." I can hear him rolling his eyes in his tone.

A more devout believer in the gods than he, I know better than to cross Ghabari, the god of matrimony and sacrifice. He is Raya's cruel but loyal lover, just as I intend to be to my queen.

"I'm only saying that no matter how brightly Ghabari may shine on you, his smile still did not stop you from rutting the poor sapling before you wed her properly. Ghabari would not be pleased in this."

"Ghabari knows what will come." I stand in obstinance, knowing that Puhyo speaks the truth. "A ceremony is only a formality. She is mine in all ways that count."

"Would that she knew that, too. You need to be clear with the girl."

I shove Puhyo out ahead of me as I approach the high table and take a seat. A thrall immediately runs to attend to me. "I did not ask for your counsel. Now find her before your king of lambs becomes your king of pain."

Puhyo smiles at me, looking every bit the mischievous boy I knew once, and I can see on his face that he is pleased, despite my threats. He gives me a subtle nod. "My lord."

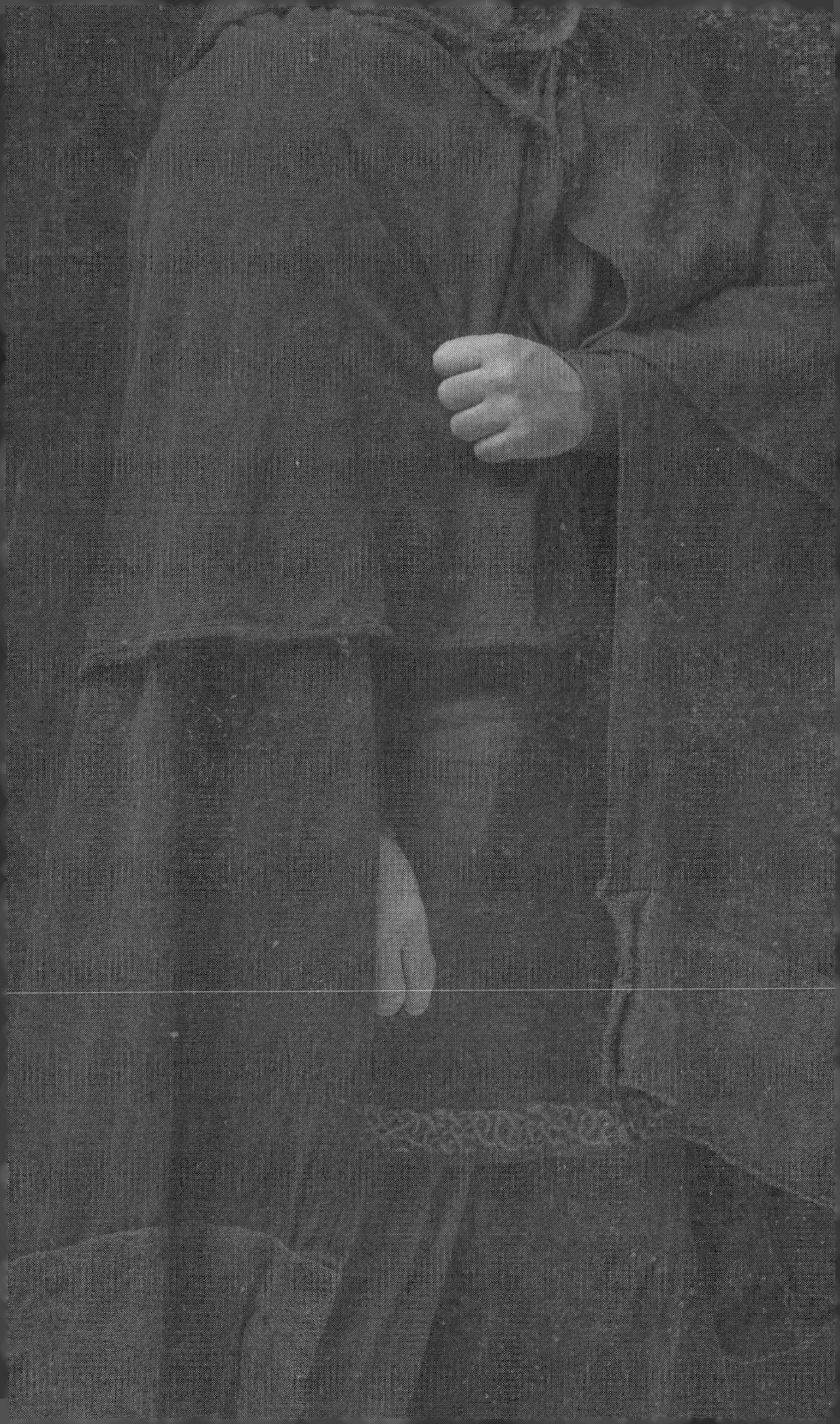

The Doomed

PUHYO

The chief's speaker may have been speaking through his arse when he told tales of the bounty of this place last night over King Calai's feast, but one thing he did not lie about was the beauty of its women. In all the years I've known Calai — since we were boys, all rough and tumble, before we trained with blades made of steel and were content to prod one another with wooden sticks, thinking we were brave — I've never seen him react in such a way to a female.

Granted, I've never seen a female who looked quite like she does, either. My first thought was that she'd been stolen from some land in a raid, brought here by a boat, but not one of ours. If she had been, Calai would have seen her then and I would have remembered. So, I asked around and learned that it was the girl's mother who was brought over by King Calai's *father* on Calai's very first raid as a boy.

Having glimpsed her in the crowd, one female among many, I'd been surprised that this was the female who'd so enchanted the king the previous night. Calai had hardly spared her a look in the light of day. I thought perhaps, he'd changed his mind. Then, dismounting his horse in the barns after completing his tour of the city, he'd turned to me and said, "She is even more stunning in the light of day."

"Who?" I'd asked.

He'd given me an incredulous look. "My wife."

I have learned as much as I can about her in the past day — knowing that females can bring males all kinds of trouble and I have no desire to see my king and friend betrayed or broken by one — only to discover a rather sad, short story about a young girl orphaned with no home. Waiting for her reward.

Ghabari is good.

He brought her a prize most sacred. For none will treat her better or protect her more fiercely than our king — that is, if he doesn't frighten her away first. His intensity and violence are devils to be bargained with and one as soft as she could fall to them if she isn't careful. If she isn't clever. I know naught of her mind and have little faith that I'll be given much occasion to speak with her privately to learn more about her thoughts than this opportunity I'm afforded now. I intend to use the moment to my advantage.

I ask several villagers for directions, and this morning, all know of whom I speak when I ask them for the female the king selected. Even those who were not in attendance at last night's feast no doubt have heard the rumors already.

I am pointed in the direction of the kitchens. Preparations for first meal are well underway, with thralls and cooks streaming in and out of the structure built opposite the great hall on the town square. It is a squat, wooden structure with a patchy thatch roof and only two chimneys.

It looks far too small to accommodate the dozens of people bustling in and out of it — quite a few more than one would expect for a village this small. But I imagine that the feast the king supplied for the full three-day period would excite many. I don't doubt there's quite a bit of thievery going on as well.

The smell of baking bread entices me forward. I duck beneath the thick curtain as a portly man exits the building with staggering steps, hefting a large steel pot on his shoulder. Once inside, it doesn't take me long to find her.

The two chimneys belong to ovens located on opposite ends of the space. I veer right and see her working diligently on her task, her long, dark hair shifting against her back in loops and curls with each thrust of her arms. Her hair looks more vibrant today than it did yesterday, oiled and glossy where yesterday her curls appeared limp and frayed. That pleases me. At least, in this small way, the king has demonstrated his commitment to caring for her.

I ignore the other people in the room and approach my queen from behind as she pulls a heavy wooden spatula from the depths of a stone oven and deftly maneuvers the much too heavy bread loaf onto the short table beside the oven.

I was seated beside the king at yesterday's evening feast and, while she was on his lap facing away from me, I wonder if she caught a glimpse of my profile and might recognize me. I do not wish to frighten her.

She twists to the side, giving me a view of her profile, and I frown. The skin of her hands and feet glistens a lovely and robust shade of brown, but...why are her feet bare? I can see how her toes curl into the packed earthen floor, unshielded and filthy. Her hair may be adorned, but the rest of her is covered in dirt, soot and grease from her labors. She has sweat staining her shift around the collar and...gods.

My gaze drops down to her midback and, when her hair shifts to the side, my heart seizes in my chest. Dear Ghabari save us all. Is that...blood?

Standing four paces from her now, far too close, I struggle not to unleash a barrage of accusations — what the fuck is on her back and please, please for the sake of my own life and the survival of this entire village tell me that the blood droplets staining the back of her shift are not hers, but belong to someone else — but I don't know what to call her. Your Highness? My lady? And confuse her likely more than she already is? I could call her by her name, but that feels blasphemous.

Instead, I settle for clearing my throat loudly once she's successfully maneuvered the loaf off of the large wooden handle, and then once more for good measure. When she still doesn't seem to realize I'm standing almost near enough to her to touch, I call out, "MISS." I sound like an imbecile.

She turns, sees me and glances around, as if seeking help though truly, she has no idea. I should be the one seeking help. Because the left side of her face is purpling and there's blood splitting her bottom lip. My gut drops through the ground directly into the depths of the underworld. Which is where I'm like to end before this day is through.

"Davral," I whisper, hating and fearing this god more than most. The rumors say that the king carries Davral's spirit and I know firsthand that those rumors are true. "Damn you."

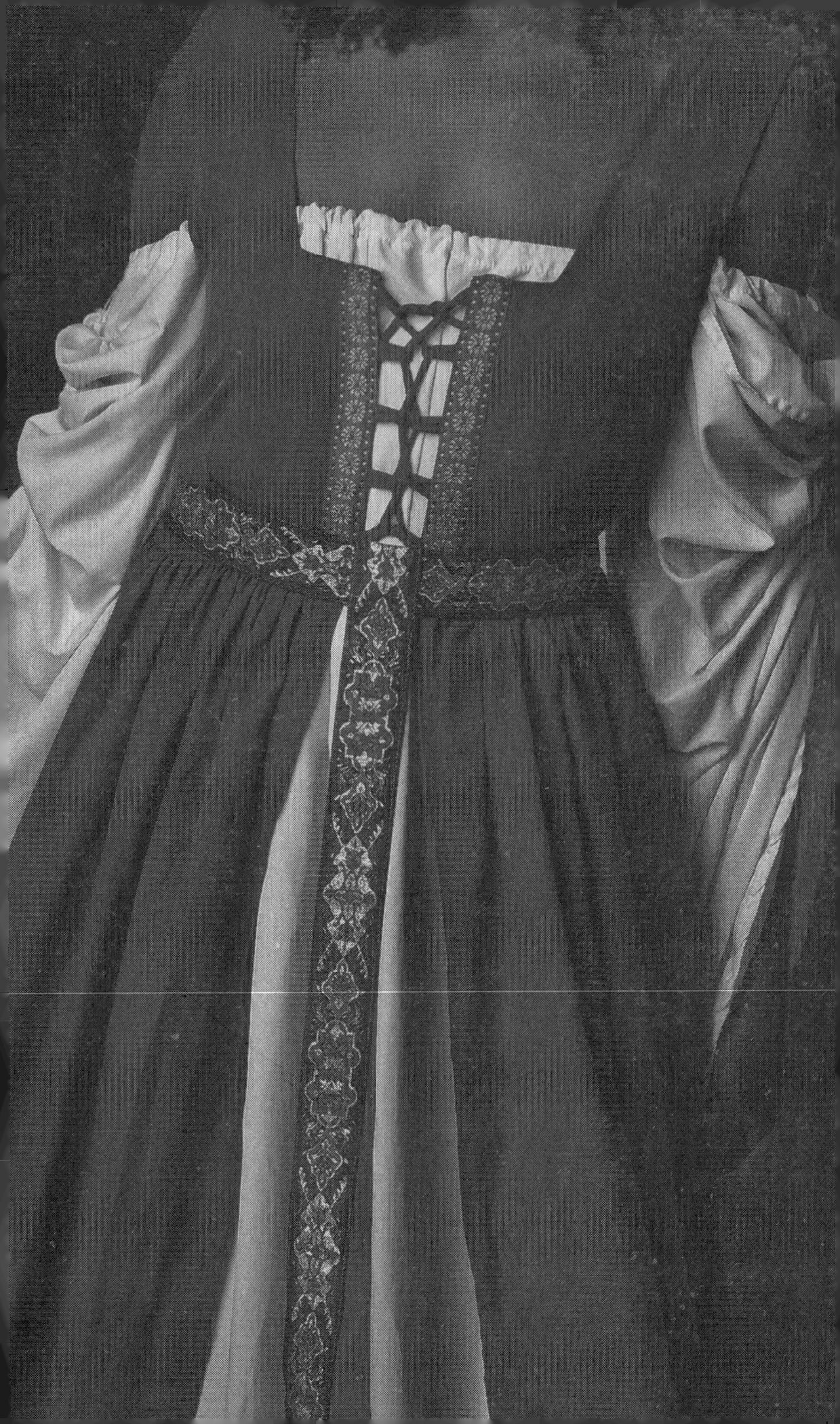

The Wounded
STARLING

The sick feeling in my stomach will not be soothed as one of the king's warriors closes the distance between us by half. He's staring at the left side of my face and horror does not begin to touch his expression. Despite my earlier fury, standing beneath this foreign male now, I am immediately embarrassed, ashamed. Even the thralls who've taken a hundred times as many lashes as I have looked at me and winced this morning when I stepped into the kitchens.

"Has the king…" His voice gives out. He clutches his stomach like he's about to be sick.

I momentarily blank, unsure of what he's asking. "His Highness did not strike my face, my lord."

His eyes round and he balks, "The king…He didn't… *Of course not…*"

Oh. The thought that it would be so inconceivable for the king to strike me fills my stomach with a strange…fluttering. As sorry as they were for me, I don't think any of my fellow thralls were surprised Rosalind struck me. They wouldn't have been surprised if it had been Olec or Torbun, either. "I'm so sorry, my lord. I didn't mean..."

He's barely listening. He all but shouts, "You said the king did not strike your face — did the king hurt you elsewhere?"

I shake my head, but I...hesitate.

"Where?"

My lips tremble. I bite them between my teeth. I don't dare answer.

"My lady, I will not be...displeased," he seems to struggle to speak. "Not with you, but if you are further injured, I need to know where and to what severity."

"I'm not injured, only...sore..." My voice is scarcely more than a whisper.

"Bruised?"

I nod.

"Severely?"

I don't know. Perhaps not, but I've been forced to work all morning and the pains that might have been soothed with a morning's rest or a hot bath are aching anew. I bite my trembling lips more firmly between my teeth and shrug.

"Fucking..." He releases a long string of curses before wildly gesturing one light brown hand at my right shoulder. I had recognized that several of the men that traveled with the king were not white, but closer to my color. Seeing one such male now so close to me is surprising. I've never encountered anyone who looked remotely akin to me, but here he is, concerned on my behalf. "And what is on your back? There's blood there. Please tell me that it is not yours."

I don't respond, merely stare at the floor.

"Gods be damned. Gods be merciful." He takes a step towards me and I immediately counter it with one of my own backwards steps. He stops his advance immediately and does not punish me for retreating from him. "Was it an accident or were you injured with intent?"

I keep my gaze rooted to his boots. "May I see, my lady?"

I don't know what I find more shocking — that he asked me permission, or that he calls me his lady. I recoil straight into the wooden table. It clips my lower back, making me hiss.

He curses. "Apologies. I am so deeply sorry, my lady. That was extremely forward. Our healer will have a look at you — she's female, if that assuages your concerns any."

"Oh, I... Please don't concern yourself, my lord."

"It is too late for that, my lady. I am already concerned."

"My friend Ebanora... Her mother can tend to me as soon as we finish preparing breakfast..."

The male scoffs like I've said something sacrosanct and comes to me. I have nowhere to go and flinch, fearing his ire, but he simply takes the staff of the large bread turner from my hands, sets it down and leans it against the table behind me.

"If I may be so bold as to ask, my lady, where are your shoes? The frost will catch you if you are walking around the village with bare feet."

He is not as large a male as the king — I've not seen any males so large as he — but he is not a small male, either.

Thinner, brawnier with hawkish, deep-set eyes and dark hair pulled back into a braided ponytail that hangs all the way down his midback, he is a fierce male to behold…but not frightening like the king, I realize. It's because his reactions he wears on his sleeve. I can make sense of them. I know what he's thinking.

The king, by contrast, reveals nothing. And it's perhaps for that reason that I say, "You…you can look, if you'd like to, my lord."

He winces and opens his mouth, but I turn and clutch my arms to my chest and bow my head forward. I shiver as he pushes my hair over one shoulder and tugs slightly on the wide collar of my shift.

He gasps, "You were *lashed*?"

I nod.

"For what?" He releases me.

I turn back around and hazard a glance at his face. I know better than to reveal anything, so I cryptically say, "For being with the king."

"He has gone about this all wrong," he spits, raking a hand roughly over his face, "and now, Ghabari is punishing him for it. And you. And me, too. The gods will have their sacrifice on this day."

I am not so familiar with the god Ghabari, but from what I know…he collects sacrifices — human sacrifices only because his wife, Raya, does not allow him to touch the softer animals. They fall under her protection. I shudder.

"Who did this to you? We will need to offer them up if the rest of the world is to remain unscathed."

He watches me expectantly but I say nothing. Because the strangest realization dawns on me in this moment. I may fear the king terribly, and his man here may intimidate me — but that is nothing compared to the sure and brutal death I know I will experience if I name Chief Olec's most favored Rosalind and offer her up for any kind of punishment.

My fingers move to conceal my swollen cheek and I wince, shake my head and whisper, "You will punish them."

"Yes. Terribly."

"But...I'm sorry, my lord. Truly. I do not mean to deny you, but if you punish them...then you will leave. And I will suffer the retaliation. I would rather you let it be. It is not so bad compared to what will happen to me should I offer someone up to the king."

My gaze has returned to the ground, but I still hear his weary exhalation. The man's shoulders sag forward a moment before he whispers, "Come. We will have this out with the king now."

"Please, my lord." I shake my head and he softens, but only slightly.

"You don't need to fear me, my lady," he says.

I glance up as he slips his hand beneath my elbow. I am humiliated and afraid. I can see the other thralls nearby watching us. Elena is closest and she watches our interaction with a bewildered look on her face.

"I am a thrall, my lord. Not a lady. And truly, I'm fine. I appreciate the king sending you to check on me. You've been very kind." I suck in a wet breath that catches in my throat, never making it past that barrier to reach my lungs. My whole body squeezes tight.

"I did not come to check on you, my lady. I came to escort you to the king. He would see you now. And since you are injured, I must insist on carrying you, *my lady*," he says loudly, placing emphasis on the term in a way that feels like it's not only for my benefit, but intended to be heard by everyone in the room. "I will not have you walking any longer with bare feet. I will endeavor to take care with your back." He does not wait for my reply, but swings me up into his arms awkwardly, supporting only my knees and my side against his chest and my opposite un-lashed shoulder.

"You weigh not near as much as you ought to, my lady," he mumbles, stomping out of the kitchens into the village square where all eyes are on us. I shiver because of the cold, because I do not know what's going on... I know only that it cannot end well for me.

I remain curled in his arms as he stomps across the town square. He hails another of the king's warriors — a woman — as she passes by the fountain. She's only one of two women that I saw traveling with the king and when she and I accidentally exchange glances, she starts.

"That's not..." She points at my face.

"It is," the male holding me says, his eye twitching. I glance at my hands in my lap, trying to focus on keeping my stomach clenched so that I can hold myself upright. It hurts too much as it is to lean all of my weight on his arms. For as best as he attempts to hold me away from him, his arms still occasionally brush my new wounds.

"Gods help us," she curses. "Have you called Hilde?"

"That's what I was going to ask you to do."

"Fuck," she says and she doesn't walk away — she runs. The male moves on.

I don't deign to ask him to explain the female. I am shocked enough by his actions and now hers and pained enough by his arms pressing into all of my bruises and wounds that it is no great burden for me to remain silent as we pass through the open doors of the great hall.

The slightly warmer space envelops us, making me shiver against the contrast. There is a fire pit in the middle of the hall that was overrun by tables last night, but that is now being lit. Rushes are being gathered and pushed back against the walls. Tables are already set up — only four this time, forming a square around the fire pit, as most villagers will take their first meals at home.

The only people in the great hall at this hour are Chief Olec, Rosalind, their two unmarried daughters, Chief Olec's top men and their families, the king and the fighting men and women he brought with him. Only the chief, Rosalind, the king and five additional men sit, at present, at the high table. They line one side, so it feels like a tribunal as the king's man carries me to them.

I don't dare look at the chief or meet Rosalind's eye, but my treacherous gaze cannot be helped when it comes to King Calai. I glance at his face, feeling so strange being presented before him like this after what passed between us last night. It was so...intimate. A rare glimpse at a man of his power and rank as he became totally and utterly wild.

Now, he has returned to a state of composure. Relaxed back in his seat, a lazy smirk on his face that fades the moment our eyes meet. He's swirling a pint of something — honey mead, perhaps? — but the motion of his wrist stills as his gaze sweeps my face fleetingly before moving to the male holding me, and then to my outstretched and bare feet.

He sets his cup down on the table, the motion deliberate, careful. His posture remains as it was, easy, not a care in the world. His expression is inscrutable as ever as it focuses on the warrior carrying me. There are muscles laced with tension standing out in his neck.

He does not speak.

"You enjoyed yourself last night then, my liege?" Chief Olec laughs in his deep chortle. I always found it pleasant. I don't now, and tighten the clasp of my hands in front of my body.

The king still does not speak.

Chief Olec leans in towards the king and speaks in a mock whisper that carries across most of the hall. "I understand if you'd like to forego any favor you intended to bestow on her. It does not seem she was robust enough to withstand your desire. Perhaps we can find you a heartier female to warm your furs tonight."

Olec's words surprise me. Not only because they are cruel, but because it seems that he does not share the same designs as his wife to barter me off to the males of the village or, if he does, he does not seem so concerned about the fee that I am alleged to owe Tori. Tori had been...cruel when he came to speak to me of it earlier. I do not look forward to any time Tori and I may spend alone going forward...but, fearing Rosalind's wrath and the quantity of coin she expects from me, I know better than to try to reject him.

The king still does not look at Chief Olec, but he does finally shift in his seat. He leans back even further, becoming more relaxed. He glances at my face, just once — at my cheek, not at my eyes — and his own expression tightens.

"Puhyo," he barks, voice harder than I've ever heard it. Hard and mean. "Explain."

"She is injured and she has no shoes. I bring her before you now to get to the bottom of it. My lady fears her attacker and will not name him."

The king shoves away from the table hard enough that every glass that had been standing falls over. Ale and wine and water pour across the table's wooden surface. The king, however, remains seated. "Where is Hilde?"

"Coming."

"Bring my little bird here."

Puhyo obeys the king's order and brings me forward around the table, yet instead of depositing me in King Calai's lap, as I believe the king intended, he sets me down on my feet a few feet away from the king. I cannot muffle my grunt as my feet light on the floor and Puhyo's arm brushes the back of my shift.

"Apologies, my lady," the male, Puhyo, says and before I can beg his mercy, he grips me by both shoulders and turns me around so that the king can see my back.

I don't want anyone seeing what happened to my back. No one but Ebanora's mother. She will care for it, because she is a good, kind woman with a healer's gift. She has taught me some, but with the positioning of the wounds in the center of my back, I cannot get to them.

"Your lady?" Chief Olec chortles, his voice surprisingly slurred even though it is early morning yet. "That is quite an exaggeration."

Both males ignore him. I don't move. The sudden rush of air around me and the events of the past day — plus, my lack of breakfast — coalesces and makes me swoon.

Puhyo catches my elbow. "She is injured."

The king says nothing, but I can hear the creak of the chair as he rises. There is a soft tugging on my hair, and another on my shift as the collar is loosened enough for him to inspect me.

"Her face was struck and here, on her back, she was lashed," Puhyo says softly. "She is sore from your attentions, too. She walks with a limp."

"A good bedding then! A maiden such as Starling here would undeniably walk askew for a few days after being roughed up by a male like you." Chief Olec laughs.

Rosalind chimes in, "As my husband said, it is common with virgins. Your concern is honorable, but not necessary, my Liege. She is a thrall and I'm sure her aches and pains are nothing a few days' time won't fix, if that is your concern."

I wince, humiliated. No one comes to my defense, not that I expect any of them to. It's just...still dehumanizing being talked about like this and I feel that icy anger swirl.

My toes bury themselves into the hard, cold ground, and then flex. I glance up at the table. Chief Olec is draining his glass. Rosalind is concentrating on her plate of food. Though I cannot see him from this angle, the king, behind me, seems frozen stiff.

"Who struck you, Starling?" I shiver as his breath caresses the curve of my ear through my hair. The pressure of enormously large, warm hands covers my shoulders — covers my entire upper arms. He squeezes me gently, grounding me and reminding me that he...he knows my name. The bone King of wrath knows of me.

Starling. That he uses it here and now in the great hall before the chief and his family fills me with confusion and a healthy dose of fear. Terrified, my body so tired, my mind drained... I do the only thing I can think to do while faced with a terrible predicament. I shake my head.

"Girl, you *dare*." Olec's voice is a thunder and he is right. To deny the king anything, let alone when spoken to directly as I've been, is a flogging offense. But if I name Rosalind, the alternative will be death. "Remove your shift and turn," he barks. "That will be ten lashes for refusing to speak to the king..."

I make a choking sound in the back of my throat and bunch the fabric of my shift in my hands. "My lord, I...I have untreated lashes already."

"You think I care about that, girl? You've disrespected our king twice now by refusing him. Take off your shift."

Tears prick the backs of my eyes, but the king's hands on my arms remain firm. "Starling." He sounds displeased.

His frosty voice is...trembling as he turns me between his hands so that I'm forced to face him. "Look at me."

I look at him and it takes great strength. A strength I feel unprepared for. My whole body is shaking. I try to keep still but I'm afraid they can all see. His eyes are black and merciless. His expression is stony. I can read nothing but darkness within it and know that I was wrong to fear Rosalind. The king looks ready to hurt me.

"Calai — my lord," Puhyo barks behind me. And then he lowers his tone and speaks in a hiss only loud enough for the king and me to hear. *"Easy."*

Meanwhile, Chief Olec says, "My liege, release the girl and I'll have her whipped to your satisfaction..." The chief orders one of his men to grab me. Puhyo surprises me by stepping in the young warrior's path. "Lower your hands if you'd like to keep them," he whispers. "No one touches the king's woman while I live."

The words are startling, but what confuses me even more is the king's reaction. He doesn't seem to see anyone in the great hall but me. He hasn't. He ignores Rosalind and Olec and everyone and everything that doesn't relate back to...me.

A tear drips down my cheek. I want to wipe it away, but the king beats me to it. His thumb brushes my cheek. "Starling." He clears his throat, looks at me while I keep my arms tightly wound over my chest, afraid to move them...simply terrified. "Will you sit with me?"

Chief Olec does not say anything more. Neither does Rosalind. The entire great hall has gone eerily silent. All I can hear are the thralls rushing in the distance and the fire crackling just behind us.

The vein in King Calai's forehead pulses. His skin is flushed red. He inhales and it lifts his whole massive chest, then he exhales softly, "Please." He clears his throat again and whispers even more softly. "Please."

Though uncertain of what I'm agreeing to, I nod and let King Calai take a seat at the high table and pull me down with him onto his lap. His gaze rakes over my body, lingering over my feet and face. His expression is tight. Everything about him is tightly clenched. "Where is Hilde?"

"Daneera is searching, but I will assist."

"No. Remain here. Daneera will not fail in this."

Puhyo nods.

The king is breathing so shallowly. His expression is troubled and I have the oddest compulsion to reach out and smooth away the wrinkles between his eyebrows. He looks...in pain. "You are cold."

He lifts my feet up over his thighs so that I'm no longer touching the ground. A shiver racks me as the heat of his chest crashes against my outer arm. I did not realize how cold I was until this moment as he pulls me close, managing not to touch my back. My face is pressed against his chest just under the column of his throat and I feel...so warm. The lie that nothing can get to me here in this place revisits me from the night before. More tears drip down my face. I don't stop them.

"Shh," he whispers. He gathers up my hands in his much larger ones and rubs them gently. One of his hands pulls my palms to his chest while the other hand reaches down to touch my feet. I whimper. He hisses, "You left your shoes in my quarters, little bird."

"Yes, my king." I gasp, the heat of his hands on my frozen toes painful.

He reaches for the leather buckle on his chest and frees it. His furs fall from his shoulders. "And you snuck out in the night while I slept."

I don't answer. I didn't sneak anywhere, but he isn't asking me. He pulls me close and I become disoriented by the sudden surprising warmth as he drags his furs over me. The swatch that covered his meaty torso is enough to shield and warm my entire body.

I gasp breathily, my heart pattering in my chest. I wonder if culture in Ithanuir is different than it is here, knowing it must be, because here to use a fur like this is an act of significance. He must not be so daft as to not know what it means and yet, he does not withdraw them.

"Better?" he breathes against my forehead. The furs are so soft that, even against my open wounds, they don't abrade. I exhale, feeling like I could simply fall apart. I close my eyes, letting the tears fall, wishing that I could just stay here.

"Yes, my king." I sniffle.

"Calai," he says in the soft space between us. "If it pleases you." His rough voice shakes.

I don't answer him, not sure what to say.

While his right hand continues to massage my cold toes beneath the fur, his left hand kneads the back of my neck. He sighs and his breath smells of honey. His skin smells of the oils he put in my hair the night before. Rosemary and eucalyptus. "Who struck you?"

He is attempting to lull me into releasing the name, I realize abruptly. I pinch my lips together, then offer meekly, "I...am fine, my liege."

"I want their names."

"Please."

"*Please.*"

"I beg of you, my king."

"I beg of you, little bird. Tell me."

"I...cannot say, my king."

"You cannot?"

"Please do not make me," I whisper, my voice so soft it could belong to a ghost.

The pressure on the back of my neck increases. "Was it the warrior male who thinks he has laid claim to you?"

My nostrils flare, surprised that he could know of Tori and the bidding when I did not know of it myself. Stupidly, I blurt out, "You know of the bidding?"

"I do now."

I wince, feeling the fool.

"Tell me of it." His hands are terrible, first on my neck, then pulling gently on my hair. I'm so tired...so tired. I've been bottling everything up as I've always done. Just going, ever going, keep going. Ignore the pain. But...right now, right here...I allow everything to *hurt* while in his care and it feels...too much. Tears wet my face and I cover my mouth with my hand, shake my head again.

"The men of your village bid on your virginity?"

"How did you know that, my king?" My voice is wet. He pulls my hand away from my face and softly, much too softly, brushes his fingers beneath the eye of my too warm cheek.

"Because I know people. And because I know people, I know that you did not orchestrate this bid yourself."

I don't respond, but sniffle.

"Who did?"

My breathing is shallow. I reach for words that I cannot grasp.

"Who, sweet Starling?" His voice is shaking. I fear I will succumb to it and to the gentle ministrations of his hand. I cannot think.

"My lord, please," I say, voice thick with tears, but he misunderstands.

"You will not be punished. Trust me."

Trust him. What a terrible thing to demand. I would rather offer him my bleeding heart, for that is what his trust would be taking from me.

"Oh for the gods' sake," Rosalind crows. "I made the deal with Tori on her behalf, and I struck her this morning, as I would any thrall who disobeyed me or failed to perform her tasks."

The king presses a dry kiss to the top of my head where my hairline meets my forehead before sliding me off of his lap. He stands and secures his furs around me with the same heavy leather and metal buckle that he used to secure them to his own skin, and then turns me by the shoulders so that I'm facing a beautiful woman with a thick blonde braid hanging over her left shoulder. In her left hand, she carries a large leather box.

"This is Hilde. She will care for you in my chambers, where you will spend the rest of the day recovering and healing before I join you. We will dine privately this evening."

I'm gestured forward by Hilde, whose severe face brokers no argument. She is shaking her head, glaring angrily past me at someone, but I do not see whom. Instead, I only hear King Calai ask, "And how much was her virginity purchased for?"

Rosalind doesn't hesitate. "Eighteen silvers and nine gold coins. Twice that for my fee, my liege. I would think it appropriate for you to pay what is owed and then some if you intend to keep her away from her duties and tending to you while you are here."

"Now, now, my lady," Chief Olec laughs. "Let's not be greedy. The king is our guest. He's brought with him a bounty and is entitled to whatever comforts he likes."

"The king has deflowered our ward. Now, we will not be able to collect a bride price for her or wed her off. The king could, with his unlimited wealth, at least pay a consolation for that," Rosalind asserts.

But the king, in what is becoming a predictable fashion, says something else entirely. "Did you feed her before or after you beat her?"

"You think I am in the practice of feeding unruly thralls, my liege?" Rosalind balks. "I think not."

"So if that is the practice of your little village then, Olaf, when do the thralls eat?" Olaf. He called him Olaf.

Olec scoffs, sounding flustered as Hilde and I walk very slowly toward the throne. My feet pause and I look back to see Olec gesturing wildly with his cup, wine spilling over its wooden edge. "You cannot possibly expect me to believe the thralls of your village eat like kings, my king?"

"You are right. You cannot, for my village has no thralls. We have those that serve and they are paid a wage as well as fed during celebrations. The god Lohr would be displeased with the care you've given his servants. They are responsible for the feasts that lead to much of the debauchery and lust he feeds on." The king has yet to resume his seat. Rather, he sits his hip on the table, his arms hanging casually down at his sides. His gaze no longer returns to me, but is focused in on Olec and Rosalind.

Olec swallows, his voice growing shrill. "My wife and I have cared for that thrall as if she were our own, my liege. She's been fed and clothed and protected, which is more than most orphans can claim. We've spent a good deal of our own coin on her. My wife is perhaps a bit bold, but not wrong in requesting fair compensation now that you've ruined her."

"And fair compensation is what you shall receive. Eighteen silvers plus nine gold pieces, times three. Puhyo? Can you *prepare* this endowment for our Lady Rosalind?" His voice does not shake with them as it did with me. But it holds an edge.

Puhyo's eyes flare before returning to their typical hawkish prudence. "Of course, King."

"And please bring it to me. I'd like to provide the offering directly."

"Of course." Puhyo leaves. Rosalind and Olec are muttering still. Hilde, behind me says, "Come, my lady. I need to get that looked at and you need to get into a bath of healing salts, bring up that temperature right quick."

I nod absently, this feeling of betrayal making me feel a little...raw. He plans to pay her after all?

"Don't concern yourself with those others now. Come with me. We need to focus on your healing. I will have some choice words with our king once he's finished with those disgusting pigs that run your village."

My body reacts viscerally hearing her speak of Chief Olec in such a way. And I'm staring at her, shocked still as she leads me to a tub filled with noxious-smelling salts where I'm carefully scrubbed, oiled, slathered in salves and then, once dried off, stitched and treated before I'm put to bed by Hilde and two thralls I recognize — both of whom are rewarded with coins when they are finished. And I am ashamed by my envious thoughts. I was promised rewards...but the thralls who care for me now have more coin than I have. And I owe Lady Rosalind so much...

I'm brought food by the same thralls and Hilde stands over me and ensures that I eat to her satisfaction and drink a thick tea that warms me from the inside. And as I fall asleep, I want to think over the strange, contradictory way the king presented himself today, but furs are draped over the bed now, weighing down my blankets and dragging me to sleep.

And as I sleep, I dream in the violent colors of terrible, terrible screams.

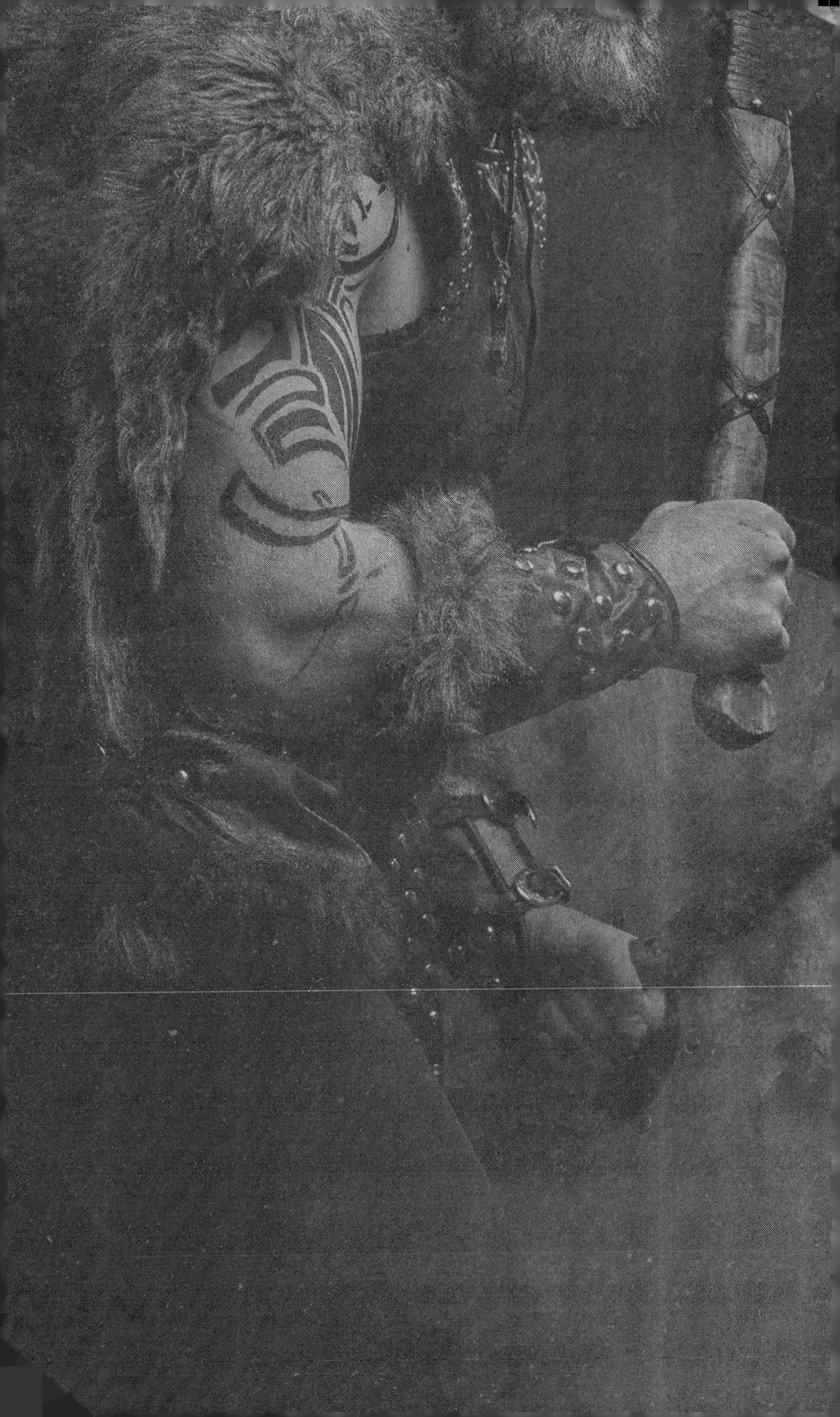

The Forger
CALAI

I watch the skin peel away from her face, smell the scent it creates, a familiar one to me as her body is remade by greed, her head cocked back, her chest caved, her mouth open on a silent scream. Behind me, her male screams a blood-curdling shriek that will be heard by the gods.

As it would seem, I was a little angrier than I originally thought.

When I first saw the bruising on *my* female's cheek and the lashes on her back, I couldn't believe it. Never in my wildest dreams could I have envisioned that a female I had claimed would be brutalized in such a way. It would seem that I have failed in all ways to stake my claim over her. To provide her shelter. I am...unused to feeling like this.

As I struggle through my feelings, my concern, my relief that she isn't more badly damaged, I watch Starling disappear behind the throne and, only when I'm certain she is out of the hall, in the chief's room, do I turn to Rosalind and drop the mask I'd been wearing. Any veneer of control slips from my grasp. I feel the veins pop in my forehead. I feel my face grow hot.

"Before you receive your payment, Lady Rosalind, I'll see the whip you used to flay my little bird's back."

Lady Rosalind is sitting up. She has hold of her fork and knife but her wrists are resting on the edge of the table. Her brow is furrowed, but there's a hesitation in her expression that was not there before. She is not so quick this time with her retort.

"Is that necessary, King?" King. Not my king, but King.

I smile. "Yes."

She extracts the tangle of wires from her skirts and I hold out my hand, taking them from her. I stand between her and Olec's chairs now. "A crude thing."

"It does the trick."

"I'd like to try."

"Excuse me, King Calai?"

"Get up. Take off your dress." I meet Rosalind's stare at the same time that Olec starts to chuckle at my back.

"You have a dark sense of humor, my liege, but I think you have taken it far enough."

"Rosalind," I say. "Up."

"Olec, are you really going to let him talk to me like this? You are a guest in my house, King..."

I grab her by the hair and wrench her from her seat. Olec shouts at my back, but he's clumsy and when he unsheathes his blade, he drops his sword. Not that it would have mattered. My men are standing, holding Olec back as I walk Rosalind around the end of the table. She is thrashing more than fighting as I take her to the center of the space near the fire and cut open the back of her dress.

"Torbun! Marek! Eli! Draw your arms!" Olec calls, but Torbun, the coward, stands from his position at the table, and points instead to his son at the end of the table.

"Viccra! You are our best warrior, son. Challenge the king now. Honor your chief!" Torbun shouts.

Viccra, a talented young fighter, is seated at the opposite end of the table from his father. I recognize the boy — trained him — and watch him stand, curious to see what he will do. He steps forward, sword drawn, and then takes a knee a few feet from me, laying his sword across it.

"My allegiance was sworn on the training yards of Ithanuir to King Calai. My king, how may I do your bidding on this day?" And thus, this boy proves my theory right. The games were not only established as a means of helping the outer villages of Wrath defend themselves, but also served another purpose. Obedience. Allegiance. Loyalty. To *me*. I grin.

"Traitor! Kill him!" Olec shouts to his guards, and they engage. I am impressed when Viccra manages to kill one and wound the other with only a few swift cuts of his blade. Meanwhile, my grip on Rosalind's hair has not strayed.

"Come, Viccra. Hold the *lady* Rosalind for me." He grabs her arms. The great hall is flooded with people now, most of whom are crowded near the entrance, not daring to enter, but for my men and Daneera, who push through and secure the space. I am easy. Relaxed in my rage. It is a place I know well.

"I call any who has ever been maimed by this female to step forward now. Thralls," I say to those gathered at the entrance. "Come forth. The time of your servitude ends now."

It takes some time for the thralls to come forward. A dark-haired, pale-skinned female is first — she served at my table the night before. After handing the whip over to the thrall, I move to help Viccra keep Rosalind upright, taking her other arm.

Olec is screaming obscenities and threats, but the female thrall meets my gaze and must be soothed by it. She acts before I can give the order, swinging the wire flail towards the exposed skin of Rosalind's back and drawing blood.

Rosalind writhes as she screams curses and threats. The female, now pink-cheeked, returns the whip to me and as she does, I rip the fat ruby off of Rosalind's finger, simultaneously breaking the digit. Rosalind screams. I hand the ruby over. The former thrall's eyes go wide.

"I... Thank you, my king."

"No. It is I who owes you an apology for leaving you at the mercy of these useless, cruel beings all this time. But their time is over now. Go. And tell the others."

A steady stream of thralls enters the hall after that, all too happy to take gold, gems and pearls from Rosalind's throat and hair and pocket and return the wounds she's delivered them. Perhaps even some she did not. One of the thralls — a beautiful pale-faced, red-haired female with large breasts on a slender frame — beats at Rosalind for some time. She uses her full body, all the violence she has within her, and when she's finished, I offer her gold coins, but she turns from them and points at Olec with her whip.

"Can I?"

I smile. "Of course."

She whips Olec in the face while Daneera and Fuzier expend what looks like very little energy to hold him steady. Even if the male weren't drunk constantly, he's so out of shape that any young farm boy in Ithanuir could best him with a blade. He is not suited to lead. That his wife harmed Starling simply makes my decision to remove him easy.

The red-haired thrall is smiling as she skips out of the hall. She never did collect her gold pieces.

This goes on for some time. Long enough for Puhyo to return with the village forger. The forger stands now near the fire, his blackened gloves on, his pocked face expressionless. He does not heed Olec's shouted curses.

Viccra and I hold Rosalind's weight. Her legs have given out. Her cries of rage, however, are ceaseless. "If you think I won't tear every thrall in this village into pieces the moment you are gone, starting with yours, you are as stupid a king as you are a violent one!"

"You raise a good point, Lady Rosalind." I drag her to the fire, Viccra moving when I move. "Are you ready for your payment for Starling, Lady Rosalind?" I ask, shoving her to her knees and ripping her head back by her hair. Blood perfumes the air, the flayed skin on her back weeping to saturate her dress.

I beckon the forger forth and watch as slow understanding trickles across Rosalind's expression. Her hatred melts into despair. The forger's mask covers most of his face, but he lifts it when she looks at him. He doesn't look smug, but he holds a frost in his gaze that tells me two things: that he is not sorry for Rosalind's fate, and is he not sorry to be the one delivering it.

"Is it ready?" I ask him.

He nods. "It will not remain hot for long, Your Highness."

I wait. Watch Rosalind's face. Listen to her pleas. "You...you can't do this... You can't..."

"Are your children here?" She is babbling, unresponsive to my question, so I continue, "I see that they are. I will ensure that, after, they are cared for with the same compassion you showed my thrall," I lie. I do not intend for anyone anywhere in Wrath to be treated as Starling was. But I enjoy the panic that flits across her face. "Now, I believe it's time." I gesture for the forger and watch as Rosalind screams and thrashes with all of her flagging might.

When I had Starling on my lap earlier, I went through the repertoire of punishments available to me given that I am here in this little village, not back in Ithanuir where I have my dungeons. However, I struggled to arrive at the correct punishment that would bring me just the right level of satisfaction. Fortunately, the clever Rosalind took the occasion to speak up about her payment. I could have kissed her on the mouth for the suggestion she provided had I not other uses for it.

Now, her mouth is opened. I stand over it, the forger holding metal tongs clasped tight around the iron cup, in which Rosalind's fee and Tori's payment swirl together.

"Tip her head back," I order Puhyo while Viccra and I hold her down.

"No! No, don't!" she screams. She is thrashing, scratching wildly at anything she can. She clamps her lips shut and I know I only have a limited time before the liquid inside my cup cools and I have to refire it.

Puhyo has his hands on her jaw, attempting to pry it open, but her thrashing is violent enough to keep him from it. So, I step down on the back of her left calf, bone crunching beneath the ball of my foot. She screams. Puhyo yanks her head back and the forger hands me his tongs. I take them, tip the cup gripped at the end of the tongs straight to Rosalind's teeth, and pour all of the liquid coin she's owed inside of her body.

She convulses as the liquid metal touches her tongue and then slides down her gullet into her lungs and stomach. I pour the cup empty and her body spasms inhumanly. Puhyo releases her when my cup is dry. Viccra and I follow suit. She tips to the side, her body struggling through its final transformation. Her face turns bright red and then purple and I crouch down and place the burning hot cup in my pincers to her cheek, marking her where she marked my Starling.

Her eyes bulge out of her head, red and veiny. Puhyo reaches to close them but I hold up my hand, wanting them open. I watch closely as she burns from the inside out, wondering what exactly it is that has killed her. From her cursed golden lips, steam wafts into the cooler air. I imagine her body will be a good deal heavier now, when we lift it. She's finally stopped moving, her bare fingers gnarled and twisted, no longer covered in precious gems.

Olec's screams are even more pitiable than those of his female's. There will be no welcome for her in the land of the strong that exists after, of that I am sure. For either of them. His screams of despair for his wife's fate turn quickly to begging for his own life. He pleads with me, offers me riches that he could not possibly pay. I ignore him, knowing that his time is coming soon to an end. But not today.

"Return the king to his current chambers," I bid my men. "Bind him to the bed and place his wife in a chair beside him, so that she may watch over him as he rests." My orders are carried out, Rosalind is carried away, too. I return the forger his tools along with a fair payment, both of which he takes with no complaint, no sign of contrition, before turning to Puhyo and Viccra and giving them orders to secure the village armory and gather any warriors and fighting-age men in the great hall so that I may speak to them directly and discourage any mutiny.

"That is all for now," I tell the hall, those that are gathered, before I return to my chambers, Puhyo at my side, and find Hilde administering to my prize.

Starling is sitting up in the bed, buried deep beneath the bedding, my furs draped across her thighs. The symbol of it makes my breath catch. I am her first defense. I am her last defense. I am her shield against the cold. I am her shield.

And the bruising on her cheek so visible to me now that she's clean, her hair combed back away from her face, the ointment shining on her skin, makes me wish that I had devised a different punishment for Rosalind. One that lasted much, much longer.

My sweet little bird looks like she's just rousing from sleep. She has sleep in her expression, but perks when Hilde slides a heavy tray onto her lap. She reaches for food, which pleases me, but on seeing Puhyo and me, she stops. Her face flushes red for reasons I'm not sure I like because her gaze is concentrated on my chest, but passes occasionally to Puhyo, too. I block sight of him with my body and he grunts — a laugh — and I hear him trudge off.

"I will be outside on guard, my lord," he says.

Hilde grunts something about despicable men under her breath. I ignore her and move to the bed, my gaze tracking Starling through each of my steps, each breath.

"How are you, Starling?" I ask her. My tone is hard. Yes, I am a *little* angrier than I thought I was. Even with Rosalind's death, that anger's edge has barely dulled. But...there will be time for more punishment, and now is not that.

I place my hand atop my furs, finding her calf through the blanket and giving it a gentle squeeze. *Gentle.* I exhale through flared nostrils, barely able to hear Hilde as she dismisses herself and leaves.

"Starling," I say in my most placating tone. "Breathe."

She inhales sharply and lowers her hands to her lap. I made sure that the thralls placed an entire loaf of sweet bread on her tray and that she was reaching for it pleases me. I feel myself relaxing. I thought I'd been on my way to relaxing before, but now I actually feel my muscles sagging slightly, my shoulders easing down my back.

"I thought you'd be asleep by now."

"I was woken, my king. I thought I heard screams."

"Hm," I say and leave it at that.

I reach out and gently, gently stroke my knuckles over her injured cheek. Her face flares with color. It rolls down her neck and is visible in the parted curtain of her tunic. She wears one of mine. I hope that it is all she wears and then curse my own thoughts. It will be some time before I can bed her properly. Days at best, at worst, weeks. My anger nips at me, but it is an anger that knows no violence. Because before I can bed her again, I need her to want to come with me.

"May I sit with you?" I ask.

"Oh, um…of course." Starling, as I expected she would, panics and worries herself with making space for me in the bed. I grip her calf firmly, and slide onto the bed near her knees. I line her leg with mine.

I nudge the overfull tray on her lap. "Eat." My fingers move over the tray as well. I gravitate to the meat, my hand hovering over the sweet bread and then quickly flitting past it. I want to eat it because it's her favorite, but I don't touch it for that same reason. Instead, I take a piece of pork marinated in something divine.

I grunt, "What seasoning do your cooks use on this?"

"I…" She's flustered. I can feel her eyes on me, glancing up. She's so small, her head only coming up to my shoulder height. I don't look at her, but nod when she says, "It's a salt rub, primarily."

"What else is in it? What gives it this darker color?"

She lists a few spices, a simple combination, but surprising. "You add a little honey?"

"Yes." Her voice betrays confusion. She glances up at me and our gazes lock. "Just a little."

"Do you usually do the cooking?"

"I help when I'm required."

Not needed. Required. "Are you often required in the kitchens?" I say, trying to keep my anger enchained.

She nods.

"Eat," I encourage, taking another morsel of meat myself. Her calf lines my thigh and I make no move to separate us, even if I can feel her feet rotating around beneath the blankets, the clearest evidence of her discomfort. "Do you enjoy cooking?"

"En...enjoy cooking?" she asks me and the question makes me glance at the exit. Perhaps, I will go tonight to Olec after all.

"Yes. Enjoy," I repeat, ceding no ground. She will tell me what she enjoys if I have to wrench it from her by force.

"I...suppose I don't mind cooking, my king."

I bite my own tongue. My king. I growl deep in the back of my throat, only once, briefly, before I catch myself. "What else do you enjoy?"

"Spending time with Ebanora and her family. Though I have not much occasion to do so, my king."

"Ebanora. Who is she?"

"She's..." She hesitates, chewing nervously on her bottom lip and whispers, "She's just a girl. Poor, but they have always been kind to me when I needed kindness. It is my hope that when you..." But her voice fails her. Her courage collapses on itself like a burning thatch roof.

"Say it. I will not be angry with you."

"It's just..." She lowers the grapes in her hands back to the tray. She's nervous. I hate her nerves. I want to scrape them out of her with a blade. "Apologies, my king, I simply am not certain what will happen to me when you leave our small village."

I could laugh. "What are your concerns?" My gaze does not pass to hers. If I try to look at her, she will look away, and I rather like the way her bashful gaze feels moving over my face, assessingly, curiously, hopefully... I will not let her down. Not after I already have.

"I worry that you have punished the chief and his wife because of me, and I will be punished severely. I will probably be killed," she says, voice the ghost of what it was before. "Tortured, first. Ebanora and her family may try to harbor me. I don't know. But I don't want to see them punished, too."

I tense. Nod. This changes things a little. A very little. "You have concerns, sweet bird, but what do you enjoy?"

"I..." She falters, likely put off by my abrupt change. I want to reassure her and I will, but I need to know this. "I don't...know, my king."

"You don't know?" I shake my head. "I understand that you may not have been given many occasions to feel true enjoyment, but I want to know. What do you want from this life, Starling?"

"What do I want?" She takes another small bite of honey bread. I smile down at her, looking at her with pure longing. "I want to be free to learn what I want."

Her words are honey riddled with thorns. I can't stand them, but at the same time, they fill me with warmth. I lean towards her and watch as her eyes widen. She looks up at me and I cannot help myself. I shift up onto my knees so that I may loom over her and kiss her temple, the press of my lips full against her skin. Gods, she tastes heavenly. Nights spent with her while she is injured will be excruciating. But I will shackle myself.

I whisper, "And you shall have that, little bird. I promise." I retake my seat with a loud grunt and resume eating. As I do, I tell her, "I have decided to extend my time in your little village by several days. There are some matters that need sorting. I am displeased with the way Winterbren has been running. Your hall is the poorest I've seen in my travels across Wrath yet your Chief and his wife, among the most finely decorated. I intend to set it right.

"There is also the matter of the games. I have delayed their start by a day, but they will begin tomorrow. I had hoped to ask if you would do me the honor of sitting beside me at the games and at the feasts to follow. It is my hope to keep you close while I remain in Winterbren." I clear my throat. "But I also understand if it...if my company... If you do not prefer my company, I will not be offended," I lie, thoughts drifting to chains and shackles should she decline.

"I... You... I'm sorry, my liege," she starts, and I tense, fear gripping me, "but I have many duties to attend to."

"I have already spoken to Rosalind and Olec. They are pleased to dismiss you from your duties if you should have any interest in spending the coming days with me." All of the days until the end of them.

Starling blinks at me brightly, looking so pretty wearing her swollen cheek like the mark of a warrior I could weep. "I... I'm not sure, my lord."

My heart sinks. "I understand." My voice is gruff and I struggle to hold her gaze, but force myself to anyways. "If I may be so bold as to ask what concerns you, I would be grateful for your response."

"It's just...I... My body is very tired and I worry that I won't be able to give you what you want from me..."

A small rage floods my spine, causing me to sit up. "Ah," I grunt. "I see. And I am sorry for not being more clear. I wish to sit with you, dine with you, speak with you, spend time with you...but I am fully aware that I will not have the privilege of bedding you again until you are well."

"That may be longer than the time you spend in Winterbren, my lord. Lady Hilde had to stitch some of my back and cautioned me against any intense physical exertion."

A slow smile creeps across my face. The warmth of the room coalesces around me and I get goosebumps. "Last night was *intense*, wasn't it, little bird?"

Her cheeks flare with color. She nods, holding my gaze this time for once. "Yes." Her voice is a little too breathless and my cock is behaving with poor conduct. Were it a trainee on the fields of Ithanuir, I'd beat it senseless. As it stands now, I still have need of it. "It was, my king."

"I enjoyed myself greatly."

And then it happens. The dawning of a small sun. She smiles at me for only the second time, the first being when I first met her. It's a small, caged thing, unlike the first time when she gave me a little more. She didn't call me by any honorific, and she didn't look down at her feet, but sought my gaze. Yet, this is still a start. My heart beats harder in my chest. Slow, steady, loud. I lick my lips. My mouth has gone dry and I am *thirsty*.

Softly, she says, "You were very vocal in your pleasure, my lord." Her grin stretches and is punctuated by a slight, breathy *chuckle*. Is she...teasing me?

I bark out a laugh so startling that she jumps, knocking grapes off of her tray. I shake my head slowly and gather them. "As were you, my lady. At least, I hope your screams were those of pleasure."

"They were," she breathes.

A growl picks up in my chest and I cannot help edging forward, closer to her an inch. "There are other males more experienced than I who could have taken your virginity. In any ways you like to be pleasured, I would like to learn."

"You were very... It was...lovely, my king."

I smirk. "Lovely?" Her breaths become more staggered and I see her gaze stray to my lap and the erection tenting my pants. "Ignore it. I want to hear more about what you liked, what you didn't like... Eat, princess."

I lean away from her and she exhales. "I liked all of it, my lord."

"You are lying. I can sense it." I can see it in the way her eyes shift left and her smile falls and she returns to fiddling with her sweet cake. She picks up a piece of it and nibbles on the syrupy edge.

"I did like all of it. Too much. I worry that..." She shakes her head. "Sorry, it's stupid, my king. I don't mean to trouble you with childish imaginings."

"Trouble me, little bird. I desire it."

"It's just...it was *intense* as you said and I doubt very much I will ever experience anything like that again. I wonder if it was not a curse, rather than a gift, to have experienced it at all."

My lips purse. I debate, hesitating, wondering if I should just tell her...ask her... But if I ask, she could say no. "Was there anything else you didn't like?"

She looks surprised for a moment before biting her lip and shifting her legs against the mattress.

"Tell me."

"It's not what you did, my king. You did... Everything you did was perfect. I've never experienced pleasure like it. It's only the bruises. They are a little painful, but Hilde has given me a milk elixir and they already are feeling..." She's rambling a little and my brows draw together. I reach for the tray in her lap and move it away for the moment.

"I'd like to see," I say, but I hesitate, wondering if I should just strip her as I like, or if I should ask her permission. I'm not used to asking permission for anything, let alone something I really want. And I've never wanted anything like this before. Her heart. "May I?"

"C-certainly, my lord." My lord again. Hm. I frown, but it does not stop the motion of my hands as I draw the blankets and furs down to her knees and then roll her knee-length tunic up to her hips.

Revealing the juncture of her thighs is a painful thing because my need roars in my ears, cut down only by the fury I feel towards myself. She has finger-shaped bruises covering the outsides of her hips and her inner thighs are red and chafed, covered in a salve undoubtedly applied by Hilde.

"Spread your legs," I bark.

She doesn't speak as she obeys. Her mound is dusted in curls and looks slightly swollen but otherwise unharmed. I reach down and try to spread her mons with my fingers so I can see her asshole, but she squirms. I let her go, drop her tunic and push the blankets back to cover her.

"Did I draw blood?"

"No, my lord."

I nod once. "And Hilde, what did she say of the bruising?"

"Only that it would be uncomfortable for a few days' time, likely less. I'm okay, my king."

I look into her eyes. "Truly?"

She smiles again, but it is shaky this time in ways that make my fists clench. "Truly, my lord. Please, let it go. This is more painful."

"What is?"

"The way you look so genuine. It is... That's what I was talking about from last night. You said things with such passion. Things that couldn't possibly be true."

I surge forward, place my hand against her unblemished cheek. Lean over her and close my eyes, press our foreheads together. "They may not be true yet, but I want them to be, so long as you want them, too." I kiss the tip of her nose then lean back so quickly she sways towards me. Rapidly, she blinks. "But we have time to talk about that over these next days." I clear my throat. "Among many other things. I will not touch you again in Winterbren. Your body needs time to heal and I do not deserve your warmth after having savaged you like this."

"You won't touch me again in Winterbren?"

I shake my head. "But perhaps in Ithanuir..."

"In Ithanuir?" Her eyes widen. Her nostrils flare.

"I'd like for you to spend these next days with me, considering."

"If...are you saying... Asking me to consider coming with you, my king?"

"No. I want you to consider coming with me, *Calai*."

She gasps just a little bit and I feel it all the way down in my toes. I smile at her softly, reach forward and tuck her curls behind her ear. "Eat, little bird. You need to regain your strength." I pluck a grape off of her tray and she watches me chew for several breaths. "You have all day to relax and tomorrow the games begin."

She picks up a piece of meat and chews thoughtfully, her gaze never straying far from mine. We don't speak, but the silence between us is comfortable up to the point that she breaks it with a whisper. "I would be honored to watch the games at your side, Calai."

My heart slams against my rib cage and I smile. "The honor, Starling, is all mine."

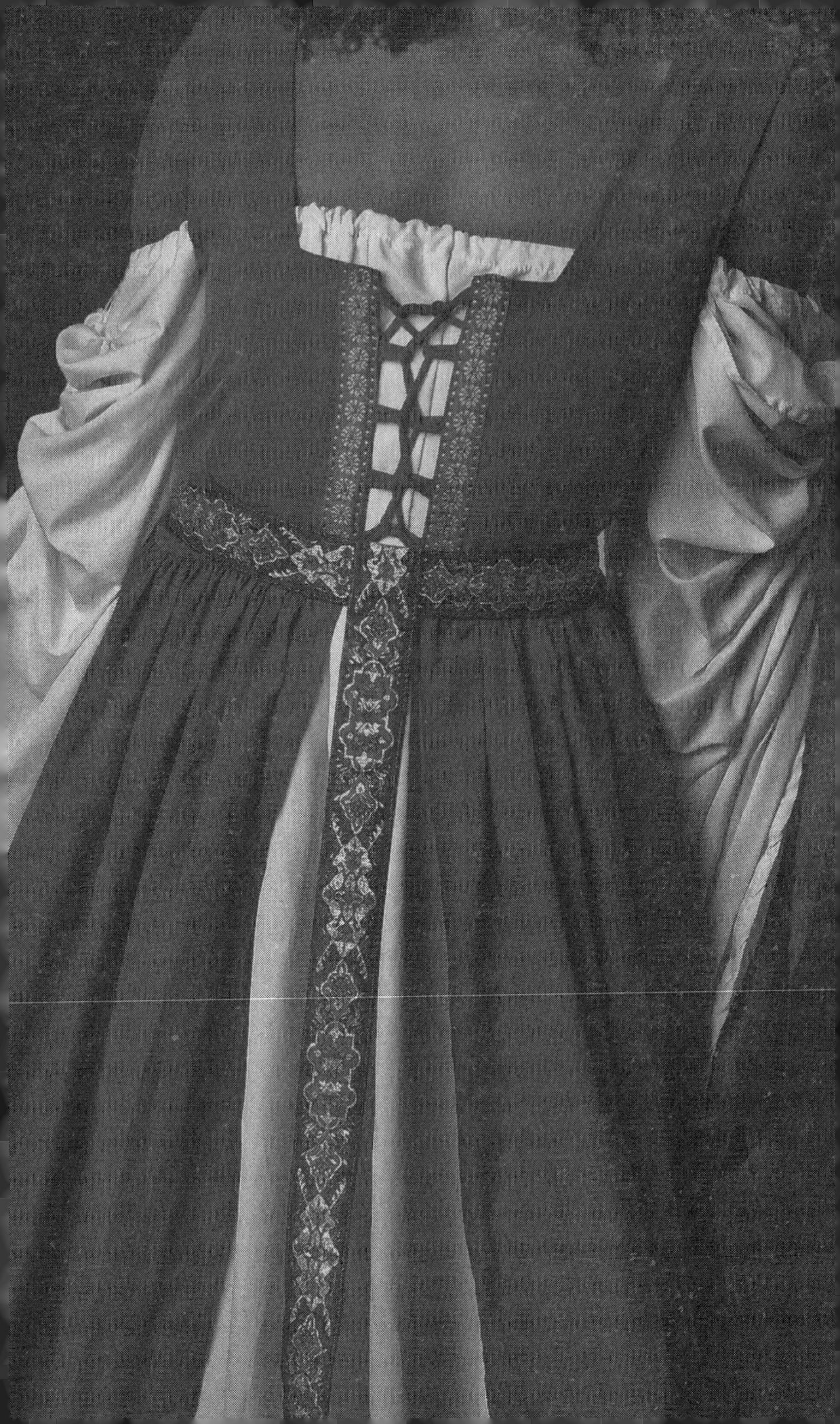

The Queen
STARLING

The king leaves me for a short time and while I hear commotion in the great hall, I can't hear at all what is being said. There's a chorus of voices though, mostly male. The sounds of trouble, a rowdy discourse, followed finally by loud cheers. The king returns to me shortly after that.

His expression is, as ever, inscrutable but when he glances at the tray on the bed, the stern expression he wore softens. The smallest smile graces one corner of his mouth, entirely transforming this imposing male into one I can almost imagine dining with every night. Almost.

"You've eaten," he breathes.

"I have."

"Good. Would you like more?"

"Oh no, I'm full, my lord. Thank you. It was very generous of you to feed the thralls and cooks like you did. I don't think many other guests would have, even those with the means."

The king grunts and pulls a seat next to the bed. He begins to eat in earnest from the tray, which is so full, it could have fed me for four days. "I think you might be surprised by the benevolence of other leaders. You have had the misfortune of having Olec and Rosalind as your only examples of leadership thus far. Among the twelve villages I have visited across Wrath in the past two years, only four maintain the practice of keeping thralls and in none of the others are thralls treated as appallingly as they are here."

He speaks so matter-of-factly, without maintaining my gaze, that I feel compelled to believe him even if his words seem so unbelievable. "Maybe, Olec and Rosalind can learn from another example," I whisper, wondering if the king speaks true on the promises he made to punish them...and that I won't have reason to fear the repercussions of whatever punishment he chooses.

The king makes a gruff sound I don't understand and sucks a piece of pork into his mouth in a way that I find oddly...salacious. His gaze flashes to mine and I start. Heat stirs in my chest. "Yes. Olec and Rosalind have learned what happens when my people are mistreated," he says cryptically. "The thralls have been released from their duties. It will take some time to restructure your village — there were more thralls than I thought — and while the former thralls have been encouraged to continue their existing duties, they have been compensated for their work and will continue to be compensated."

My eyebrows pull together, my chest feels hot. "From what coffers, my lord?" I immediately bite my bottom lip, aware that this knowledge is so far beyond the scope of my duties and my rank. I go to apologize, but the king seems to think nothing of it.

He answers right away. "To start, from Olec and Rosalind's *personal* coffers. Additionally, the grain you produce in your village is substantial. You are my second largest grain supplier and Rudabeth, my largest, is a village with ten times your population. The success of their production draws many to the city. Winterbren appears destitute and derelict by contrast, and yet, Rosalind and Olec were in possession of many precious gems and quite a bit of gold."

"Truly?" I gasp, shocked. Though...perhaps not *that* shocked. Perhaps, I shouldn't be shocked at all.

He nods. "They removed the gold and gems from these chambers before I took them. They were moved to Olec's man, Torbun's residence, where Olec and his wife have been staying. Those gems alone will be enough to fairly compensate all thralls for many months. Possibly a year or more. And then profits from the grain supply can be used to supplement when that runs out. The farmers, however, should be the recipients of that profit, minus a small tithe — much smaller than the one they were offering up to Olec and Rosalind before."

My brows scrunch, my fists clench. That same cold rage I've only felt in recent days crawls up my back and covers my head. "B-but Rosalind always maintained that the tithe was so large because *you* requested it."

"A fact that I have corrected. I didn't bring my books but I offered enough history to repudiate that claim to your townspeople. I hope that you may simply take my word for it." He smirks.

Shock. I can't believe it. His easy way with me, or his words.

Our village has always been poor. I thought...that was simply our lot. I did not know that Rudabeth, a thriving city I've heard spectacular stories about, was what we *could* have looked like. I swallow hard and reach for the cup of murky liquid on the table beside the bed. "I believe you, Calai," I whisper.

His ensuing smile is worth the nerves using his true name costs me. He pours himself a large cup of ale, takes a draught, sets it down on the table beside my bed with a loud thunk.

"Since maintaining their duties is not a long-term solution, I have encouraged the thralls to rethink what it is they would like to contribute to the economy of this place. I've set Elnis, one of my men, in charge of offering small loans to those who believe they may have competitive ideas for new businesses. He helps run the coffers in Ithanuir. Is there someone in Winterbren who might help him? It's good to know the characters of those interested in applying — those who are serious and capable compared to those who intend to take the money and squander it."

I... Is he...asking for my...advice? My jaw works and I momentarily flounder before finding my voice once more. "Rosalind is our village treasurer. She's very secretive." The king grunts, his face twisting in distaste as he lifts a cup of water this time, drinks from it, then offers that same cup to me. I take it, feeling unbalanced, as I do around him perpetually.

Finished, I add, "Moira might have the most useful experience with balancing books as she runs the inn just outside of town. It's the most successful business in Winterbren and from the girls I've spoken to that work there, Moira is a good, fair employer.

"However, if you're looking for someone who knows the people and can speak truthfully to their character, none would be better suited for the work than Elena, though she is — was — a thrall herself. She's also a very talented baker. While the cooking may be best suited for someone else, if she were given a chance, I don't doubt she'd run a successful bakery for the village."

The king is nodding at what I'm saying, continuing to eat. And when I've finished speaking, he meets my gaze in a way I find frightening in its intensity. His dark eyes move to my face. He exhales deeply, the rise and fall of his chest so large it makes him look as big as a ship's sail. Then his cheek softens, his mouth quirks to the side and he says, "Do any in this village know how bright you are?"

I feel my face heat and look away. "Thank you, my lord," I answer on instinct.

"Calai, please."

He sounds so sincere, so soft. I cannot imagine that this is the male they call the bone king at all. I offer him a gentle smile which causes the skin at the corners of his eyes to crinkle. "Calai," I repeat.

"I have another predicament I'm puzzling over. I wonder if you might have some thoughts, my little queen." I start at the moniker, but his gaze is unwavering. I don't know what that means. "What do you know of Viccra?"

"Viccra is Torbun's eldest son. He is our best warrior and slated to wed Ella, Chief Olec and Lady Rosalind's eldest daughter, though..."

"Though?"

"It is nothing. Petty village gossip."

"I'd like to hear it."

"Well, it isn't important. The marriage was planned at the time of their births, so there isn't anything either of them could do about it. Viccra is known to be in love with Mirabel, Elena's daughter, also a thrall. Mirabel has been beaten many times by Rosalind for the love she has for Viccra. Rosalind always felt it a slight to her daughter."

"Pale face? Red hair?"

"Yes," I say curiously.

"That explains it, then." The king grins.

"Explains it?"

"Nothing. What do you think of Viccra's character?"

"Oh. He's a good man. Nothing like his father. Viccra has always been defiant to Olec, but more so after he returned from his year training in Ithanuir. He's always been kind to me when many weren't."

"Do you think he is someone the villagers of Winterbren would follow into battle?"

I nod. "Yes."

"Do you think Olec is someone the villagers of Winterbren would follow into battle?"

I smirk. "Olec would never lead anyone into battle. He'd be in the back, issuing orders, not from a horn but from a pitcher of wine."

The king laughs, loud and bright. It's shocking, but I don't jump at the sound of it this time. Instead, I laugh a little with him. "Good, very good." He shakes his head and sits back in his seat, regarding me with affection of the purest kind. No one has ever looked at me in such a way in my life. "The gods have truly blessed me."

I don't answer, but track the king with my gaze as he stands, moves the tray out of his way and takes a seat at my side. His chest is very close. He is very close. He brushes his hand over my cheek and tucks my curls behind my ear. He is so gentle. And he smells so wonderful. I've never been stimulated by the scent of a man before, but the scent of his skin is divine and takes me straight back to the *intensity* of the previous night.

"I am to be a good boy today," he huffs, gaze scanning my face. "But I'd still very much like to taste." He leans down and his lips feather over mine in a way that has me tilting my head back, seeking more. I tilt my chin up and open my mouth, my tongue sneaking out to meet his. He moans.

His hand on my cheek hardens, a stern reminder of his size and the power he has over me, and yet, I don't feel as frightened by it this time. Especially not when my own hand tentatively reaches out to touch his chest. It lands on his pectoral, over his armor. He wears no furs for they are spread out over my bed.

"Gods," he gasps and in a daring moment of insanity, I use the moment to plunge my tongue into his mouth. He sucks. Pleasure and desire zing through me. I stiffen and pull myself up using his shoulder strap. My other hand fumbles, finding purchase around his thick, muscled neck.

"Oh," I mewl. "Calai," I wheeze.

Our lips are moving frantically against each other now and my hips are doing everything they can to try to create some semblance of friction between my legs. Calai starts to push me back into the pillows, but I cry out at the awful feeling of fabric rubbing against my stitches through the bandages.

"Fuck." He pulls back and keeps pulling, revolving our bodies until I find myself on top of him, my legs spread and a flurry of cool air tickling my bare behind beneath the short hem of my tunic. "Does it hurt like this?" he says and I rise on the motion of his heaving breaths.

"No." I'm frantic, pressed close to his body, forearms braced against his chest. I keep kissing his bearded cheeks, working my way in towards his mouth where I suckle and peck at his lips.

His tongue enters my mouth and our kissing turns open-mouthed. I angle my head in an effort to find the most effective way to sear our mouths together. I want to keep my eyes open to watch his pleasure, but continue to lose myself to mine. His fingers are gentle as they move over my behind, touching me through the thin fabric of this tunic. My hips are behaving scandalously, humping, gyrating, craving friction, but...he's too tall and my body can't reach the place I feel the greatest need.

I break our kiss on a gasp and shove myself down his chest. Sitting up, I place my bare core over the bulge in his trousers. "Augh!" His head flies back. His hands on my hips tremble. "I'm supposed to be a good boy, Starling." His voice is so strained, he sounds like he's being tortured. Which seems only fitting. I feel the same.

I shake my head. "I...made no such...promises..." I gasp. My legs are shaking as I suddenly find the pressure I need and start to rub myself in earnest up and down his groin. The madness from last night has taken me and it has not faded with the daylight. I cannot seem to extract myself from it, despite the wounds on my back and the fear I still have for him.

"Starling, no exertion...remember..."

But I'm so close, already. I want to feel what I felt again, that spike of pleasure. I feel wild in ways I've never felt before. The fear I felt last night slipping from my fingers, denuded by his words...his kindness...his faith in me...his promises... I want to believe him. I want to trust. And I've never felt that want before. It's too much to catch in my hands.

"Calai, I've never felt like this. Your kindness...your care..." I meet his gaze as mine starts to grow fuzzy around the edges. My hips jerk. My sensitive mound erupts in lightning. My head tosses back. I gasp his name as I come for him and I spasm as his pelvis jerks up. We moan together. I come down from my pleasure to see his face twisted in rapture. His hooded gaze is on me. He's reaching for my breasts, fondling them through my tunic. I shudder wildly and collapse onto his massive body, meeting his hungry mouth with mine once again.

In between the taste of his lips, I utter, "I would be a fool not to go with you when you leave this place, my king."

I kiss him desperately. "I'll be your helper, your mistress, your whore...whatever need you have of me..."

King Calai grunts, his own body twitching beneath mine. He reaches between us to adjust himself and looks a little angry as he meets my eyes. He holds my face in one of his hands — from cheek to cheek, his massive hand wraps all the way around my chin and jaw. He starts to speak, then stops. It doesn't matter. Over the sound of my panting, I can't hear him anyway.

"Whatever need," I repeat.

I feel embarrassed by my declaration, but it is true. To feel like this again, even if only as a hidden secret the king keeps tucked away behind his throne...I would do it. For a time, as long as I had with him, I would take it and I would not regret it. Hopefully. I just don't know what it would be like to know that he was this way with other females...

"My little bird," he breathes hard against my forehead and then slowly plants a kiss right between my eyes. It is searing. "I would not take you away from Winterbren as anything less than my queen."

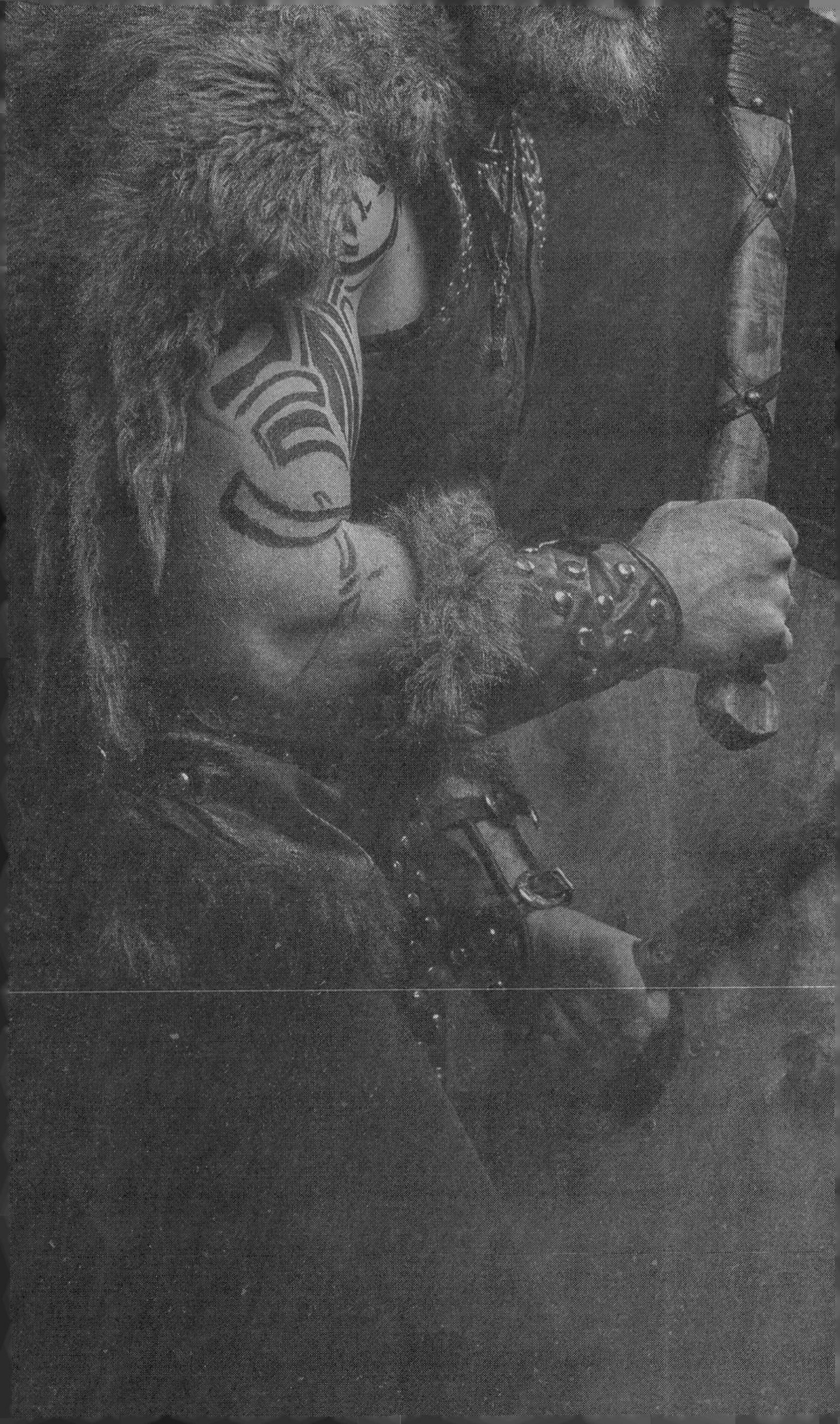

The Temptress
CALAI

The surprise on her face wounds me, but I release her and let her push herself up on my chest. She looks thoroughly fucked even though she still wears her tunic and I still wear my pants. My cum-covered pants. I cannot believe I emptied inside of my trousers like a young lad... Then again... My gaze runs over her face, its luminous color, her voluminous curls, her lush breasts and hips...and I chuckle.

"You tempt me too greatly, little bird," I say, laughing outright. "You've made a liar of me." I slide out from beneath her body and resettle her on the bed while she stares. Quickly, before I can command the obedience of my own limbs, I spread her legs at the knees, duck my head between her thighs and press an open-mouthed kiss onto her lower lips.

She gasps and I pull back as soon as I feel her fingers light on the back of my head. I cannot stand the feel of her touch. It sends me to places I find difficult to crawl out of. Dark, dangerous pits where there exists nothing but our bodies, nothing but flesh and want and lust. And she needs rest.

Fuck.

"Fuck." I groan and tilt my head back, separating our bodies by the length of the bed. Standing at its foot, I grab hold of my lengthening cock through my trousers and watch her sitting there, her brown shoulder gleaming in the torchlight as her tunic slips. "You are a temptation too great for a poor, weak man like me. I want to fuck you like a filthy whore every night, but that is not all that I want from you. I want so much more."

Cheeks flushed, eyes aglow, she still looks so...uncertain. "But..." She shakes her head, her curls twisting and glistening in the light. She is stunning. Stunning is even too trite a word. "But I don't...You *cannot* want me for a queen..."

"Not *a* queen. *The* queen." I feel uncomfortable, and not only because of the semen drying in my pants. "I want you for my wife." My voice breaks. Does she hear it? I hope, for the sake of my own pride, she does not.

"How...many wives do you keep?"

"One."

"So, I would become your second?"

"No, little bird."

Her lower lip trembles. "I...I cannot do that."

I clench, my entire body tightening. "Why not?"

"I'm a thrall..."

"*Were* a thrall..."

"I just..."

"What?"

"I cannot..." She shakes her head.

"Why?"

"Why?" She sounds shocked. Her lower lip trembles. "Why would you...make such an offer to *me*?"

"Why do you care?"

"It frightens me."

Our exchange has become slightly more heated and I find myself riled and wanting to ravage, knowing that I have found a wife with whom I can spar, yet annoyed that our sparring over *this* subject — the subject of her worth — is so constant. I try to ease my tone as I speak next, Puhyo's words ringing in my mind over again. *Easy.*

"The gods placed you in my path. When I saw you, they spoke."

But she's still shaking her head. "If that were true, you would have made me an offer before bringing me to your bed."

I find myself unable to counter what she has said with anything but the truth. I rush her, returning to where I sat at her side at the head of the bed. I slide both hands around her neck, tilt her torso back until she's forced to give me her weight and move in to kiss her. She yields to me, her lips opening like a gift, but I manage restraint like I never have.

"I am weak." I deny her mouth and instead, plant small kisses over her cheeks. "I have waited a long time for my wife. To have found her, yet be unable to touch her until our return to Ithanuir was too great a torture to imagine. I have..." I falter, knowing this confession will cost me. "I have not taken another before."

She stares between my eyes, disbelieving. "You are...king..."

"And I am first a believer in Ghabari and Raya. Would he have disrespected Raya so?"

"But...but you..." She shakes her head, seeming to shake off the shock of hearing that hers is the first body I've claimed for my own. Her voice grows shrewd as she asks, "Why then did you have Torbun suggest...that I would be offered riches in exchange for my body? You could have simply asked me... You're the king. I wouldn't have said no."

Anger licks up and down my spine, hot and hard to contain. I wrench back, pacing away from her once more and running my hands through my hair. "You would have said yes to the king, but what would you have said to Calai?"

She bites her trembling bottom lip, temptress that she is. I grab my cock. She glances at it and I see that she's holding her breath before she exhales words meant to torture me. "You frighten me, Calai. Not just the stories I've heard of you as king but your intensity...the way you seem so sure about me."

"Since when is *conviction* something to be feared?"

She fists the hem of her tunic and sits back onto her heels. "You don't even know me. And I don't know you. We've known each other a day."

"Two."

She cocks her head.

"I saw you first in the darkness, at your town square. You were strong, tough, even though you are not a warrior and were being intimidated by a much larger boy. That is what I first admired about you. The ferocity I saw in you."

She touches her mouth. Understanding sunrises in her eyes. "You...were the stranger in the square?"

"I was."

She touches her chest. "You were very kind. I..." Her cheeks flame pale pink beneath her beautiful brown skin. She glows with her sheepishness, making me want to coddle her to my chest and keep her all to myself, forever. As I will. "I dreamed of you that night. I hoped I'd see you again."

I smile. "The gods crossed our paths for a reason, Starling. I know that I ask much of you, wife, but even if you still fear me, do not fear the gods. They would not have laid your path over mine for no reason." I cross the room towards her, knowing I have lingered too long and need to return to the hall. I can hear the rising sounds of commotion, the higher-ranked villagers likely fearing destabilization. Some may even want to challenge my edict. I will need to swiftly put a stop to that. Bloodily, perhaps.

Yet, this is more important.

I wait and watch my little bird make swift calculations in her mind. I know not if she is a believer in the gods, but when she finally issues me a curt nod, I smile. "You believe me? Believe in the gods?"

She returns my grin with a tentative, hopeful one of her own. "I've never had much reason to believe in the gods. They've never given me much — a terrible father and a terrified mother — and the little that I was given was always later taken away."

I inhale rage, and exhale brighter rage. *Easy.* "Is that what you fear? That what might be offered will later be stripped from you?"

"Not wholly, but a little. I think…my greater fear…is disappointment. I am no great warrior, no great beauty. You will tire of me in days, or weeks, or even years. Even Olec is known to bed the thralls and the farm girls and he loves Rosalind…"

"Shh," I say. I return to the bed, ignoring thoughts of her father, of Olec, of the males and females who've wronged or disappointed her, made her feel unworthy of me. I take her hands in mine and I offer her a simple vow, one I should have offered her before Ghabari had I the strength to do things properly.

"As I've told you, I am a believer in the gods. And I fear Raya as I do Ghabari. When I say I marry once, I mean that in all ways. Our binding, should you accept, will be the only one I'll ever have. And I do not fear disappointment. Because you are a warrior, I have seen it."

I tuck her hair behind her ear. Watch her face turn up to mine. Her eyelids flutter at my small touches, like she's never been touched with any degree of kindness before in her life. "And you do not understand beauty if you do not see it in your own face," I whisper. "I had not seen you yet when I decided to help you with Tori two nights ago, but when the moon shone on you in the square, I knew I had never seen anything so lovely. Do not deface or demean that which I hold in so high regard."

"You speak too kindly to me. It would be easier to accept your offer if you were mean."

I chuckle and press my lips to her forehead. "It will not be easy. We will need to learn each other. But I can tell you already I like all that I've seen."

She looks up at me, such hope, such shaky, tenuous hope in her eyes, and says, "As do I. I think...I think I could make you a fine wife. At least, I will try."

Her words are aloe against the bright burn across my chest. My heart swells. I feel the magic of the moment coalesce around us. I kiss her lips tenderly, then roughly twice more. Wrenching back, I clear my throat and try to speak through the glass that has embedded itself in my throat. "You do not need to try. Come as you are."

She grins so wide, it hurts me in my bones. I know in this moment, I would do anything for this female, anything to guarantee her smiles. I drop my hand to her throat. "I am making some changes here in Winterbren. You have helped navigate me and I need to communicate some of these new thoughts you've given me to the others. I will be back for dinner. We will dine privately tonight and you will rest in the meantime, join me for the games tomorrow and sit beside me, as my wife. My queen. For the rest of our lives."

"Y-yes, Calai."

I fight to not say the words, fearful of scaring her again with my intensity, but the words still ring in my mind as I exit her chambers and return to the bedlam of the hall. *I love you, Starling.*

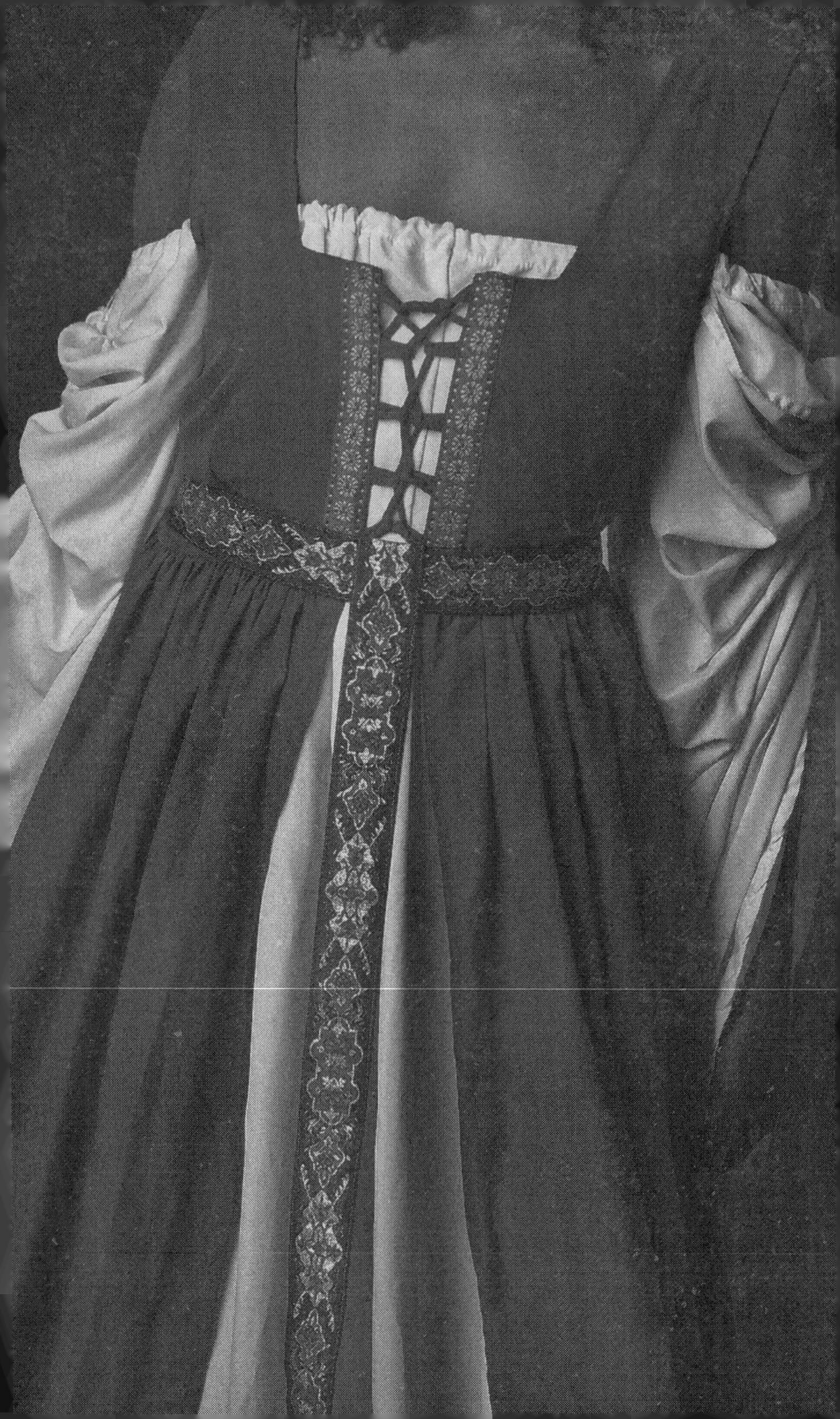

The King of Bones
STARLING

The king of bones is tremendously sweet. I giggle as he finishes removing his leather armor and flings it against the chests in the corner. "Fuck! Finally, I can be with my wife. At peace, in our room." He crawls over the foot of the bed to completely cover me on all fours. He kisses me.

It's dinnertime and he's come with a small feast to dine privately with me as he promised. And as he vowed, he doesn't touch me once all night. He kisses me passionately and offers me scandalously titillating touches any chance he gets, but he never moves to strip off my clothing and mount me, even though…the slickness between my thighs wishes he would.

My back still stings and I'm grateful when the healer returns with more milk of the poppy and salve. The king insists on applying it himself and actually obeys the shrewd, blonde healer when she instructs him on how to handle me properly.

"It's healing well. The minor scratches should be better by tomorrow, the rest by next week. It'll be important we keep you dry and warm on the road — you will be joining us, won't you, my lady?" Hilde asks me.

I know I'm blushing as I nod. "I will."

The king beams. Hilde just grunts and nods. "You will enjoy the road. It is beautiful this time of year. The leaves of the forest of Dorn are changing," she says, speaking of the lush forests known to surround Ithanuir's northern border. "And you will enjoy Ithanuir, I'm sure of it. It has something to offer everyone."

I nod, smiling and feeling so light as Hilde finally leaves and the king turns to me, eats with me, converses with me all through the evening and well into the night. He speaks to me of his mother, strong woman that she is, and his fallen father. He tells me a little about what it was like to become king at such a young age and, before that, how hard it had been to live in exile. How he owes his mother so much and, interestingly, how he sees some strengths in me that he believes she will admire.

And in turn, I tell him a little of my sordid history... My abusive father, my cowed mother... How the village did nothing to help her, short of Ebanora's mother who occasionally helped heal her wounds for free, as she now does for me. The king asks me about Ebanora and her family, her brother in particular. I tell him that he's a farmer, but has been pushed to enter the games though he would rather not. I tell him about the other villagers, warriors and anyone he seems curious about, until my voice gives out.

He's so curious about everything, everyone. It surprises me. He's king. I would have thought that our mundane little lives would be beneath him, and yet, he asks me about things that even I find trivial. How far the walk is from the silos where we store grain, why the kitchens are set so far off from the hall, how often we have out-of-town visitors and how they're treated, where they come from…why so few move to Winterbren and why so few born here leave. He seems to value my opinions on so many things…

I'm satisfied, a little tipsy on wine, and smiling as he blows out the torchlights and slides beneath the sheets and into the bed beside me. I sleep on my belly now that Hilde has removed some of my bandages to let the shallower wounds air. I keep my face turned towards the king and fall asleep to the feel of his hand tracing patterns across my hair.

Waking is just as pleasant.

I wake before the king and see that his eyes are still closed and his lips are parted in sleep. He has no lines in his forehead, but his beard is disheveled and his hair is in knots. It makes me giggle.

"I'm not sure whether to be pleased or offended that I've woken to the sound of my wife laughing at me," he grumbles, which only makes me laugh harder.

Getting out of bed, I procure a basin, oils, water and a comb. He has several. One of them is made of bone and perfect for detangling the kinds of knots I often get in my thick, tightly coiled hair. It looks newly made and I feel a tightening in my chest at the sight of it, knowing that, among all the other things he has to do, he prioritized this.

I use the finer comb now and apply oils to his beard before combing it out while he continues to lie on his back. He smiles as I work and sits up when I get to work on his long hair. I unbraid it, comb and oil it, then apply a few braids in a Winterbren fashion. They sit tight to his scalp on the sides and fall behind his ears. I add a few larger braids to keep the rest of his hair from falling over his forehead, still allowing for the length while not using half so many ties as he had the first time.

"Shall I braid yours?" he asks me when I've finished and I'm shocked enough that I agree. "I used to braid my mother's hair when it was just the two of us, and I still braid my own. Though, you are much better at it. I could get used to the feeling of your fingers on my scalp daily."

I bite my tongue to cage my moan. The low pitch of his voice, that rumbling brogue, moves through me. "Likewise," I respond.

He finishes my hair, leaving me with a crown of braids atop my head while the rest of my curls flow down my spine. "Are you ready, my queen?" he asks me. And I'm so surprised and touched by the style he's given me, and the grace with which he gave it, that I have tears burning the backs of my eyes.

I nod and smile.

"I have a dress for you. It was difficult to find one suitable, but I believe this one is close to your size." He goes to the outer room and what he returns with makes the breath in my lungs seize. The tears that I'd successfully stoppered well once more and several roll down my cheeks. He looks distraught as his gaze snaps between the dark green fabric and my face. "Starling..."

"That was my mother's."

He stills. "Why is it not in your possession if it belonged to her?"

"Rosalind took everything of value from my parents' house when they...died." When my father killed my mother and himself on the same night. "I thought Rosalind would have sold these off. I didn't know she still had them." I approach the dress and drag my fingers over the intricate darker green embroidery stitched onto the front bodice. I stifle my tears and glance up at the king, happy. "Thank you."

The king's lips, however, are hard. His eye tics. There are muscles standing out in his neck. He mumbles something under his breath as he helps me dress, first in the softest shift I've ever worn, and then in my mother's dress. It was one I last saw her wear the day Viccra and the other warriors returned from their year in Ithanuir.

Three warriors had gone that time and only two returned. The third, the spice-maker's son, had stayed and married a merchant's daughter he met there. They were with child last time they came to visit. And I remember hating myself a little at the sight of her rounded belly and happy husband. I'd been so envious. Not only because of her family, but also because after she came to Winterbren for a few days, she'd gotten onto the back of a wagon and left. She'd been able to leave, to go back to a better life than this.

The king's mood still does not improve as we take first meal in private, and then leave for the great hall. Most who took their meals here have already left their tables, likely vying to get a good spot to witness the games, which will be held on the barren wheat fields, freshly harvested, just south of Winterbren. The king surprises me by declining to ride a horse, but asks if I'm well enough to walk there.

In my new fur-lined boots, I've never felt more up for walking in my life. And my good mood will not be anchored by his displeasure, not when walking through Winterbren now, today, with the king holding my hand, everything feels so different. I see the world so differently — I'm *able* to see the world so differently unburdened by status or station.

People wave at me when they see me now — the same people who may have wanted to wave at me before, but couldn't. The thralls are smiling at the king as they pass him and I notice that not one of them walks with their face pointed at the ground. They walk with their chins tipped up. They aren't scrambling to serve and to clean.

I peek into the open curtains of the kitchens and see that it's, surprisingly, in perfect order, even without the threats of punishments guiding the cooks within. Instead, cooks and helpers and workers of all kinds are crowded in the streets around us as we all walk together to the impromptu practice field south of Winterbren, where the hopeful warriors — a dozen this time — await the king and his verdict on whether or not they are fit to fight alongside him.

My good mood is improved by the weather. It's beautiful today and I'm the perfect temperature in my mother's dress, swaddled by the king's fur. The sun is shining. The raised platform where the king and I will sit is already erected and, from this distance, I can already see the silhouettes of Olec and Rosalind occupying their places upon it.

My mood is elated even though I'm nervous to see Lady Rosalind, in particular, as I know her anger with me will be of catastrophic proportions. Still, I refuse to bow my head as King Calai grips my hand tight and leads me up the platform. He has to help boost me onto the ledge before he follows me onto it with a single sweeping leap of his own. I take my seat and it's only as he takes his place between Olec and me that I finally look up and boldly meet Lady Rosalind's eyes.

My good mood dies like the leaves of a sunflower at winter's first frost. My eyes may see, but my brain does not process. I can...cannot believe... What am...I seeing? What...

Lady Rosalind, pale of skin and fair of hair, is known to be one of the most beautifully adorned women in Winterbren. Always put together. Always composed. As smart as she is mean, as shrewd as she is vicious, she is untouchable. She is the chief's wife. His favored woman. Any who'd dare cross her knew already that the consequences would be as long as they were terrible...

But now, under the puffy white clouds, drifting so lazily over a baby blue sky, Rosalind sits in a position of honor at the high platform overlooking the games, her gold-crusted lips hang open, just like her eyes. Rolled back, she stares unseeing at the gods.

Rosalind's limbs are all twisted, caught in terrible positions, like she's been frozen mid-seizure. What looks like gold and silver paint crusts her mouth, her chin...

Droplets stain the front of her dress. Her throat is...it's *missing*. Part of it has been...melted...and the hole merely sits there open to the wind.

Her immaculately coiffed updo has fallen to the side and her dress is tattered, stained in blood. Her collar is split open wide, like the back of her dress has been torn, and there is blood seeping through her seat, swirling around her hem, coating her hands, which are reaching for her neck like she died trying to stop whatever happened to her from happening.

The contents of my stomach pitch and I taste bile. A weak grunt and a shifting blur drag my attention to the seat beside Rosalind where I meet Olec's gaze directly. I stutter something unintelligible. His normally bloodshot eyes are bright red and the bags beneath them are pink and puffy. He has blood on his cheeks, some smears that I don't believe are his and other lash marks that certainly are.

Aside from those few marks — marks I recognize, as they match the wounds on my back — he looks otherwise uninjured. A surprise, considering I would have thought that, if Rosalind were truly under threat, he would have tried to fight. Then again, on closer inspection, I can see that his forearms and ankles are bound to the seat beneath him. Perhaps, he couldn't.

Holding my gaze from the other side of King Calai's seat, Olec starts to thrash against his bindings. "You stupid, evil whore!" He roars. "You brought doom upon us! You did this! You filthy, ungrateful little girl, spreading your legs for..."

But Puhyo bounds up onto the platform behind Olec and shoves something into his mouth. It isn't a cloth, but appears hard and painful, judging by the way the chief wails when a tie affixes it between his teeth.

The king, all the while, stares forward. He doesn't acknowledge Rosalind or Chief Olec in the slightest. He simply continues to hold my hand and, at Olec's outburst, brings it to his mouth. He kisses the back of my hand, rolls his lips around on my skin in a way that, this morning, might have made me pant. Now, it makes my skin shrivel.

"Why, my dear Chief Olec, that isn't any way to speak to your future queen, now is it?" He speaks calmly, but loudly enough for all nearby to hear. And they are listening. The field is quiet, I realize, and though many are pointing and staring, none are objecting to this. It makes me wonder...if this was not a surprise to them, as it was for me.

In between tender touches and words that were saccharine sweet, did King Calai torture and murder Lady Rosalind, mere feet from where I was sleeping?

The king of bones...is a madman.

Chief Olec starts to weep openly and the king makes a condescending, pitying sound that elicits laughter from many of his warriors standing near the base of the platform. The king pats Chief Olec on the cheek with the same hand he used to braid my hair so deftly and tenderly. Then he gives my hand a little squeeze. "Do not trouble yourself with Olgar, my queen. As I told you before, repercussions from the two of them won't be delivered to you. They are simply paying their penance now for what they have done to you and the others in this village for decades. I am simply acting as the hand of the gods."

King Calai's mask is impenetrable. He is not the same male that he was in the privacy of our chambers. *This* is the king. Calai is nowhere to be found here.

I sit and am bone cold. The king's fur I wear does nothing for me anymore as the crowd rushes with excitement and seemingly ignores Olec and his wife seated high above them, one dead, the other tortured. Olec moans while the king whistles loudly enough to command attention.

"Let the games begin!" he roars.

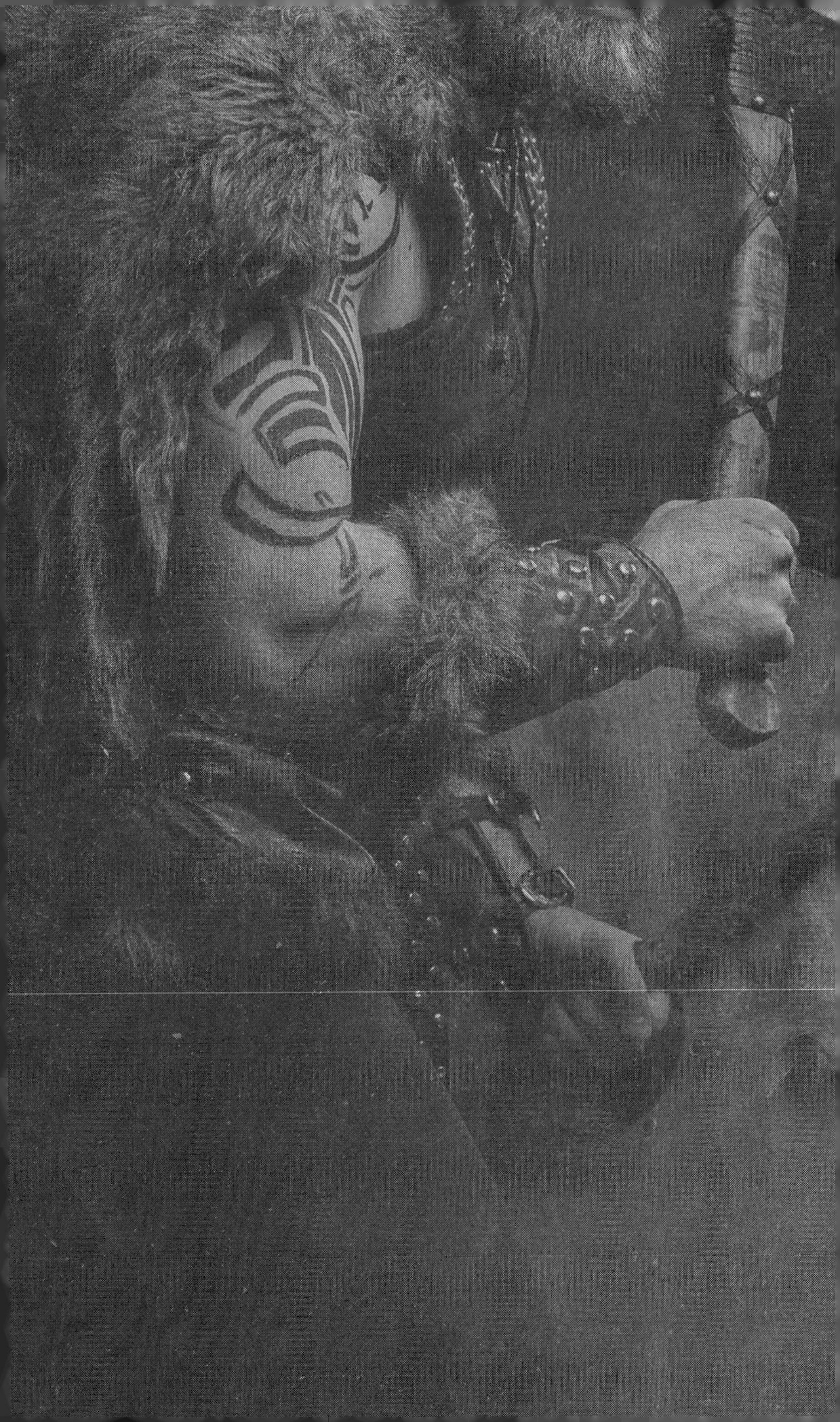

The Fighter
CALAI

I sit upon the elevated square looking down at the rowdy cluster of fighters as they battle in small contests. There are pitiably few fighters here, and I regret that I cannot take more of them to train and return, but Innara, who organizes the trainees and sees to it that our ulterior motives in bringing them to the capital are fulfilled, will not allow me to bring more than six from a village as small as this.

A cartographer and expert city planner, she is responsible for aiding me in much of Wrath's design — where new roads are built, where we must erect new dams, where cities and villages sprawl dangerously, where they need to expand and where we need to better refine our borders.

She keeps a census of the populations of Wrath's villages and has been concerned for some years that the smallest villages will suffer from too much inbreeding. Inland villages such as these do not raid often. It is her imperative that any warrior who comes to train finds a mate, and with the help of a small, conniving team, she has a high success rate.

There are eighteen who fight now, though only eleven true contenders. The others are either too young, too old or too small, likely coerced into participating in the games, as Starling's friend's brother was. It is a pity that he is a satisfied farm boy. Had he a bit of bloodlust, I'd have enlisted him into my army. As it stands now, I will take him for a year and make him capable of picking up arms to defend his town, in addition to matching him with whatever bride Innara chooses.

Of the eleven contenders, I can already pick out two or three that might make suitable warriors for this village. The brother, a small male who fights with speed and cunning who I may even need to keep at my side in Ithanuir, and…Tori. It is a pity he is a rotten boy who will not survive these games. He may not even survive the day.

Yes. As it turns out, I am *still* a little angrier than I initially thought I was.

I glance to my left. Chief Olec sits fuming beside me, his rage almost as large a presence as his grief. He weeps like a miserable drunk every few minutes, but he never glances once to the seat beside him where his wife sits. Coward. Filthy, miserable coward. I still have yet to decide, among a short list of tortures, which one will be most suitable for him. I wonder if my queen has an idea.

I glance to the right and am surprised to see her staring straight out at the field where the young warriors are battling, her face oddly ashen. I glance at the sky. The sun is shining, glittering over her hair. But her skin seems to lack its usual light. I release her hand and gently trail my fingers across the curve of her cheek. She jumps.

"Little bird, is everything alright?" I ask her as the groups break up into pairs under the administration of Daneera, Puhyo, Fuzier and Hektor.

She nods, but she doesn't look at me. The easy way we walked to the training field is dead. We are back to where we were two nights before, when I had my little bird backed into a corner. When she thought herself a whore.

I lean over towards her, take her chin between my fingers and force her to look at me. She sits lower in her chair than I do, and she looks utterly dwarfed by my fur, which is sure to be keeping her warm — if not hot — but when she meets my gaze, she still shivers. "What is wrong?"

She glances past me and I am immediately caught off guard. Olec and Rosalind. She is *displeased*. I'd have thought she would appreciate the suffering of those who wronged her, yet she seems utterly shaken by the sight of them.

"What did you do to Rosalind?" Her voice is thin as ash, brittle.

"I gave her the payment she was owed for your virginity." I take her hand, lacing our fingers and giving her palm a squeeze. She does not squeeze back.

"You...m-m-melted the payment? And fed it to her?"

"Yes. On both accounts. First, I let your fellow former thralls repay the kindnesses she bestowed onto them using the same wire cords she took to your back. They were very vigorous." I chuckle and then my laughter fades. I realize...perhaps, I made a slight. "I did not think to rouse you from bed to exact your own vengeance. I am sorry for that, though I would be pleased to let you take your rage out on Olec by proxy."

Olec is clearly listening to me and shouts at my back, voice muffled and mangled through the gag he's been fixed with. I reach over and give his shoulder a firm squeeze, one hard enough to make the grown man whimper.

Meanwhile, my hand on hers remains utterly tender.

I smile in her direction, but she's shaking her head quickly and sputters out, "N-no. No, please no."

"You don't have to..."

"Thank you. Thank you, Your Highness." Your Highness. We're even further from Calai. She does not even address me as lord... "I just...I think I need to relieve myself. I'm suddenly not feeling well."

She leaves, escorted by three of my men and Hilde. It takes them a while to return and, when they do, Hilde joins my queen on the platform. She gives me a dark look I do not understand before unfurling a large black sheet and using it to cover Rosalind's body. I don't know why. The outline of her shape still clearly shows her golden mouth, forever opened towards the sky above. This seems to settle my young queen a little, but she still doesn't eat when food is offered to her.

By now, the pairs have switched three times, and Tori has proven to dominate all three of his partners. My fists clench. My desire to jump down and meet Tori's blade with my axe is strong, but that would be an insult to me, to fight one so small and pathetic.

No, I have more creative plans for Tori. I clap my hands. The fighters break for water. Those that are performing well are congratulated. One older warrior is attended to by a healer and removes himself from the battle.

"I am impressed," I tell the crowd. My words are met with cheers. The pride of this small town is not to be dismissed or scoffed at. It is important. It is what will keep this town together when Rosalind and Olec are removed from the mortal plane forever and returned to the dirt.

"There are many among you with fighting skills strong enough to protect your people in times of hardship. There are several of you even who might make warriors strong enough to raid with me." More cheers sound. My wife's is not among them, but when I glance at her, I see a similar pride shining in her eyes. Even if the rest of her is clenched tight and oddly leaning away from me.

I wonder if it is the sight of Tori that vexes her. That doesn't seem quite right, given the way she spoke back to him that very first night when my life changed forever. Still... Perhaps I should get on with Tori's punishment, then, just to be certain it is not the sight of him breathing and winning at these games that causes her such stress.

"There is one among you, however, who has stood out to me most of all. Tori, come forward!" The cheers resume and Tori struts forward, arms outstretched. He approaches the raised dais with a broad grin and bows. He has the audacity to glance at Starling as he does. I do not dare look to her reaction. After all, I am *already* angrier than I thought I was.

"Tori has bested all three of his opponents. I say Tori is ready for a rally! Any who are able to draw blood from Tori will advance to the next round automatically, and Tori, if you are able to remain standing all day, you shall receive a special reward."

Tori smiles broadly, confident boy that he is. Overconfident. This will be *fun*. "Bring it on!" he shouts up to the gods.

I organize the challengers, giving Tori the small man with the cunning arm first. He is ambidextrous. I wonder if Tori has realized that. In earlier battles, he fought only with his right arm, but based on the way he carries himself, I do not doubt he would be just as adept at fighting with his left.

I order their training swords swapped out with real ones and place the challengers in order of strongest to weakest. I want Tori to tire quickly. I want *every* challenger to draw blood from him. This is not about pain *today*. Today is about humiliation. There will be plenty of time for pain tomorrow and the final day of the games when I truly decide to unleash the full power of my creativity.

"Begin!"

The first challenge begins slowly and my respect for the slighter male grows. He seems to understand Tori's fighting style well, understanding Tori's strengths relative to his own. He never allows Tori to get him on the ground, or on his back, choosing to retreat again and again, rather than engage too strongly.

Tori is an athletic male. There will be little chance of tiring him completely so early in the bout. The smaller male knows this. I lean over as he makes his first parry, one which Tori only just manages to block, and ask my queen, "What is the smaller male's name?"

"That's Elia," she whispers. "He's Viccra's younger brother."

Ah. That explains much. "Viccra must have been training with him."

She glances at me, her face creased in worry. "You think he is going to beat Tori?"

I only smile. She winces. I frown. "Do not question my instincts, little bird, not in this." I reach out and take her hand. She is stiff. "I promise it will all work out in a way that will please you."

She nods, her cheeks glowing pink. She turns her face forward, but...she does not watch the battle, choosing instead to keep her gaze on the cup of wine in her other hand, or on her knees.

The battle rages on and Elia's strategy rapidly becomes apparent. He is not aiming to wear Tori down physically...but break him mentally. He taunts Tori with poor jabs and halfhearted advances. He keeps moving all the while, dancing circles around the larger, stronger male. He's fast and Tori has to expend incredible focus to remain guarded, to counter each block and attack again and again and again.

He is not wearing Tori down...but frustrating the mean-spirited boy.

"Ough!" Tori shouts, heaving his sword overhead and bringing it down with incredible force. Elia slides out of the way, his entire right side lined in mud as he lies on the ground. Tori advances on him. I smile at the bloodlust in Tori's eyes. He thinks he has him. And then...Elia switches sword hands as Tori brings his blade down.

Elia bats Tori's blade out of the way and, shifting onto one knee, spins in towards the bigger male. Elia takes his sword in a backwards left-handed grip and sweeps the sharpened edge of the blade across both of Tori's shins.

Tori falls back as Elia rises amidst a chorus of gasps and cheers. Tori's defeat was unexpected. Even Elia looks half surprised to have defeated him. He raises his sword arm above his head and looks up at me. He does not see Tori rising from the ground behind him.

"Oy!" I shout, hailing his attention. He turns and jumps back just as Tori swipes for him. Tori manages to draw blood from his shin, but not as much as he had intended. Tori had meant to take the leg, that I don't doubt.

The crowd goes quiet. Eyes turn to me as Elia falls back. "See to his leg," I tell Hilde. She moves off of the platform and I squeeze my queen's hand. She is sitting forward in her seat, strained.

"Well done! What a first contest," I say, pitching my voice loud enough to be heard above the whispers. There are a few claps, but nowhere near the cheers there were before. I am sure these people are surprised I do not reprimand Tori, but there is no need for that now. "Tori, well done. Up on your feet. Your next challenge begins now."

"Next...challenge?" He scoffs as he uses his sword to clamber upright. "You cannot be serious, my lord. I need medical attention..."

"You would not receive medical attention on the battlefield for a little scratch like that," I say, flicking my gaze down to his shins where bloody tendrils mix with mud and weep down his pantlegs. "And it is your intention to become a raider of mine, is it not?"

Tori nods after a brief hesitation.

I grin. "You'll be on the front lines on the battlefield, charging into unsuspecting villages. You'll have first pick of loot and females. Perhaps, you'll even find one that looks like my queen to make up for what I've stolen from you."

Tori's expression turns sour as he glances briefly to Starling. He cannot make sense of my light tone and I want to laugh at the trust he has in himself here. That I value his sword arm more than the disgrace he's brought to my female, the hate he's brought to this village. That he would dare to attack a fellow warrior in a petty contest such as this makes me wonder how he could ever think I would take him for a trainee, let alone a full-fledged warrior on a raid. Warriors must be able to rely on one another for any raid to be a success. If Tori cannot even be trusted to lose a simple challenge, then how could he ever be trusted to support his fellow warriors when the heat of bloodlust came over him?

"On your feet. Come on. There are storm clouds on the horizon and there is feasting to be had tonight, Tori. You will be celebrated for what you've done here today."

Tori fights and wins the next battle, much to my dismay, but loses the next three. He is rewarded with light cuts to his cheek and left thigh, and a deeper wound to his abdomen. "Next!" I shout when he asks for reprieve.

He wins again twice, then loses every other battle he fights and by the time the sun has moved closer to the horizon, he has cuts decorating most of his body. What a beautiful thing. I cheer and congratulate him while his village's healer takes a look at his wounds. He shoots me looks meant to scathe as I clamber down from the platform and reach back up for my wife. There are no steps to this platform, so I have to fit my hands around her waist and lift her down. Her gaze remains on my chest all the while.

She is silent as we return with the tumultuous crowd to the hall where the feast already is spread among the tables. This time, there are extra places — two entire extra tables have been laid out in the town square. It is a cold night, but there is no rain and, to ward away the chill, several bonfires blaze bright. Plates are stacked high with food across all the tables. There are no servants. Former thralls take their seats for the first time tonight.

My queen eats at dinner, but excuses herself early, claiming she's unwell. I follow soon after, but find that she's already asleep in bed. Something about her attitude vexes me, but I hesitate to wake her to demand answers to her mood. Instead, I lie down, foul-tempered myself, only for sleep to elude me.

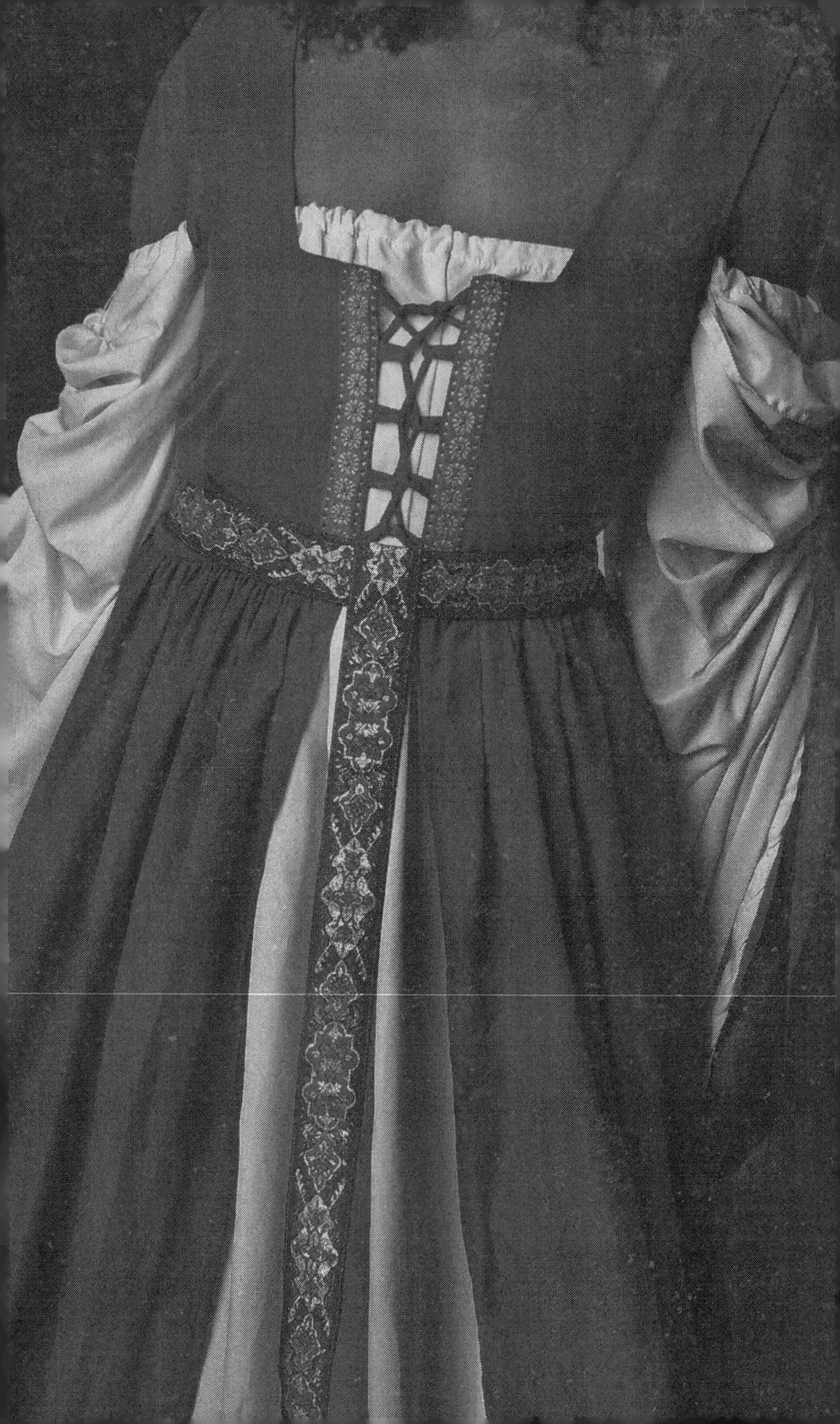

The Victor

STARLING

I don't feel well. I haven't felt well since I saw what the king did to Rosalind. Olec's foul mouth didn't disturb me. I understood his rage, his misdirected anger — besides, I hardly heard the words. Instead, I watched the king's apathetic — nay, his *pleased* — expression as he looked glibly over Olec and his ruined wife. And then I spent the rest of the day watching him torture Tori, though Tori seemed largely unaware that he'd been set up to fail, and all I could think to myself was that this king is a male steeped in violence, so saturated with it he is no longer even aware of it.

And he wants to be my husband.

He wants to share my bed. Raise my children. Keep me at his side as his queen. Place me in positions where I'm meant to constantly see the bloody madness he's capable of. And somehow, never fear that he might turn that violence to me.

I was raised by a violent man. I've felt the sting of a man's palm against my cheek, against my back, against my belly. I've felt the rake of wire against my spine. I've felt the belt, the paddle. I've endured it all. But when he took me to his chest and told me words I now know a male of such violence could not possibly mean, I believed him.

You do not need to try, he told me. *Come as you are.* But what if who I am displeases him? Maybe not today, not tomorrow, but five years from now? What will he do to me?

I will make mistakes. I have no idea what becoming queen entails. And if he depends on me for things outside of my control — heirs, particularly — and I'm unable to deliver...how will I be punished? Will I be cut into pieces like Tori? Like Rosalind, will I be doused in flaming gold?

I lie quietly all night, worried that he will touch me, ask me what's vexing me. I worry that this will begin the fall. I cannot begin to dictate to this male how he should punish those who have wronged him. I can't even dictate to this male how he should punish those who have wronged *me*. But must I...be forced to watch? I don't want to watch. Does that make me a coward? Will he think me weak if I don't?

I glance at the king from the corner of my eye as we settle in our seats for day two of the games. Rosalind remains seated in the final chair on the end of the row. The sheet that Hilde covered her with yesterday has been removed and I am horrified to see that several flies have been drawn to her. They flutter in and out of her mouth, smaller flies swarming the open wounds on her back.

Olec sits beside her slumped in his seat. His eyes are closed. He appears to be sleeping. I wonder...if they left him out here tied to his seat all night. He is still gagged. I don't know if he's been given water and have to fight the urge to cry. The king glances at me. I turn my face quickly forward.

King Calai leans in towards me and his lips brush my earlobe as he whispers, "We will speak tonight, little bird. You will tell me what has upset you. Why you are ignoring me." He lifts my left hand and drags his impossibly smooth lips over my knuckles. "You need not fear me."

That's what he says to me, but when he turns to the crowd and announces a new game for today, one not part of the original program, I know he is wrong.

"Tori did so well yesterday, did he not?" he shouts and the crowd claps and cheers. Tori does not grin, but stoops a little lower than he did when he first stepped onto the training field yesterday morning. His shoulders are no longer rolled so far back, his chin no longer so high.

The clouds have returned today and the temperature dropped overnight. I have chills. I hate this male, yet I still fear for him.

"I would love to see Tori compete again, this time in an even more daring contest. How about you?" His tone, pleasant and light as it is, riles the crowd. They cheer and shout and stomp their feet, whooping loud. "Warriors. You will fight Tori again, the strongest among you. This time, you will only advance to tomorrow's games if you are able to take something from him."

That causes a stir. It is Ebanora's brother, Matthias, who surprises me by stepping forward, out of the cluster of combatants, and asking, "My liege, could you clarify? Do you mean, disarming him? Taking his sword or his shield?"

"Sword or shield, certainly, but I actually had something more permanent in mind. A hand, an ear, the tip of his nose, perhaps?" The king smiles.

The crowd gasps and goes wild. Laughter mingles with shrieks as the bloodthirsty among us are given the opportunity to see a show for the ages. I close my eyes and swallow the disappointment and bile in my throat. When I open them, I see Tori's mother step forward. "Your Highness, please. Tori is our eldest son. For whatever way he has slighted you or your intended bride, he begs forgiveness..." But her pleas die when Tori's father pulls her back into the crowd.

"Let the boy fight. Do not disrespect the king," he shouts gruffly, yanking his wife to his side. Tori's father is not a cowardly male, but a mean one like his sons. I know he has always been hard on his boys. I wonder if he is not among those who enjoys this...even though the boy is his own.

"If that is all, then let us begin. As Tori wounded you yesterday, Elia, I offer you the chance to fight first."

Elia steps forward, a grim look on his face, and for a moment I dare to hope that he might decline and defy the king. Then he says, "I would cede my place to Vale, if it please you, my king."

The largest of the trainees is a brown-haired male I've seen around the village but have no personal connection with. He steps forward, his broadsword in a tight grip. "I would be honored to fight Tori first in this challenge, my king."

The king looks between the boys. I watch Tori's mouth tighten. I don't know what passed between this lot, but I can feel a certain mad and dangerous energy emanate from Vale as the king gives his assent. The boys square off against one another, but Tori is already weakened from yesterday. He doesn't stand a chance.

Vale is perhaps the third best fighter here, based on what I saw of his performance yesterday. He's strong, but he's not as quick or agile as Elia, and Tori had him matched in strength yesterday when they battled each other. But not today. Today, Vale manages to get Tori onto his back. From there, he punches Tori in the face several times and removes both of Tori's ears. Tori's screams make my stomach clench and toes curl. The wind carries the scent of blood. Real or imagined, I'm not sure. I taste my breakfast in the back of my throat and grab for the king's arm as Vale stands, boasting Tori's ears to the bloodthirsty crowd. He tosses the ears onto Tori's body.

"My liege, please," I all but gasp. "No more."

The king looks at me and light flares in his dark eyes. His grim expression pans over my face, no softness to be found. "Do you favor Tori?"

I want to laugh. "No. No, my king. Of course not. I just..." I want to cry.

I can no longer speak. The sound of Tori's screaming has rattled my insides. I get up from my seat and run to the back edge of the platform. I purge everything I ate that morning.

I distantly hear Hilde muttering under her breath as she approaches me from below. The king, however, holds my hair and smooths his hands over my back. "I am sorry, little bird. Are you alright?"

"Of course she's not alright," Hilde grunts. "I told you last night, your queen has a soft heart. This violence is too much for her. She should not be required to watch the games if this is how you plan to conduct them."

"I am doing this for her," the king argues as I finally find my feet.

I tilt my head back and look up at him, all the way up, admiring the way the light silhouettes his massive shoulders in glory. And then a thimble of confidence drags itself up my throat and makes itself known on my lips.

"No, you aren't," I whisper. "I did not ask for this and I do not want it. You do this for yourself."

The king glares down at me, his expression stony and severe. And I know, as Hilde wheels me around and escorts me back to the village, two things with absolute clarity:

I cannot be King Calai's wife.

And I absolutely cannot stay here.

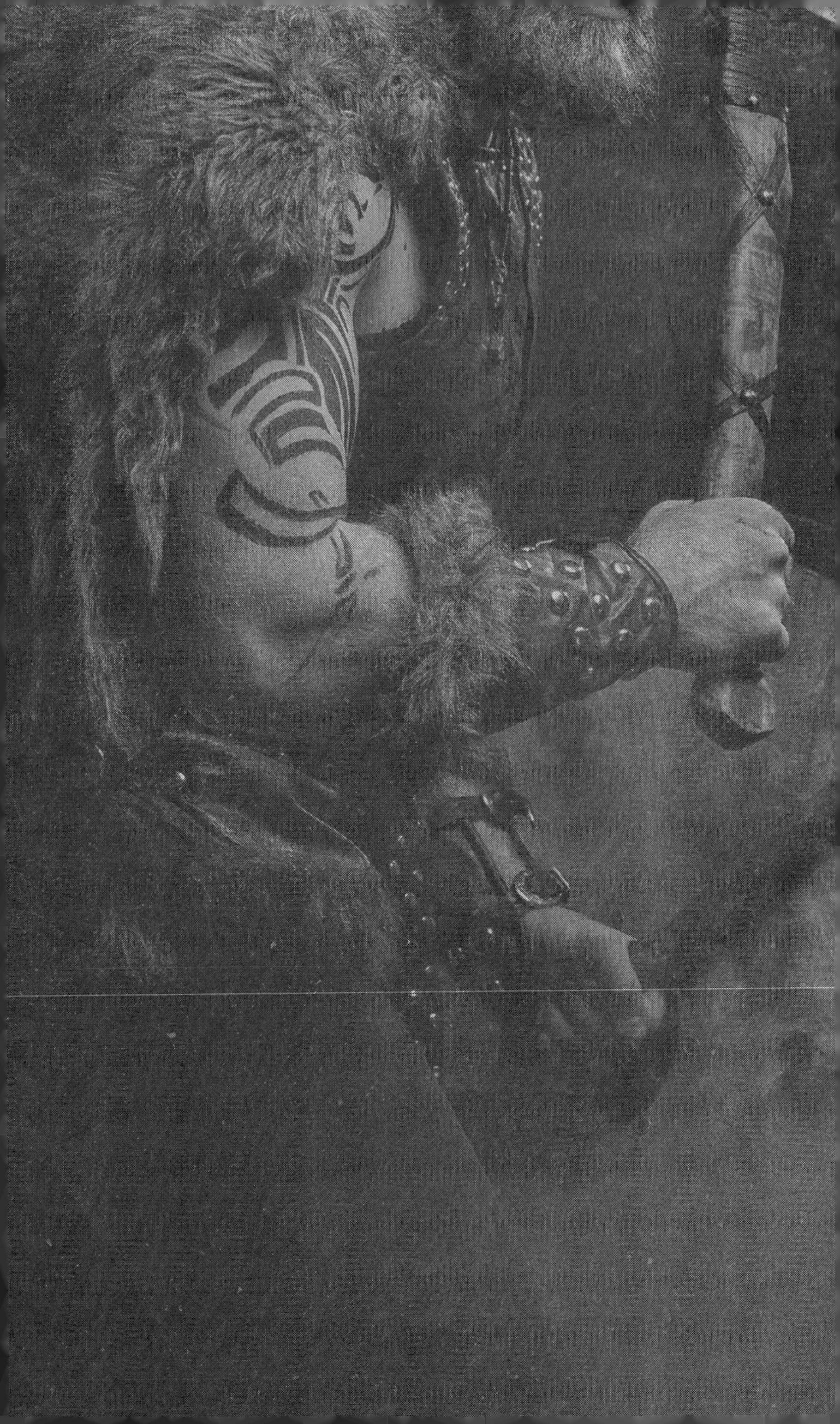

The Little Bird
CALAI

I am displeased. After my wife fell ill, Fuzier came to me and provided me with advice that I did not like.

"Let the boy go and kill Olec. Be done with this now. Show your wife that she is more important to you than your rage."

It was…advice that I knew in my heart was the correct advice to take…yet it still pained me to take it. Releasing Tori to the healers was the most difficult thing I've done in my long years as king. Killing Olec in a ritual sacrifice right there on the training fields is easier and helps appease some of my displeasure, as I know that his blood will appease the gods of war and mischief.

I finish marking myself with his blood, painting it across my pectorals. I mark my cheeks. And then, I mark each of the men who will advance to training tomorrow. I choose eight of them, Vale and Elia among them. Tomorrow I will narrow it down to six. The next day, I will finish sorting the affairs of this town. The following day I will appoint Viccra as chief and exile any who dare dissent, including his father. The final day, I will be off, my lady at my side.

But before any of these things can happen, I need to return to my chambers here in this small village. I need to see to my queen's wellbeing, ensure that she's alright and reassure her that she is my priority. As much as it pains me to admit, it would seem that yesterday, Hilde was right. My little bird is not a little violent thing. She is not the shield maiden to sever heads at my side, but the strong planks of a house to ward away the rain. She is my shelter, as I wish to be hers. She is not my blade.

I am displeased as I return to the village, the villagers all gossiping like children around me. My own warriors are no better — I hear the way they speak in hushed whispers of my failings. Of how I frightened my precious Starling. I am a fool for not realizing it earlier. And I am twice the fool for daring to think, for even a single moment, that Starling wanted to stop the violence because she favored Tori. Because she does not want to see him bleed does not mean that she likes him. But does seeing him bleed mean that she likes me less?

I frown, stopping before the hall without entering it. People pour around me, but I turn to Fuzier and shout at him above all of it. "Will my queen be upset to see me in such a state?"

Fuzier smirks. "That you ask should be indication enough, my king."

Grumpily, I make my way to Rosalind and Olec's last quarters — where they have been hoarding and guarding their precious commodities — and command a bath brought to me. I soak myself thoroughly, making sure to wash away the blood. I don't want to mess up my hair, but that can't be helped at this point. I have to pull out the braids she gave me. As I rise from the steaming waters, I hope only that I have not ruined things so irreparably that she will not braid my hair once more. Every day for the rest of our short lifetimes in this world, and then every day for the rest of eternity in the world that comes after.

Hair long and unkempt, I don a simple tunic and trousers and return to the great hall where the day's final feast is underway. Feeling strangely nervous, I round the throne and enter the chamber where my wife rested for the rest of the day. I rehearsed several times what I intend to say, but now that I am here, I suddenly can remember none of it.

My wife is not in bed.

The pit that takes up residence in my stomach starts small, but widens as I move from room to room and find traces of her — my tunic neatly folded, a tray of food entirely empty, a flagon of water missing, a single bejeweled dagger of mine gone — but not my wife.

No.

Horror and rage flood my bones.

My little bird has flown.

I immediately shed my clothing and opt for armor. I dress my belt with axe and sword. I hail six warriors to ride with me, sending the entire hall into a stir, and then we mount our horses and take to the road. We hunt.

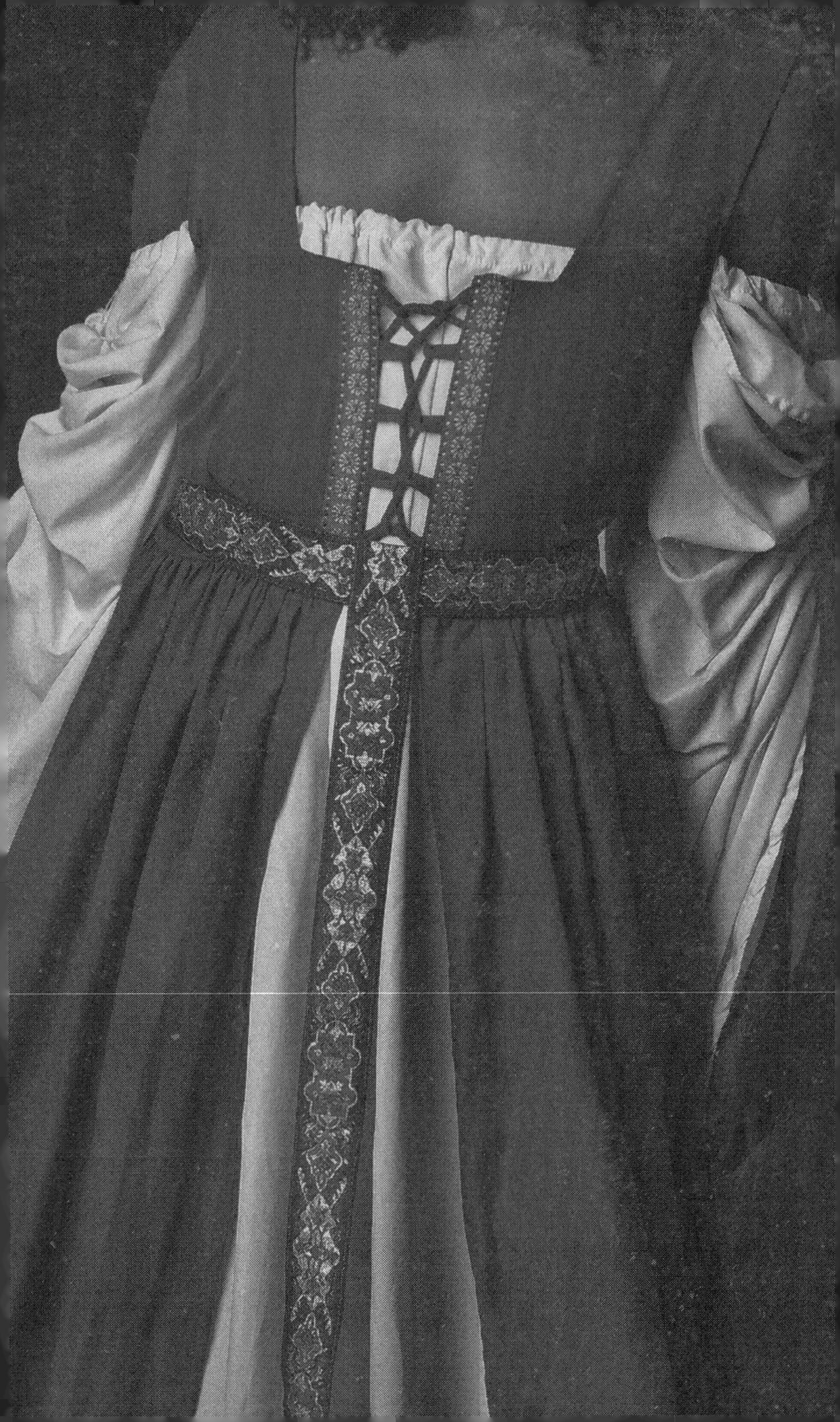

The Warrior
STARLING

It took me all afternoon to reach the woods. A risky path, I know, but I have no doubt I'd be caught on the road by Calai's men...or worse. I took none of the riches I found in Calai's chamber with me, opting instead to only bring Calai's dagger to defend myself with, and my mother's dress to trade. I didn't want to steal from him...at least, more than I had to. And I know neither dagger nor dress will get me very far, but my hope is that I might be able to reach the inn outside of Winterbren and barter passage beyond Wrath.

I don't know what I'll find. Ebanora told me stories of stone cities built like staircases to reach the gods, but that seems too unbelievable. I suppose I'll have to see them with my own eyes. I do not feel as excited as I thought I would, though. Instead, I feel only frightened.

As the woods close in around me and I step through thick patches of mud that soak my new boots up to the ankle, I wonder — not for the first time — if this was, perhaps, an impulsive choice. Too impulsive.

The king frightens me more than the unknown. But the unknown cannot be reasoned with. Could Calai have been brought to reason if I'd merely stayed and had the courage to try to talk to him? At least…told him the reason for my malcontent and hoped — prayed to the gods — that he didn't carve my tongue out for it?

I shiver at the thought. I'm shivering in my boots, a gift from Calai. The cloak I stole from his chests along with the dagger. I am ashamed to have taken anything at all. I left his furs. That…fills me with sadness. The first furs I ever wore, given to me in one of my very first, unexpected kindnesses. The only kindness I ever saw before was from Ebanora and her family. But they are too fine to wear for a thrall on the run and would arouse suspicion. So I left them behind. I hoped they would serve as a message to the king, because I left him no note. Coward, that I am. Yet, what was my other choice? Live the rest of my life tongueless for daring to suggest that he stay the blade of his sword and deliver those who have wronged me more merciful punishments? I like my tongue where it is.

I trudge deep enough into the woods that I can still see the road, but cannot easily be seen from it. Mostly, I follow the sounds of horse hooves and horse carts. This road is well traveled. And as night descends and frightening sounds start to make themselves known in the forest surrounding me, the gods finally see fit to show me mercy. *Mercy.* The word curls my toes and makes me think of the easy way he smiled at me, the soft way he stuttered when he said *I want you to consider coming with me, Calai.* But is it *Calai* that is Davral's incarnate, or the king?

Lights flicker in the trees ahead. My mud-soaked hem is weighing me down, as is the pack on my back. I took very few possessions, but as much food and water as I could carry, unsure if I'd be able to barter the few coins I've amassed over the years for a roof and food or just one or the other. It's cold tonight. Not a night to sleep in the stables, if I can help it.

As if to press that point home, the wind whips through my cloak, flinging my hood back from my face as I step out of the woods, finally emerging onto the packed dirt road. The bank is still muddy and I hear the slap of my hem against my boots with every step I take to the front doors of the tavern. I'm halfway across the road when two women burst through them.

"Can you believe it?" The one slurs, drunkenly falling over the other. Both women have bright blonde hair piled high on their heads and very low necklines revealing large breasts.

The other answers, bringing a wine pitcher to her lips. "The king of Wrath — here at this place?"

I stop walking and hold my breath. The lights reveal my face fully and I rapidly pull back up my hood as I watch the two women who don't even notice I'm there.

"You think he'll take me to bed if I'm real sweet on him?" The women are walking around the tavern now, crossing the short square between the tavern and the inn. Three sides of a square, the horse stalls making up the third side that connects the inn and the tavern together. Their boots make clacking sounds on the cobblestones.

"Maybe, both of us. A male like that would have a ravenous appetite." They make lascivious sounds that honestly make me smile a little — would have, had the female not immediately followed by adding, "Have you heard the rumors?"

"About him taking a wife?"

"Yes. But I don't see a woman with him now."

"I think we should fix that..." They both devolve to laughter as they push open the inn doors and disappear inside the large, squat two-story structure, their keys and coin pouches jangling at their hips.

I remain frozen on the walkway, unsure of what to do. I need to go into the tavern to make payment for a room from Moira the innkeep, but if what the women were giggling about is true, then Calai is already here. *Of course he is. And I'm the fool.* I can't risk being seen by him.

The doors open and three men with deep hoods step outside. I quickly avert my gaze to my feet, tug my own hood lower, and start walking around to the shadowy back side of the tavern.

Along the flat wall of the back of the structure, several doors hang open. They lead to the kitchens, workers — paid workers — moving through them rapidly. I recognize one of them — an orphan girl who was once a thrall in Winterbren until Moira purchased her freedom from Rosalind — and quickly rush forward to grab her arm before she can go back inside.

"Dimitra," I whisper, pushing my hood back so she can see my face. "It's Starling of Winterbren. Do you remember me?"

The girl's panic dissolves and a smile comes to cover her pale, freckled face. "Starling! Of course I remember you. You were always so kind. It's lovely to see you, but what...what are you..." And then her voice gives out. Her hand moves to cover her mouth, diffusing the visible clouds of her warm breath. "Are you... You are the king's woman now. That is what everyone at the inn tonight is saying. The king made a large pronouncement when he arrived an hour ago that anyone who has information as to your whereabouts should come forward and receive a reward..."

I wince, my lower lip quivering. After making it all this way, I'm already found out. I was a fool. A stupid, silly little girl who thought she could outrun shadows on foot in the dark. "I..."

She frowns and leans in very close to me. Two men move behind her carrying a large tun of ale and she quickly pulls me further around the building until we stand at the corner of the tavern and the stables beneath a low hanging eave where light cannot touch us.

"You do not wish to be discovered?" she hisses.

I wince, then nod. It feels like a confession.

"Has the king been cruel with you?" she asks, sounding so sincere, her eyebrows pulling together.

I shake my head. "Just cruel. I'm very afraid of him and I don't...don't..." Don't know how to say what I mean to say next.

Dimitra nods, her face setting. "Wait right here. I will fetch Moira. She will help you, don't worry. She has helped many women in your position before."

Dimitra leaves in a flurry but does not keep me waiting long before returning with Moira. She was the first person I'd ever seen as a young child with a skin color to match mine and my mother's. She'd been kind to us, the few times we'd had occasion to cross her path, and had always gone out of her way to speak to me when she traveled to Winterbren.

She frowns down her straight nose at me now and pushes her waist-length curly braid over her shoulder. Then she takes my hands in both of hers.

"Your hands are cold, Starling." And when her frown clears she looks like an entirely different woman. "I had hoped to see you again." She wraps me in a warm hug that I don't understand until she says into my hair, "I don't know if your mother ever told you, but she and I are from the same land. I tried to help her flee with you, but she was too afraid to leave your father. When I heard of their passing, I sought to purchase you from Rosalind but she would not sell you for a fair price."

She pulls away from me, holding me out to look at me with straight arms and a brilliant smile that lights up the darkness. "You are a beautiful woman now. It is no wonder."

"She fears the king, Moira," Dimitra says just behind her. "We should provide her shelter."

I'm surprised by Dimitra's boldness, and by Moira's ease. Moira simply nods. "Of course. I'll sneak you in the back. There is a spare room on the ground floor on the opposite end of the building. The king is on the second floor. You should avoid notice. Come. Dimitra, can you go ahead and prepare the room?" She nods and runs off towards the inn while Moira takes my hand and guides me around to the back of the stables.

There, under the shadow of the building where moonlight does not reach, she pushes me down onto my knees so that we sit below the half wall of the horse stalls. Inside, I can hear them happily braying. "Wait here and stay out of sight. I will come get you when the coast is clear and I'm certain none of the king's men are roaming about."

I nod. She turns. Before she can gather her skirts and leave, I tell her, "Thank you. I do not know what I've done to deserve such kindness."

Moira smiles and crouches down in front of me. She takes my face between her hands and says, "We women have to stick together. It's a cold world out there. Even colder alone." She hesitates, but doesn't leave and when she drops her hands to catch mine, she clutches them firmly. "Are you certain?"

"Certain?"

"I am assuming you mean to leave Winterbren, maybe even Wrath, entirely. I can help you secure passage almost anywhere you like, and I still have family back in the old land that could harbor you, but I will tell you it isn't an easy life. No life is easy for a young woman, or woman of any age. You could stay here, as an alternative, work for me. I would pay you a living wage..."

"No. No no no no no, Moira, I couldn't. The king... He would find me eventually and you would be... He would kill you for harboring me. I didn't even say goodbye to my friends in Winterbren for fear of what he'd do to them if he ever discovered they knew of my plans." I shiver and shake my head again, emphatically. "No. He is a violent man."

Moira's mouth falls open and her eyebrows crease. She touches my cheek. "Violent towards you or violent for you? There is a difference."

"I..." I shake my head, confused by her words. Rattled. "I just...can't stomach it."

She nods in understanding. "You are a grown woman of sound mind. If you've made yours up, I will not question it. The king will never know that you were here tonight, though I will tell you that he does not seem like a male who's come with the intent to punish. He seems more like a male who's come with the intent to plead..."

"The king's men are everywhere," Dimitra says, huffing as she rounds the corner at a sprint. "We won't be able to sneak her inside, even through the back entrance."

Moira curses and stands up. "Let me see if I can't give them some motivation to leave the inn. Wait here, Starling. I'll return for you when it is clear."

Quick as the wind, they turn and flee leaving me alone with my thoughts, with my concerns...maybe even, my regrets. *He looks like a male who's come with the intent to plead.* What does she mean by that? Does she think him not as violent a male as I do? Is he only acting in his capacity as king? Or does he enjoy the blood and the agony? Will he direct it towards me should I fail or upset him...as I've already done by running? Or, is his violence only an act of the care he seems to feel towards me?

I shiver. There is no chance he wouldn't have my back flayed far worse than anything Rosalind could have ever dreamed up. Though to know now that I had a chance at a free life years ago and Rosalind denied me makes me feel a little less charitable towards her. Not that charity will save her. I'm not sure King Calai left enough of her soul intact for even the gods to salvage.

As I sit huddled against the wooden wall of the stables, my nervousness mounts. Time passes. Moira and Dimitra don't return. The temperature has dropped and I'm even colder now as all this insecurity brings the temperature of my blood down. I want to scream. I want to weep. I want to ask the gods if they can allow me a small glimpse into the future so that I can know the king's mind and be sure that the violence of his hand does not affect his heart.

And then a voice as familiar to me as my father's and just as mean tears my thoughts out from under me like a rug. "He's in there now," Tori says, voice sounding ragged and enraged. His voice is clear, frighteningly so. I clap my hand over my mouth and glance at the wooden half wall. He's in the stables. There is only this flimsy wood separating us. I don't breathe. I don't move. "Let's go. I'm not waiting anymore. He needs to pay!"

"That disgrace of a king destroyed Winterbren." The second male's voice comes to me as an even greater shock. It's *Torbun*. Torbun may be many things, but a devout loyalist to Tori or even Olec, he is not. Torbun's character was never easy to puzzle out. He is devoted only to power. I'd have thought his allegiance would fall easily to the king now.

Torbun prattles on, "We will exact our revenge for what he has done to Olec and Rosalind. And to think, he will install my own *son* as chief in Olec's absence, overlooking my claim entirely." Ah. I understand now. Even though I understand, Torbun's inability to be happy for his eldest son surprises me. Perhaps, I truly am not meant to be queen. I do not have the ambitions of these petty, jealous men. I yearn only for kindness, only for love.

"There you are. What did you find?" Tori says.

Another voice I don't recognize answers. "It's time. The king has ordered a bath and the servants have brought his water. He should be bathing now. We should go."

"Are we enough?" a fourth voice says nervously.

Tori is quick to respond. "We're seven." *Seven? Seven against one?* The king is said to be a formidable warrior, but seven seems far too many. I cannot fathom who else would have joined this crusade, but I suddenly feel fear for the king. Despite his violent hand, I can say that the changes he proposed to me in private would make Winterbren better. Already, releasing the thralls was a wonderful gift. I can't let them kill the king. My feelings towards Calai aside, I can't let them take these new freedoms away from so many people. I must warn someone. The consequences to me be damned.

Careful not to make any sound, I shuffle along the edge of the wooden wall until I round the end of the building. Here, the wooden stable walls turn to the stone walls of the inn and I burst into a sprint. My hem and pack weigh me down, but I fight the strain in my shoulders and neck as I pass by startled employees who try to stop me from entering the squat, two-story structure.

"What...what are you doing?" Dimitra says, rushing out of the lit building and grabbing my shoulders. "You shouldn't be here. You'll be seen! Moira has just convinced all of the king's men to come to the tavern for free ale. Only the king remains in the building and she's plying him with wine while he bathes."

"He's alone?" *What have I done?* They will surely kill him now.

She nods, expression confused and concerned. "That's what you wanted..."

"It is, but I believe someone may be going to try to kill the king! Go get his men! Urgently!" I push past her, unsure if she's listening to me at all. I remember Moira saying he was on the second floor, but I don't know which room. "Where is he?" I shout over my shoulder.

"In the room just at the top of these stairs!" she shouts after me. "Are you not worried about him punishing you for running from him?"

Of course I am, but I cannot let Tori, of all people, be the one to slay the king, ambushing him when he is weak. *A male who's come to plead.* I will have to take my chances with Tori first, the king second if I am successful. And if I'm not...then we are all doomed.

It only occurs to me as my feet hit the narrow, weathered stairs that Tori is still living. I thought the king would have killed him during the second bloody round of the games. I wonder what stayed his hand and a momentary ache fills my chest at the thought that perhaps...the king might have been willing to see reason.

Fear has been my only constant these long years. But perhaps, I should find a new ally. One called courage.

The inn is a simple construct. Two floors with a single hall running the length of each, rooms on either side of the hall. There are two staircases. One for use by guests, the other a narrower staircase for the inn's employees. I take the latter and it brings me up to the second story at one end of the hall. The other, wider staircase brings guests up in the center of the room-lined corridor. I reach the second floor at the same time Tori does.

He is turned away from me at first and I can hear my heart in my throat, even louder than my voice as I shout, "Calai! Tori is here to kill you!" My hand fumbles in my skirts. I slide the straps of my pack down my arms and it hits the floor behind me with a heavy thud.

Tori turns towards me while Torbun and five other males crowd the space behind him. They are all brandishing swords except for Tori, who has an axe. He has bandages over both ears and his face looks like it's been bashed many times, but he isn't missing any other appendages, as I expected him to be. He meets my gaze before dropping his own to the ornamental dagger clutched in my fist, and then he does the most terrifying thing he's ever done. He smiles at me and raises his axe to point it at my nose.

"The things I'm going to do to you in front of your precious king."

There are two rooms at the end of the hall, the one behind me and the one before me. The one before me is utterly silent but I hear a thud from within the one behind me and place my body before it. I hold my knife aloft and all of the men laugh.

"A disgrace," Torbun hisses.

"Let's go. Tonight is the night for killing kings — but not whores. Leave this one for me," Tori says.

"Calai!" I shout — no, I don't. My voice abandons me. I barely whisper his name as I fall back against the door. I rap on it frantically with the knuckles of my free hand, hoping, praying he'll come out and somehow get his army up here to defend him in time. But then I consider that he might be inside, drunk on the wine Moira plied him with — at my behest — and asleep in the bath as Olec would have been. Then again, Olec would never have gotten off of his behind to chase down anything — let alone a woman. I'm such a fool. And now, I'll die as one. But at least I won't die a coward.

Tori charges down the hall and is on me in a flash, despite his multitude of injuries. "Stay back," I gasp. But he only comes closer until we're toe to toe. He reeks of blood and hate.

His men move to flank him, all of them turned towards me, towering over me and crowding the hall while my back remains pressed against the door. I hold out the king's dagger. My grip is tight, but shaky. I know realistically that I can't stop all of them — maybe, any of them. But I won't simply lie down. I've laid down too many times in my life to do it here. I lay down every time Rosalind told me to turn for her and drop my shift. I lay down every time my father raised his hand to me. I lay down every time my mother looked at me with hollow eyes full of apathy.

But...I stopped lying down when the king's violence made me afraid. Against his sadism, I found strength. Ironic that it should be the king to make me strong enough to run, that it is for the king I return. I will be strong for him now. I will fight for the king and the promises he's made to my village and people like me. But also, I will fight for Calai and the small mercies he's shown me. And most of all, I will fight for me.

"Turn away, Tori," I whisper, tears pricking the backs of my eyes. I'm afraid to die. I feel like...my life has only just begun. "You don't have to do this."

Tori simply reaches past me with the blade of his axe. He smashes the blunted top of his axe against the door, letting the blade lightly skim my shoulder — a threat as clear as the bloodlust glossing his gaze. "Open up, my *lord*," he sneers. "I have your precious queen."

"Tori, don't make me..." I say, pressing the tip of my dagger against his abdomen.

He looks down at me with blue eyes ringed in purple. His bruises are pronounced and grotesque. His nose looks broken. Dried blood crusts his nostrils. The men at his back are clamoring to break down the door, to hurry, but Tori takes the extra moment to bend down and whisper with blood-stained breath against my cheek, "You will leave this inn alive, but with no arms, no legs, no eyes, no tongue. You'll be a simple carcass I'll keep with me like a chest, one I can fuck whenever I like. You'll breed me bastard after bastard and I'll tear them to pieces in front of you. You won't be able to see, but you'll be able to hear their screams. I'll keep you alive like that forever. You'll be my special...little...toy..."

The door swings open at my back. I exhale, both panicked and relieved at the same time. "Calai..." I turn but the door slams shut again on a squeal. One of the blonde women who I heard speaking about Calai in front of the tavern is who shut the door. And there was a man with her. I caught a glimpse of him and, though I couldn't make out his features clearly, I could see well enough that he stood a foot shorter than Calai and had a round belly and brown hair.

I jolt as I stumble back against the door and turn to look at Tori. My eyes are strained against wide lids and in this moment, I manage to find it amusing that Tori and I share the same expression. The men behind Tori have started to turn, but they are too slow... Because the door across the hall is open and a bare chested Calai is filling up its breadth.

Two of the men hit the floor before the rest can turn. He holds no weapons and I don't understand how he's felled them. One of the men releases a battle cry, turns with his sword raised and stabs it towards Calai. I cry out, as if I might stop him. It is a senseless thought, for Calai is the bone king, used to the feeling of bathing in other mens' blood.

Calai grabs the man's arm at the wrist, not even blinking as his attacker's sword stabs mere inches from his right eye. Calai outmuscles the man, twisting his arm back, and then drives his forehead into the man's nose.

The man collapses and Calai raises his other arm, driving his fist into a fourth man's nose. He takes his elbow to the man's chin as he starts to fall and I hear a loud crack as the man falls back, collapsing into the servant's stairwell. The man's body makes terrible sounds as it falls down the stairs, hitting every one. Torbun, meanwhile, takes off down the hall, heading towards the guest stairs, but Calai rips a dagger from his next attacker's hand and tosses it almost absently down the hall, hitting Torbun directly in the center of his back.

Calai has already moved on to his next attacker. The man punches Calai in the stomach four times, but Calai seems hardly affected. He doesn't block. His muscles, shimmering with oils from his bath, simply contract as the man does his worst. And then Calai grabs the man by the head. He snaps his neck in one swift motion.

Two men lie grunting on the floor now, three more lie dead, the one in the stairwell I assume is either dead or sure to follow. That leaves only Tori — Tori, who lifts his axe. Calai's arms are down. He has blood spatter on his face. I gasp.

And then my arms jerk. Tori grunts. He looks away from the king, twisting to slowly look at my face. He blinks at me, anger and rage swirling in his gaze, but sprinkled with surprise, too. It's an honest sort of surprise that makes him look, for the first time I've ever known him to, quite boyish.

I imagine that this is the man he could have been, and for a moment, I feel deep sorrow...and anger...not only at his poisoned character, but at the fact that he's been poisoned from his childhood, as we all have been, by Winterbren and the terrible way the people have been treated within it. The select few very wealthy taking all the spoils and stepping on or over the backs of those with so little. I didn't realize there could be another way, that there was another way all along. That people could be treated with basic dignities. That the weak could be protected, rather than beaten, by the strong.

"It didn't have to be like this," I whisper, the burning in my eyes abating. I will not cry, not for Tori, though my entire body shakes beneath the magnitude of what I've done.

Tori looks down. I drop my gaze, and then drop my hand from the hilt of the beautifully ornamented blade. It doesn't move. The blade remains embedded in Tori's side, between two of his ribs. I don't think it will kill him, but it's enough to stop him. He drops his axe.

It lands hard on the ground between us, embedding itself in the wooden floor. I jolt at the shocking sound it makes and, when I step back, hit the back of my head on the door. "You should have been mine," Tori hisses, his hands lightly closing around my throat. But King Calai grabs Tori by the back of his hair and rips him off of me easily, tossing him down the hall as if he weighs nothing more than the dagger I stabbed him with.

"She was always mine. As I was hers," Calai says simply, following Tori down the hall and dropping to one knee. "Before you were born. Before time."

I hear a horrible gurgling sound and then silence, before Calai rises. He turns and I notice his fingers look like they've been dipped in blood. We stare at one another, unmoving, for what feels like a dozen lifetimes. My gaze scours his massive frame, his unbraided hair falling free around his shoulders, the blood on his face, the oils gleaming on his skin accentuating the lines of his muscles and the hard planes and ridges of his body made for killing.

And for loving, when the mood strikes him.

He watches me in return, his gaze lingering over the top of my head, my hair, my chin and throat. His gaze drops lower, to my hand — my blood-stained hand. I follow his gaze down and, seeing the bloody pads of my fingers, I quickly twist my hands in my skirt.

His gaze returns to mine and his mouth opens, but he doesn't say a word. Instead, I watch in fascination as his cheeks flush the brightest pink. He comes forward, towards me, and I don't back away. Not even as he stands less than half a pace away from me and brings two of his blood-coated fingers to my right cheek. He makes a single downward stroke from my temple to my jawline before repeating the motion on the other side of my face.

I know the mark and its meaning. It's a warrior's mark. I've only seen it delivered once, when Winterbren was raided when I was young and a then-young Viccra killed one of the raiders. He hadn't been to Ithanuir then, but he still managed to best a male. It was his first kill and Olec had given him this mark. Viccra had been celebrated that night. To receive a similar mark now makes me feel a little horrified but also...so seen.

I've never... A warrior? Me?

I begin to stutter, but stop when I feel something hard touch my hand. I look down to see that he's returned my dagger — his dagger — to my fingertips. I take it.

The king's hands then move to my face and mold around my ears. He grips me tightly and moves our foreheads to touch. His breath caresses my nose and mouth and chin, smelling of the wine Moira gave him, yet it did not seem to impede his fighting abilities at all.

I wonder if it's me or if it's him that shakes.

"Calai," I say in a rush.

He sucks in a breath as if he'd been holding his, waiting for me to speak. "You ran from me."

"Yes," I say, starting to shake. I cobble together a thousand apologies in my mind, but I can get none of them past the gate of my teeth. "I know you..."

He cuts me off, his voice a deep and loud boom that acts as a hook in my stomach, pulling everything up. "And then you came back," he whispers.

"Yes."

"To save my life." His hand moves down the side of my body, fingertips trailing over the outside of my arm until he reaches my hand. He squeezes my fist around the dagger and when he exhales, he sounds even shakier than I am. "Thank you, little bird."

Thank you is not what I expected to hear from him now, and the terror it lifts from my bones is enough to make me fall to my feet. He catches me. His hand slides around my lower back and he pulls me up against his body, not seeming to care at all for the dagger I still hold in my fist. I release it, knowing that I would never — could never — use it against him. This man isn't here to hurt me. How could I have ever thought he was?

"I couldn't let him hurt you."

He presses his mouth to the edge of mine, tasting me, but not enough. Not enough... "You were so brave."

His beard brushes my much softer skin, almost too roughly as he seeks to be closer, ever closer. He's pulling at my low back, at my face and neck, pressing his cheek to mine. I breathe him in and though I'm frightened, I feel a sudden...desperation. For him. For this. It may just be my crashing nerves or the battle lust the men speak of when they fell their opponents, but I need...everything.

"I was so scared..."

"But you were more afraid for me than of me." *Violent towards you or violent for you? There is a difference.*

I nod, tears I didn't know needed release crashing down now. "Yes. I'm sorry, Calai. I didn't..."

"No, no, shh... Shh." He gathers me to his chest, lifting my feet off of the ground and bringing me entirely into his heat and his shadows. He wraps his arms fully around my low back and shoulders, encasing me in his warmth as he is careful not to touch my center back. "It is I who am sorry, little bird. My queen. I should have taken better care. I exacted a revenge I wanted for acts committed against you. I revenged for *me*. It was wrong. I should have asked you what you wanted. I will not make that mistake again..."

"I just... When I saw your violence... You reminded me of my father, of Rosalind, of everyone who's ever raised a hand to me. I feared you'd just become another... That if I ever displeased you, you'd cast me aside or worse. I have nothing, Calai. I cannot stop you."

"You can. You always can. We come from two worlds, just as Raya and Ghabari do. But it is Raya who turns Ghabari's head and stays his hand, just as you can mine.

Do not allow me to displease you, little bird, and I vow that I will not ruin your tenderness with violence."

I wrap my arms around his neck and squeeze him with all the force that I have. He squeezes me back to the point that I can scarcely take in more breath. He says to me gruffly, "You are strong, and you are powerful and I am yours to command, my queen."

"I'm so sorry, Calai. I should have found courage earlier..."

"You found it when it counted."

"I should have trusted you..."

"Shh." He strokes my hair. "There will be time for that." And then his voice breaks. "If you'll still have me?"

I force distance between us and look up at him, our faces so very close together. I hold his cheeks between my hands and smile, choking on my next laugh. This is not at all how I expected this meeting to go, and I am so grateful to the insidious Tori for having ruined my earlier plans.

"I'll have you, Calai, if you'll still have me?"

He smiles and shocks me by betraying a gloss to his gaze that was not there before. "I will have you every day, for the tender, beautiful, strong, courageous, brilliant and bloodthirsty thing that you are. You are my queen and you have my heart."

"I promise I will be careful with it from now on."

"As I will be with yours." His gaze flits between my eyes before briefly sobering. "And do not run from me again, my warrior. I cannot survive the pain of your loss again in this lifetime. I want death to be the only thing that separates us going forward."

I nod, seeking strength, mining for courage and finding both. "I will not. I will speak to you and make my demands as a queen should."

He grins. "And what are your demands, my lady?"

I glance around the hall, the desecration of so many bodies, and then at the small army of men and several women crowding the hallway, staring at us with one of two expressions — wearing smirks, or in utter shock.

"Take me away from this carnage, my king," I say, circling my arms around his neck tighter and planting a kiss on the lobe of his ear.

The king shudders and hoists me up against his chest, his hands underneath my bottom. He takes three backward steps putting us inside his room, then kicks the door closed behind him, blocking all his violence out, and trapping only my tenderness within.

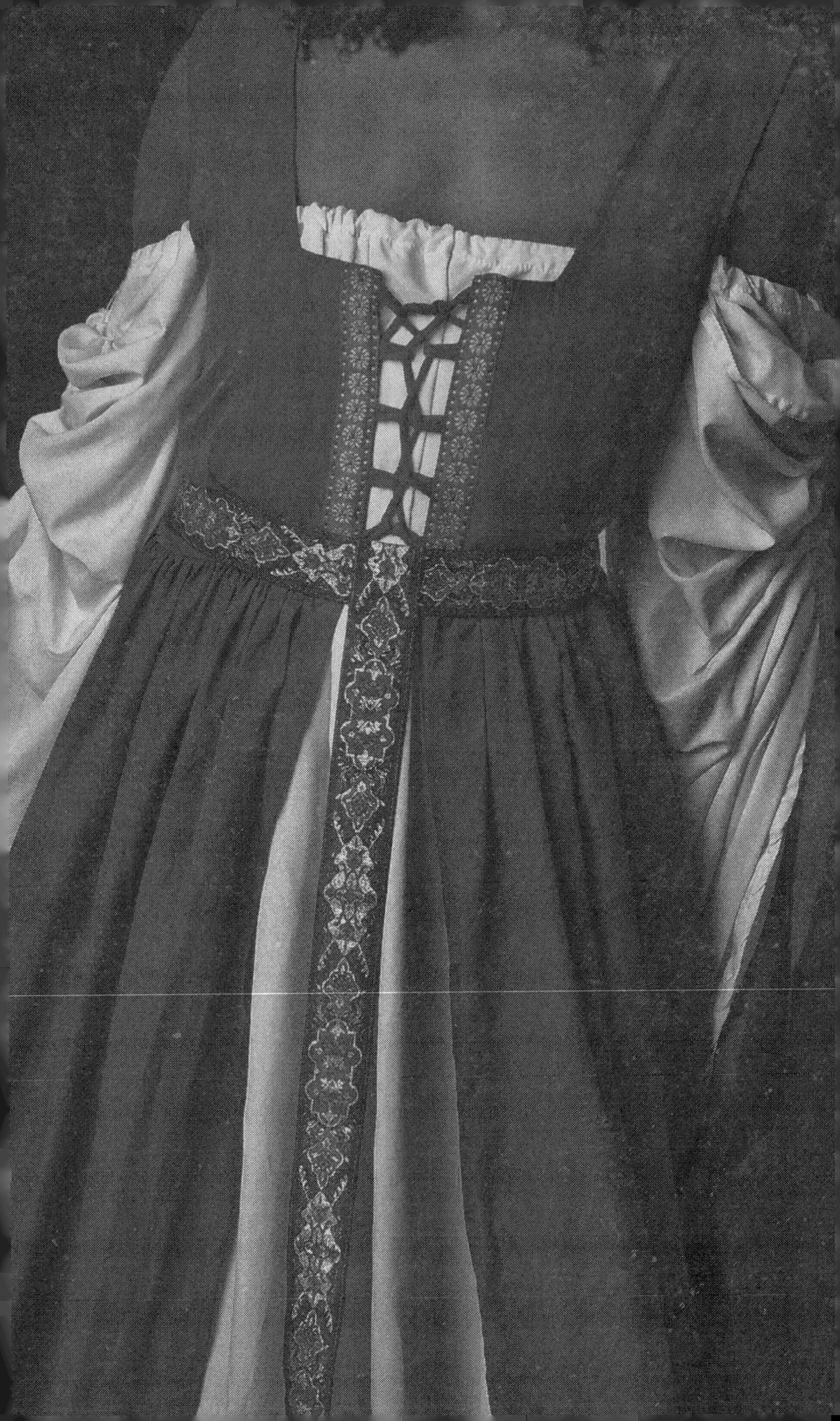

My Husband

STARLING

My eyes burn with delight as I take in marvel after marvel. Ithanuir is everything Ebanora said it was and even more she didn't. She stands beside me now, her brother having accepted a trainee position with the king.

It was not his interest to take the position, but he could scarcely refuse when the king also invited his family to join them — us. Considering that Ebanora's mother is a healer and her father works the fields, only her mother came with Ebanora as an escort. She'll leave after six months and for these six months that she's in Ithanuir, she'll take up training with the midwives' guild. Winterbren has only one midwife and she's an older woman whose practices are out of touch and out of date. A real midwifery practice in Winterbren would make it a very attractive destination to visit for those who live in neighboring villages and on the outskirts of Wrath.

She grips my wrist and points off into the crowd. "Do you see that!"

I nod, my face scrunching up. "I don't know what it is…"

"It's a mammoth," Hilde says from the row of women warriors who've assumed the position behind me. "A spoiled creature, there are six who live near Ithanuir. They are harmless creatures and the children love them. They wander as they please."

A shaggy, four-legged creature with massive tusks, it wanders lazily through the square, sucking water from the fountains it passes and spraying itself as well as passersby. It draws nearly as much attention as the king does and makes me laugh loudly and freely. I have never felt so unburdened in my entire life.

I stand now at the mouth of Ghabari's temple, surrounded by Ebanora's family, the female warriors closest to Calai, Moira and her two daughters. Wind whips through my curls, which have been twisted into intricate braided patterns atop my head, only a few curls falling down my spine and around my ears. I inhale deeply, the scents as foreign to me as the sights of Ithanuir. Spices and sunshine, honey and unfamiliar trees.

The temple is open to the elements, wooden beams draped in white and red fabrics that catch even the slightest breeze. It's beautiful today. The sun is shining. Even though it is entering the cold season, I feel nothing but warmth in my white dress, the color of pearls, shrouded in one of the king's furs that is just as white. I clutch a bouquet of blood-red lilies in my hands.

The mammoth meanders past the town square and the people who'd been distracted by it crowd back into the temple just in time for the priest to call me forth. Calai has completed his part of the ceremony and waits for me now at Ghabari's altar in the center of the space.

I walk confidently, my head held high. I am no longer the woman I was in her entirety. Calai and I spoke at length and he made me promises that I no longer feel such fear he will keep. I learned in myself that I would do terrible things to keep Calai safe and that helped me understand a little more how he must have felt seeing others do terrible things to me.

I know better than to think him a tender man. Yet, I now have every faith that he will always be tender with me.

I take soft steps down a green petal-lined path. Hundreds of villagers crowd the atrium steps that rise up on my either side. It is enough to make my fear spike, but I look up at Calai, groomed and washed, wearing white trousers and a white fur draped over one shoulder. My pulse settles. I exhale and smile.

He had me braid his hair today and right now, the red looks wild and vibrant. He looks beautiful, if a man so savage ever could. I smile. He returns my smile with one that is blinding and I ignore all of the hundreds of people who've come out to watch their king take a queen today — even if he did *take* me and wed me in the wrong order.

"Little bird," he mouths as I ascend the final steps to the dais and come close enough to touch him. He takes my hands in his and yanks me into his chest, causing a ripple of laughter to move through the crowd.

The priest begins his ceremony and I accept the bloody chalice when offered. This is not a tender life, but a violent one, I think as I sweep a stroke of blood down Calai's right cheek. I hand him the chalice and he does the same to mine. But I know better now than to think myself powerless against it. I can be a warrior too, when required.

The ceremony is over in a blink. I can scarcely believe it when the priest finally binds our wrists together with white silk and has us step over Ghabari's pulpit together, as one. The priest says in a booming voice that somehow manages to carry over the increasingly boisterous crowd, "And I present to you all, people of Wrath, the king's new bride, your new queen."

The cheer that goes up is deafening, a call to the gods to show me favor. I cast my gaze around and see my people cheering loudest of all, and laugh alongside them. Calai sweeps me off my feet and kisses me deeply enough I can feel it in my toes. As he carries me away, I wrap my arms around his neck, feeling for the first time in my life truly safe, treasured and powerful.

And loved most of all.

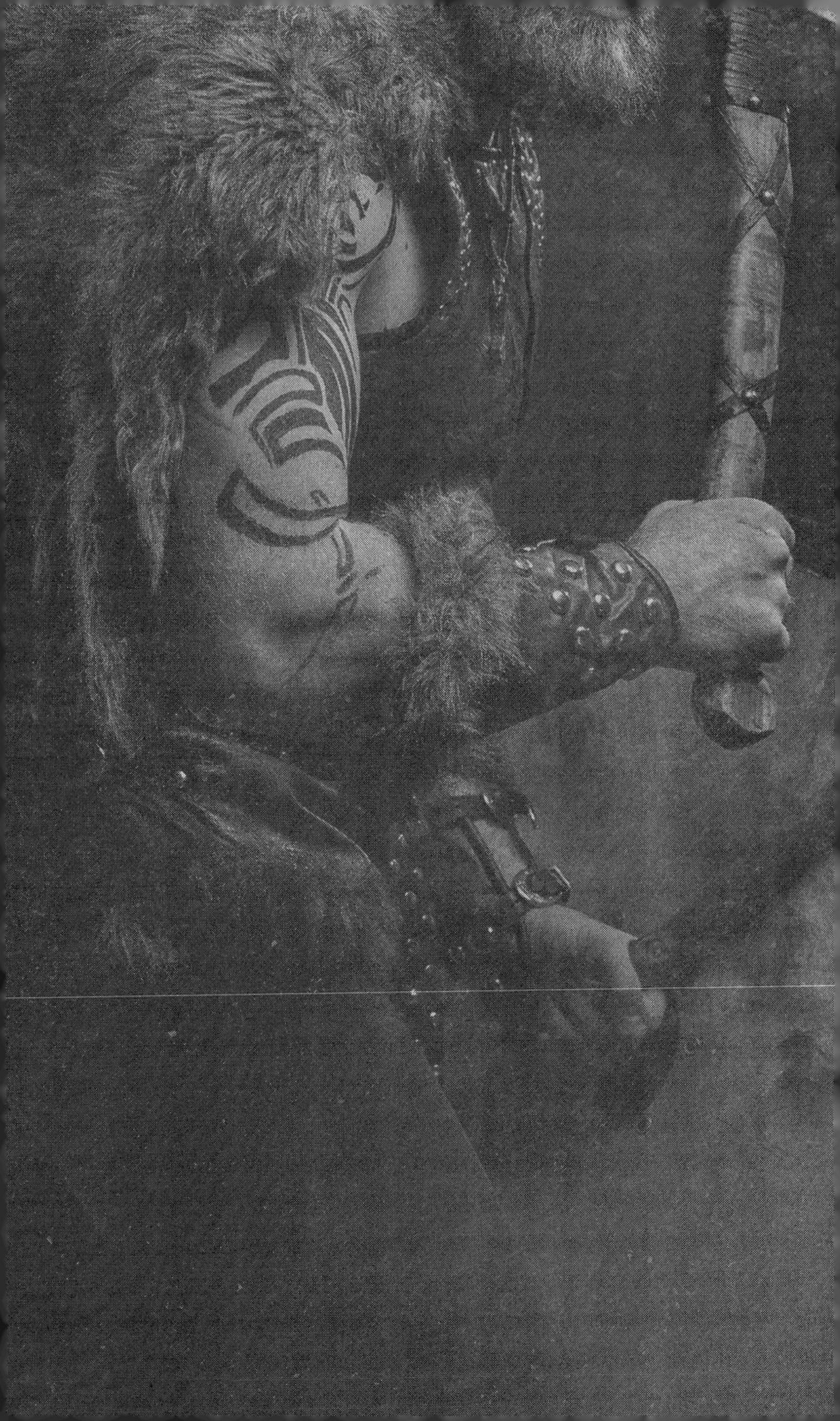

My Wife
CALAI

"My lady looks so beautiful in white. It makes the color of your skin look even more vibrant." I prowl over her body, covered in that scandalous dress. "Some unholy combination of sunlight and starlight."

She smiles up at me and smooths her hands over the sides of my face. She tucks my hair behind my ears. "I love you, Calai."

My heart nearly bursts at the seams. I flip up her skirts and kick off my trousers and I waste no time in breaking in the marital bed of our new home. Now that she is well healed, I enter her dripping heat roughly, unable to escape the range of emotions raging through me. Her body yields to my cock, making space for me to take her how I like. It's incredible. Sensational. Tenderness and violence at the same time.

I hang my head and shake it slowly. "Starling, you have no idea the gift you've brought me. I love you, little bird, more than anything."

Her mouth opens on a silent scream. She licks her lips. She grabs my neck. Her nails dig into my skin and her thighs quiver around my hips. "Gods…Calai…fuck me."

I grunt out a laugh and rock my hips against hers even harder, the sound of our flesh meeting both salacious and wild. She bounces along the bed, her hair a cascade of curls across our pillows. My hands spread her knees. I look down at her wreathed in white and toss my head back, knowing that the gods are great.

"Who would have thought?" I moan up to the roof of my quarters in the great hall — quarters that will be expanded to accommodate my expanded family. My queen will have anything she wants and everything she desires. My trust. My love. My ear. My kindness. My devotion and protection forever.

"Thought...what..." Starling moans, her voice giving out as I start to grind my pelvis against hers, hoping to strike sensation in the place she likes best. At the same time, my hands move up her chest. I draw the neck of her dress down, exposing her breasts. I bend over and suck hard on her nipples.

"That the bone king would be tamed by a starling," I moan.

She breathes, "Or that the starling...would protect...her bone king...with her claws..."

We moan together as we each near our first release on this most sacred of nights, our wedding night. I have no doubt that this release will only be the first of many to come this evening. Against her supple mouth I moan, "Yes...who knew my little bird would be such a violent, tender thing..."

"Or that my king of blood and bones would have such a soft heart."

"For his queen, always. Always."

Our passion can be heard across Ithanuir as I cradle my queen to my chest, grateful to her for coming back to me, and grateful to have been led to her by the gods.

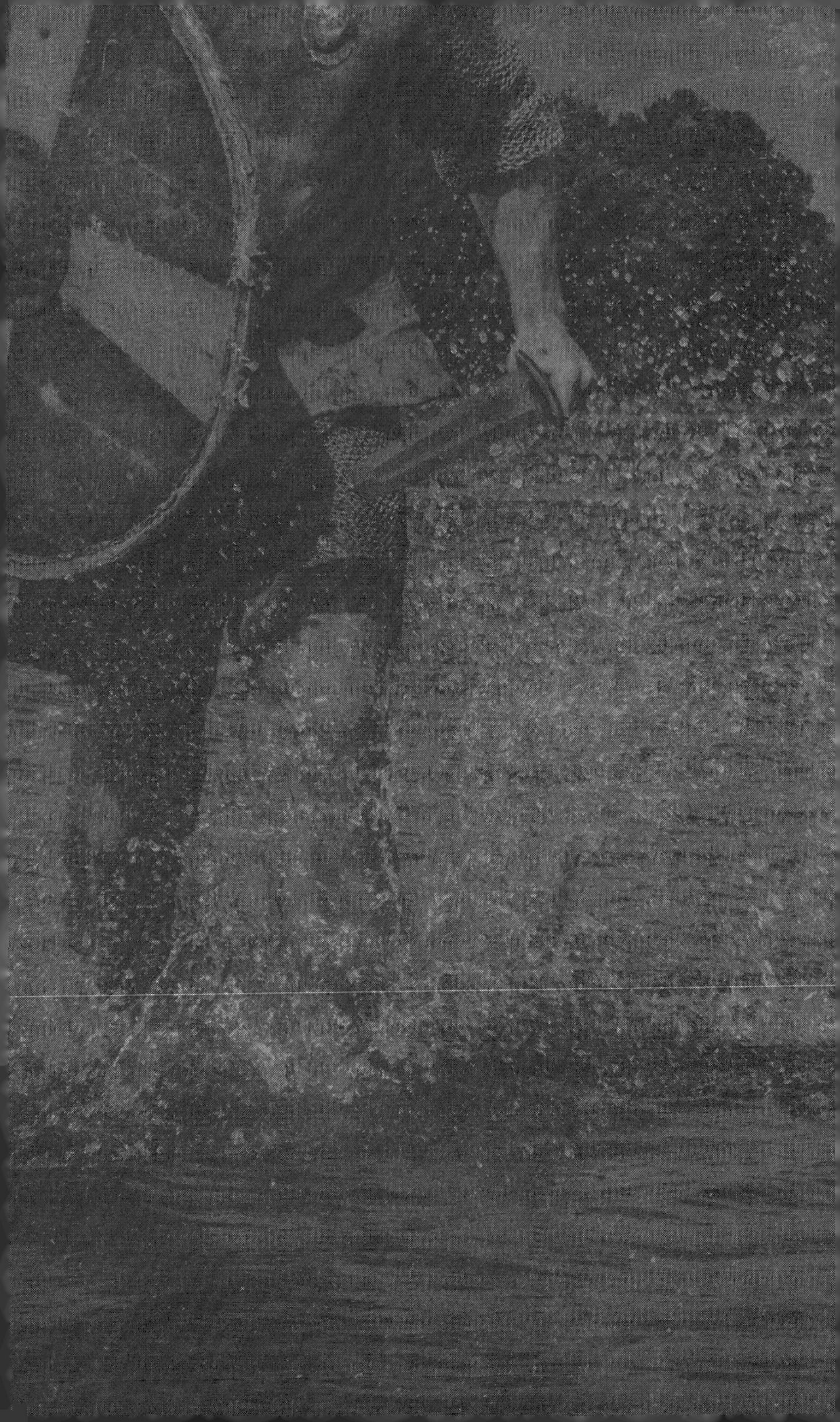

THANK YOU

Thank you for reading The Bone King and the Starling! If you enjoyed the read, a review on your platform of choice goes a long way in supporting the work of indie authors like me! If you're eager to shout about it online, feel free to tag me, or write to me personally.

You can also read more of my dark fantasy romances by checking out my other series.

ALSO BY ME

Supers in the City – Montlake, June 2025
Enemies to lovers superhero romances

Beasts of Gatamora
Dark omegaverse romantasies

Population Series
Dark dystopian vampire romantasies

Xiveri Mates
Scifi alien monster romances